RAVE REVIEWS FOR PENELOPE NERI!

"Penelope Neri proves again that she is a splendid writer of historical romances."
—Phoebe Conn, on *Enchanted Bride*

"Ms. Neri's romance with Gothic overtones is fast-paced and sprinkled with wonderful characters . . . a really good read."
—*Romantic Times* on *Scandals*

"Neri is a genius at creating characters that readers will love, and for spinning a magical tale that will leave readers longing for more."
—*Writers Write* on *Scandals*

"This entertaining, sensual story . . . [will] satisfy readers."
—*Romantic Times* on *Stolen*

A TRICK OF LIGHT

The murky green ball gleamed in the moonlight, full of mystery.

"I see a beautiful, heartless innkeeper—and a dark-haired man who is desperate for her love!" He grinned. "Catch, Miranda! Take my future in your hands. Do with it as you will!" He tossed the glass ball to her. "Now. Your turn. Tell me what you see in the depths of the crystal ball?"

"I see a dark-haired man. A very handsome man who is a mystery to me," she began hesitantly, but truthfully. "A man who confuses and pleases me at the same time, for he is like none of the men I have met before."

"Being different isn't always bad. Remember that, before you go on," he urged softly.

"This man claims to be one thing, but everything about him says that he's another. He is a man who. . . ." Here her voice wavered a little, " . . . who attracts and . . . and—frightens me, because of my unanswered questions about him."

"What is it you'd like to know?" he said huskily, catching both her her hands between his. "Ask away."

"Very well," she agreed, looking up at him. "Who are you, really, Morgan St. James? And why did you come to Lizard Cove? Are you truly a lighthouse keeper, as you claim? Or . . . something else entirely?"

KEEPER OF MY Heart

PENELOPE NERI

LEISURE BOOKS   NEW YORK CITY

With love to
Lenora Kim Ishihara and Wendie Rhody,
For Auld Lang Syne.

A LEISURE BOOK®

December 1999

Published by

Dorchester Publishing Co., Inc.
276 Fifth Avenue
New York, NY 10001

ISBN 0-8439-4647-4

KEEPER OF MY Heart

"Nail to the mast her holy flag,
Set every threadbare sail
And give her to the god of storms
The lightning and the gale."
                    —Oliver Wendell Holmes

Prologue

August 2, 1792
Off Lizard Head, Cornwall, England

"Where the devil's the blasted lighthouse?" Geoffrey Christopher bellowed over the howling wind. "We should have seen her beacon by now!"

As the mate opened his mouth to answer the captain, the decks of the schooner *Lady Anne* canted violently. The sudden steep angle brought both men to their knees. Clawing desperately for a handhold, they slithered down the sloping decks, terrified of being pitched headfirst into the boiling black Atlantic.

The terrible nor'wester had begun lambasting the Cornish coast soon after dusk. What had started out as crackles of purple light on the horizon was soon followed by deafening clatters that could have been cannon fire, but proved instead to be thunderbolts that threatened to split the heavens asunder.

Soon after, rain came roaring down as if emptied from a vast celestial bucket. The deluge had drenched the already sodden shrouds and left slippery decks awash in several inches of water.

As Captain Christopher and the mate, Walter Maddox, strained stinging eyes for a glimmer of light in that terrible black void, the *Lady Anne* sailed gamely on, rising and falling like a cork on the towering black swells.

The storm's ferocity quickly extinguished the lanterns that swung from the yardarms. In the blackness between the lightning flashes, terror and confusion now ruled the crew.

Captain Christopher could hear the deck hands muttering that the *Anne*, named for her owner's dead wife, was cursed, while the swearing of the old salts mingled with the frightened sobs of poor Ben, the cabin boy, who had claimed fourteen years when signing on, but whom the captain suspected was really closer to twelve.

"There!" Maddox suddenly sang out. The exultation in his voice rose above the noisy clatter of another thunderbolt. "Off the port bow! A light! D'ye see her, Cap'n?"

A single quick flash, three seconds' pause, then another quick flash.

Every lighthouse on the coast of England had its own "characteristic," or pattern of flashing. This one belonged to the Lizard light's warning beacon to be sure! They'd seen her in the nick of time. . . .

"Aye, by God, Mr. Mate! I see her! Starboard, helm. Starboard hard, Mr. Helmsman! Hold her off! Turn her! *Turn her, damn your hide!*" Christopher roared at the helmsman, who had lashed himself to the ship's wheel.

And against all odds, by some miracle, the schooner responded.

A ragged cheer went up as the *Lady Anne* obeyed her master's commands and veered away from the warning beacon.

Slowly yet surely, the valiant little schooner came about, turning her bowsprit from the treacherous coastline known as the "ship's graveyard," toward what appeared to be the yawning blackness of the open sea, like a greyhound putting her nose into the wind.

Hope surged in Christopher's heart. Out there, in the vast Atlantic, far from the Lizard's deadly

11

fangs, there was a chance. At sea, they'd be able to ride out the storm in safety.

And so, disoriented by rain and darkness, Captain Christopher placed his trust in the measured flash of the Lizard's familiar beacon. As a consequence, he was ill-prepared for the grinding shudder that tore through his ship seconds later, shaking her from stem to stern like a bone in the mouth of a massive pit-bull terrier.

Shattered oak screamed like skinned cats. Ruptured timbers cracked like pistol shots. The *Anne* groaned and moaned like a dying whale as the rocks impaled her proud keel.

Through the terror and chaos, Christopher realized that the *Lady Anne* had run aground! But how could that be, unless—dear God in Heaven!—unless the lights on shore were false!

Some murdering bastard had lured them onto the rocks!

Wreckers, he realized, damning their black souls! Blasted wreckers had lured his lovely *Anne* to her death. And, with her proud breast impaled upon the jagged fangs of the Point, there was naught he could do but give the order to abandon ship.

Perhaps it was too late to save the St. James' cargo from the marauders who waited on shore, but he could still save his crew, and, God willing, himself!

As Morgan St. James had reminded him before he sailed for the Indies, ships and their cargoes could always be replaced. Good men—friends and husbands—could not. And so, he would not go down with his ship—no, none of that old-fashioned nonsense for him. He would take his chances and swim, by God! Save himself for his darling Nanon, and the babe she was carrying.

Their babe.

His son or daughter would need a father.

It was only a matter of time now, he thought as he steeled himself for what was to come.

As he expected, other timbers shrieked and popped as the trapped vessel fought to drag herself off the Lizard's jagged teeth. The awful groaning, shrieking sounds were the *Anne's* death rattle.

Masts splintered and toppled, carrying sodden canvas and line into the boiling sea. Boxes of tea and hogsheads of tobacco bobbed free of the ragged, gaping holes in the splintered hold to join the casks of brandy, puncheons of rum, and other flotsam and jetsam bobbing violently about in the water.

Terrified sailors slithered down the sloping decks, shrieking as they toppled over the streaming gunwales, into the foaming blackness.

When the final mast head toppled, a sodden

13

ribbon of torn canvas that was still attached caught Christopher about the arm and upper torso. Like a stone launched by a slingshot, he slithered down the ruined decks and was hurled headfirst into the cruel arms of the sea.

Surfacing, he spat water from his mouth and began swimming for shore, where the silhouettes of several men in yellow oilskins waited for the first survivors to come ashore.

Rescuers? The captain was filled with sudden foreboding as he thought of his lovely Nan and the babe they had made together. *Or bloodthirsty scavengers?* . . .

On a rocky shelf just above the high-tide mark, a man lifted to the lantern's light the pocket watch he'd stolen from one of the bodies.

In its amber glow, he saw that an elaborate design of mermaids, sea serpents and scrolling waves had been engraved upon it. And, when he dug a broken, dirty fingernail into a small mechanism, the lid opened and a tinkling melody played. *Greensleeves*, he thought, humming along.

"Alas, my love, you do me wrong. . . ."

A grin split fleshly lips. It was a fancy piece, if ever he'd seen one. This treasure he'd keep for himself, by God.

With a furtive look about him, he made to slip

the watch deep into his coat pocket. But before he could do so, a familiar voice rang out.

"Now, now! What is it you have there? Take it back out, where I can see it, hmm? We'll have none of your pilfering! Show me what you've got!"

Scowling ferociously, he opened his hand.

The gold watch gleamed in the lantern light.

"Well, well! A pretty piece, indeed. You have expensive tastes—for a grubby little thief!" The golden eyes filled with pleasure and spite in the flare of the lightning. "And its owner will never have to worry about time again, hmm?"

The speaker laughed and contemptuously nudged with a booted foot the corpse that was draped over the rocks before them.

The dead man's head lolled limply to one side. The matted, fair hair at the back of his skull was dark with blood, the blue eyes permanently open.

"I'd say that makes the timepiece mine, since I killed him, wouldn't you? Hand it over!"

Snarling a curse under his breath, the man did so, just as another shout rang out.

"Hallooo! The cliff! Starboard away! Get hiiiim!"

His head jerked around at the sound of his father's voice. His eyes narrowed when he saw the scrawny spy crouched on the rocky ledge,

15

high above them. Though battered and bloody, Billy Ashe was swaying unsteadily as he watched them. And even from this distance, he could see the horror in the keeper's expression . . .

Damn his eyes! They'd left Ashe for dead, but not only was he still alive, he'd seen what they'd done!

"After him, lads! After him!" roared his father, his bellow snatched away by the howling wind. "Don't let the bastard get away! A rope awaits any man he names!"

With a roar of rage, he turned and ran back the way they'd come. Back toward the path in the cliffs. Back toward the looming tower of the lighthouse beyond.

Back to find her blasted keeper, and silence his wagging tongue—forever!

Chapter One

The St. James' Residence
Dorchester Square, London
Two weeks later

"Mr. St. James? There's a person to see you, sir. On a matter of some importance, or so he claims."

"Does he indeed, Phillips? And did this person mention what this important matter might be?" Morgan asked the butler absently, pausing in his inspection of the documents he was holding to look up at the man. His dark brows narrowed. "Well, man?"

"I'm afraid not, sir. When I inquired as to the

nature of his call, he said he would speak to you or to his lordship, but no other. Myself included."

"Then show him out, Phillips. I have pressing business here." He would be up until the wee hours as it was, going over the stack of papers before him, despite his heavy heart.

Just two days ago, Lloyds of London had completed its investigation into the wrecking of the *Lady Anne*, a schooner of the St. James' Shipping Line owned by him and his father, Sir Robert St. James. The investigators had convened a hearing for ten tomorrow morning, at which time they would disclose their findings regarding the wrecking.

Morgan did not intend to miss that hearing.

He was, however, anxious to go over Lloyds' original appraisal of the schooner before he retired for the night. Consequently, distractions were unwelcome.

"Very good, sir."

Phillips' tone drew a sharp glance from the master of the house. The man was about to draw the study door shut behind him when he paused expectantly.

Morgan sighed and flung down his pen. "Oh, all right, Phillips! I give up. What the devil is it, man?" he snapped.

"I know it's none of my business, sir, and I could very well be wrong, but—"

"But what? Out with it!" Morgan barked. He had neither the time nor the patience for ditherers. Not tonight. He had too much on his mind.

"There's something about the fellow. Call it instinct, if you will, sir. Or intuition, perhaps? But I think he has something to do with the *Lady Anne*, sir."

Morgan's dark brows shot up. "Do you, by God? Then I shall have to see him, after all, won't I? Show him in." His butler's instincts were sound more often than not. If Phillips thought he should see the man, he would.

A pleased smile softened Phillips' implacable expression. "Very good, sir."

Morgan was standing before the marble fireplace, warming his coattails and enjoying a brandy, when Phillips ushered the fellow into the study.

He immediately could see why his butler believed the man had something to do with shipping. Shabbily yet tidily dressed in canvas bell-bottoms, a worn navy fisherman's jersey and a reefer jacket, his visitor had the look and bearing of a sea-faring man. In fact, his rolling sailor's gait was reminiscent of Morgan's own, for he had spent several years at sea himself, before returning home to start the St. James' Shipping Line with his father.

Obviously ill-at-ease, the man waited, cap in hand, until Morgan threw down his papers and acknowledged his presence.

"So," he began. "My butler says you wish to speak with me, Mr. . . . ?'"

"The name's Ashe, sir. Billy A—I mean, William Ashe."

"Mr. Ashe, a very good evening to you." Morgan nodded cordially, trying to squelch the excitement that was rising through him.

Ashe was a wiry fellow with faded, fair hair and a long gaunt face that appeared to be covered with fading bruises. He was, Morgan estimated, in his late forties, although his eyes were decades older. Oddly, Ashe was trembling violently—not, Morgan thought, from any fear of himself, but from a lingering weakness or fever. Malaria, perhaps, from the tropics?

"You are unwell, Mr. Ashe," he observed. "Please, sit down, before you fall."

"Thank ye, sir." The man sank gratefully onto a straight-backed chair set against the wall. There he perched, like an ungainly, leggy bird about to take flight.

Morgan splashed brandy into a small balloon

glass and pressed it into Ashe's hands. "Drink it down, man."

Ashe took a sip, then another, coughing and sputtering as the strong spirit went down. Obviously not a drinking man, by any measure.

Ruddy color seeped into his waxy complexion like red ink seeping into a blotter.

"God bless ye, sir," Ashe whispered hoarsely, but with obvious gratitude. "That did the trick!"

"I'm glad to hear it. Now, why don't you tell me why you're here?" Morgan suggested in a kindly fashion.

Going around to the front of the leather-topped desk, he propped himself comfortably against it, one lean thigh hitched over the corner, both arms folded across his chest.

"Very well, sir. I'll get straight t'the point, shall I? I've come t'tell ye what truly befell your ship, sir. The *Lady Anne* and her crew, that is," he explained in a rush.

A thrill skittered down Morgan's spine. Who was this man who, while so nervous, nevertheless seemed determined to speak his piece?

A survivor of the sinking, he decided at length, although Lloyds had claimed there were none. Would he expect some monetary reward, in exchange for his account of the tragedy? Probably.

"I would like very much to know what befell

21

Penelope Neri

her, yes. Continue, Mr. Ashe. Speak your piece."

"Well, sir, as you know, on August 2nd, the *Lady Anne* ran aground off Lizard Point during a storm."

"The devil's own storm it was, too, from what I've been told."

"It was a right bad 'un, aye. But the cap'n could have saved his ship, if the Lizard light had been lit, and no false lanterns set to confuse her."

"What's this?" Morgan asked hoarsely. "False lanterns, you say?"

Ashe gave a grim nod. "I did, sir, aye. And then, after she ran aground. . . ."

Apparently unable to go on, he wetted his lips. His eyes slid away, unable to meet Morgan's, but not before Morgan realized they were red-rimmed and brimming with fresh tears.

"I . . . I saw her crew murdered, sir." He shuddered, his eyes closing as if he were reliving the horrible sight in his head. "When the poor devils what survived the wreck tried t' crawl ashore, they murdered 'em! Every last one of 'em!"

Morgan's expression was grim indeed now, pale beneath its windburned tan.

"These are serious allegations, Mr. Ashe. Murder is a hanging offense. Surely you were mistaken?"

"No, sir. I was not. Murder it was, and no mis-

22

take. Half-drowned, those poor lads were, God rest their souls! Yet they managed to crawl ashore, never dreaming death was waitin' for 'em there. When they reached the shallows, they clubbed 'em t'death, sir. Brained 'em like seals, then left 'em t' die!"

"Sweet Lord Almighty! Then there were survivors of the wrecking?"

Ashe nodded. "Four that I'm sure of. Probably more. All murdered by the same foul rogues what killed their cap'n."

The blood drained from Morgan's face. "Geoff Christopher survived the wreck?" he asked. He was holding his breath as he waited for Ashe to answer.

"Aye," Ashe said heavily. "He did. And when the poor devil pleaded with them not t' harm his men, they went for 'im, sir!"

"Can you identify these men?" Morgan demanded, almost overcome by emotion. "Could you point them out in a court of law?" His green eyes blazed.

Ashe's scrawny shoulders slumped beneath the reefer jacket. "No. I'm afraid not, sir, though I wish to God I could. I'd dearly love t' see the bastards hanged for their crimes! But . . . it were dark, ye see? And the storm was still raging. Truth is, I couldn't make out their faces, sir. All I can give ye is a name. *Killigrew*. That's what

23

one o' them shouted. *Killigrew*. There's a family by that name in Lizard Cove, sir. I heard tell they're involved in the . . . er . . . the free trade, too, if ye take my meaning?"

The "free trade." Smuggling. It was common enough up and down the English coastline when times were hard, as they were nowadays, Morgan reflected.

Under cover of darkness, contraband goods brought from the Continent were ferried ashore from small vessels that hovered off the coast. In this way, the excise tax the Crown levied on such luxuries as brandy, lace, tea, tobacco and rum was avoided, and a hefty profit could be made from their sale.

Morgan nodded gravely. Ashe's story explained the bruising to the man's face, the scabs and poorly healing cuts. Rocks could batter a man mercilessly, and cut his body to ribbons. He had seen similar injuries many times, in his years at sea. "And what of you, Mr. Ashe? How was it you had the good fortune to escape your fellows' fate?"

"My fellows?" Ashe frowned, then slapped his thighs. "Oh, Gawd love ye, sir, I weren't one of the *Anne's* crew. Why, I ain't been to sea in over ten year, I ain't, on account of me weak chest!"

"No? Then why were you there that night,

man? What business had you in Lizard Cove?"

"Why, sir, I was the lighthouse keeper, for all the good it done those poor devils, Mr. St. James. I kept the Lizard light."

Chapter Two

The Black Gull Inn stood where it had been standing for over three hundred years: at the end of sandy Gull Lane, which, in turn, led to rocky Lizard Point.

Its two long wings of whitewashed Cornish stone formed an L-shaped building with mullioned windows that were framed by smart black shutters. Its upper casements boasted lacy curtains and overlooked a cobbled inn-yard that was the official end of a road that reached west from London, across Bodmin Moor, and deep into Cornwall.

Stage coaches had rumbled over her cobbles for almost two centuries now. More recently, mail coaches from London had begun delivering the penny post here, using the Black Gull as their final stopping point, before returning east to London.

Guests who stayed at the Gull found their rooms swept and polished, their rugs beaten, their beds made with fresh linens, the food tasty and plentiful, and the ales, wines and spirits the very best her landlord's cellars could provide.

It was, in all, a very fine hostelry, despite its remote location on the westernmost edge of the moors.

By the door that led into the taproom at the front of the inn were several weathered half-barrels, each painted black to match the shutters. In them, huge scarlet geraniums nodded vivid heads, basking in the dazzling golden light for which Cornwall was so justly renowned. And on the holystoned doorstep lay a big black-and-white cat, sunning itself.

Beyond, at the crossroads, where the London Road, little more than a rutted cart track, met Gull Lane before turning back up onto windswept Bodmin Moor, the painted sign of a black gull hung from a tall post.

The sign swung back and forth in the wind that blew inland from the sea, shrieking like a hungry gull.

Miranda Tallant, innkeeper, made a mental

note to have Big Jan see to it as she marched up the lane at a brisk clip. A drop of oil would soon silence that awful screeching.

A quarter-mile away began the straggling line of fishermen's cottages that was the village of Lizard Cove. Each little cottage was different, each one clung like a limpet to its side of the steep, high street.

Centuries ago, the fishing village had been carved by wind and will from the granite cliffs of the Lizard Peninsula. The cottages had been built to house the fishermen and their families who made their livings off the shoals of pilchards found in Cornish waters.

Pretty window boxes and washtubs set before each cottage held yellow and orange marigolds and dark-eyed pink daisies. The fallen petals splashed vivid color over weathered wood and stone.

From the rugged point across the bay reared the Lizard Lighthouse, a tower of whitewashed brick crowned by a black "witch's hat."

The Lizard light, as she was known, had been abandoned three weeks ago by her wretch of a keeper, Billy Ashe, Miranda reflected. Consequently, for the past several nights, no beacon had flashed a warning light to vessels sailing the ships' graveyard off the deadly point. Those that sailed there risked running aground on its rocky teeth, hurled there by pounding breakers or a fierce nor'wester.

But then, thanks to unscrupulous keepers like Ashe, the Lizard light had rarely served her intended purpose, Miranda reflected as she pushed a lock of brandy-colored hair from her eyes and squinted against the dazzling light.

Unfortunately, there were others like Ashe. Unscrupulous men who preferred that the warning beacon remain unlit, so that they might claim the cargoes of the vessels that ran aground off Lizard Point.

It had been just such a night three weeks ago, Miranda thought as she followed the mossy path between the even mossier gravestones of St. Breoch's churchyard. A playful wind teased streamers of long, bright hair from beneath her spotless lace cap and flattened her skirts against hips and thighs, revealing a glimpse of petticoat and a pair of slender ankles in the bargain.

That night, a terrible storm had blown in from the Atlantic. But instead of lighting the Lizard's huge lantern, Keeper Ashe had abandoned his post to guzzle smuggled rum. Once drunk, he had left the beacon both empty and unlit. His negligence had caused the death of the *Lady Anne's* captain and crew.

Billy Ashe's dereliction of duty had so angered some of the village men, they had taken it upon themselves to see justice done in the form of a beating, then run Billy out of the village.

The man had not been seen since that night. Nor would he ever return to the cove, Miranda suspected. At least, not if he knew what was good for him!

His drunkenness that night had cost a score of men their lives, for, with no warning light, the schooner *Lady Anne*, bearing a fine cargo of brandy, tea, rum and tobacco from the Continent and the Indies to her home port of Plymouth, Devon, had run aground off Lizard Head.

She had quickly broken up, pitching her crew and her cargo into the foaming deep, where, to the last man, they had tragically perished.

In the days that followed that dreadful night, Miranda had seen countless bodies carted up to St. Breoch's churchyard for burial, sewn into simple shrouds of canvas. One, she recalled with a shudder, had been very small—no more than a young boy, surely.

She shook her head, saddened by the thought of so many women left widowed, so many sweethearts left unwed, so many children left fatherless by the storm and one man's negligence that night.

Had Ashe done his duty, many of those poor devils might have been saved.

Still, while it had been a tragic night for many, others had profited from it.

The shattered ship, her fittings and rich cargo had been fine pickings for the wreckers—ghoulish villagers Miranda was sometimes ashamed to call neighbors, let alone friends.

Like the noisy gulls that swooped low over the fishing boats looking for fish heads and guts, they had appeared within moments of the ship's running aground, as if summoned by some preternatural call.

With little ado, they had eagerly laid claim to whatever washed ashore. Indeed, no item had been deemed too small to be overlooked.

Miranda's lips thinned in distaste. Still, abhorrent as it was to her, unlike smuggling there was nothing illegal about "wrecking." Far from it!

A royal charter, granted the people of the coastal villages of England several hundred years ago, allowed the villagers to salvage the cargoes of any vessels wrecked upon their shores by right of "Custom and Descent," so long as the Crown was paid its portion of the pickings, and the Customs' House received its revenues.

Even the village parson, the Rev. Boreham, had been known to participate when the fancy took him, man of God or nay. In fact, she had seen him picking through the booty himself by the gray light of dawn the following morning, rather than ministering to the dead. Still, lawful or no, it was not a tradition in which Miranda's family participated.

Fishermen themselves, as well as farmers, her father and two brothers knew firsthand what a fickle, deadly mistress the sea could prove, smiling one minute, snarling the next.

To profit from the deaths of fellow sailors, however legal, left them with a foul taste in their mouths. After all, it could so easily have been they who had drowned that night, and their own families the ones left to grieve. . . .

Smuggling, however, now, that was another matter entirely.

Before a headstone that was newer than most, one only lightly marked by moss and weather, Miranda sank to her knees on a tussock of grass, her skirts and petticoats billowing about her.

The pale gray face of the headstone bore the legend:

DANIEL JOHN TALLANT
b. 1758–d. 1790
BELOVED HUSBAND

The wildflowers she'd gathered earlier that morning were wilted now. But, Daniel, God bless him, had gone past caring about such matters, she thought, gently placing the limp flowers on the grassy mound. Besides, it was the thought that counted. That, and the caring behind it.

"I miss you, Daniel," she murmured. Kissing her fingertips, she touched them to the headstone.

He had been a good and affectionate husband. And if the love between them had not been the exciting, grand passion she'd read of and once dreamed of finding, it had still been love. It had been a love rooted deep in friendship, like a sturdy sapling rooted in rich dark soil.

There was nothing wrong with that. In fact, it was a great deal more than many women had.

What sort of tree would she and Daniel's marriage have grown into, over the years, she wondered idly as she plucked a tiny weed from the grassy mound. A strong and lofty oak that offered shady comfort to all who sought the shelter of its branches? Or a supple willow that bent, but never gave beneath the winds and other onslaughts of time?

She would never know now. Daniel's life, like a great tree felled before its prime, had ended abruptly, cut short when his appendix burst and spilled its poison through his body.

It had taken Dr. Hardee, who was attending a

farmer's wife in difficult labor eight miles from the inn, two hours to get to him. And by then, it had been too late.

"He was a good man, aye, your Daniel? Solid. Dependable. The salt of the earth."

She looked up to see St. Breoch's parson standing only a few feet away. Like a cat on velvet paws, he'd approached so quietly she had not heard him approach.

There was something about the man she couldn't warm to. Those tawny eyes were too knowing, too worldly, somehow, in the way they looked her over. Too sly for a man of the cloth. And all that thick black hair, those swarthy cheeks! It just didn't seem right for a parson, somehow. . . .

"Mistress Tallant? Miranda?"

"Hmm? What is it, Rev. Boreham?"

"I said, your Daniel was a good man."

"Indeed he was, sir. The very best."

"You must miss him, I'm sure? Perhaps more at . . . some times than at others?"

His words were innocuous on the surface, yet the tone in which he delivered them made her squirm with discomfort. Her chin came up. Her eyes flashed. That wretched man! He made her suddenly very aware of how deserted the little churchyard was this afternoon. There was not a

sign of the sexton, nor any other mourners
about.

"On the contrary, sir," she said firmly, turning
and marching determinedly toward the low gate
in the iron palings. "I miss my husband dread-
fully—*all* the time."

Boreham nodded, plastering on a smile that
she was sure was meant to be one of sympathy
and compassion. "Oh, I'm sure you do. But if
you should ever find yourself in need of a sympathetic ear, my dear, please, come to me at the
rectory. I'd be more than happy to offer you
whatever comfort I am able to share. Of the spir-
itual sort, of course."

"Of course. Thank you, sir. I'll have to remember that," she murmured, bobbing him a sketchy
curtsey. "A good day to you, sir."

"And to you, my dear," he murmured, wetting
lips that were somehow too red—almost carnivorous, she thought with a shudder of distaste as
she hurried away.

Still, Boreham was not the only man
hereabouts who had shown a keen interest in
her since Daniel's death. And, parson or no, Boreham was still a man beneath his parson's garb,
with as much interest in women as other men,
if the rumors about him were true. She supposed she should not think any the worse of him
for it.

As she walked back down the lane to her inn, with its six brick chimneys that rose above the treetops, she couldn't help wishing Daniel had lived long enough to enjoy its newfound prosperity.

The mail coaches recently had extended their routes into the farthest reaches of Cornwall by way of Bodmin Moor. Miranda was flattered they'd chosen the Black Gull as the hostelry where they changed their weary teams before carrying the post east, back to London.

How Daniel would have enjoyed hearing the rumbling wheels of the smart red mail coaches that clattered down the track and over the cobbles, flying into the inn yard at all hours of the day!

The coaches' arrivals were always noisy, showy ones, heralded by loud blasts of the posting horn. Liveried coachmen either clung smartly to the rear of the coach, or were seated high on the box. Dressed in showy scarlet trimmed with gold braid and wearing high black hats, the men of the royal mail were as fancy as their matched teams of high-stepping, prancing horses.

Aye, like a gust of fresh air, the mail coaches had brought excitement and progress to their sleepy little backwater. How sad it was that Dan-

iel had not lived long enough to enjoy his inn's
success.

For as long as anyone could remember, *The
Black Gull Inn* had belonged to the Tallant family.

Nathaniel Tallant, Daniel's great-grandfather,
had boasted that his ancestors had settled the
West Country long before her own family—the
Tallants' rivals!—had ever set foot on Cornish
soil, let alone farmed an acre of it, or fished its
waters.

There were those in the village who still believed that Miranda had married the last surviving Tallant for his inn and his coin, rather than
for love. But those who believed such spiteful
nonsense believed a lie.

Perhaps she and Daniel had not been giddy
sweethearts, like some she could name. But she
had nevertheless loved her husband dearly, quietly and deeply. Just as he, God rest his soul, had
loved her.

Loneliness washed over her. And restlessness.
If only Daniel had given her a babe before he
died, she thought, missing him badly. A sturdy
little lad with a shock of wheat-blond hair and
big sky-blue eyes, just like his Da's. A son could
have carried on the Tallant name and someday
run the old inn in his stead.

But alas, he had not.

Three weeks after she'd buried him, Miranda had woken in the middle of the night to find her belly knotted with cramps and her nightgown soaked with the blood of her monthly courses. Tearfully, she had been forced to accept that her womb would never quicken with Daniel's child.

In the end, as her father Thaddeus so cheerfully, and so frequently, reminded her, it was his daughter who had inherited the old inn, lock, stock and barrel. *His* blood that had triumphed over the Tallants' by the simple means of outliving every last one of them.

Brains, blood and breeding had little to do with it, in the end, her Da had declared with a crafty wink. Longevity was all!

Smiling at the memory, Miranda took off her fringed Spanish shawl and went inside.

As always, her nostrils flared with pleasure as the familiar smells assailed them. Ale, beer and the scent of the fresh sawdust that was sprinkled over the floors of polished wood which, like the rafters above, had long since grown dark with age and smoke.

It was gloomy inside. Little light managed to find its way in through the inn's mullioned windows. Her eyes had to adjust after the brilliant light of outdoors.

She had gone behind the hinged counter of the bar, hung up her shawl on its peg, and tied her bibbed apron over her skirts before she even noticed the newcomers at the bar.

Judging by their curious stares, however, the same could not be said of them! They had certainly noticed her. Or rather, one of them had.

"Well, now. A very good afternoon to you, gentlemen," she greeted as she briskly tied her apron strings. "Sorry to keep you waiting. Can I draw you both a pint?"

"You can indeed, lass. We'll take two of your best ales, and whatever hot fare your mistress is serving today," the taller, younger of the pair declared. He fished a couple of coins from his inner pocket and tossed them onto the bar. "Rode all the way from Bodmin, we have. Aye, and a hot, dusty ride it was, too!"

He was, she noticed, very dark-haired—and very handsome! His eyes—she could not discern their exact color—twinkled wickedly beneath straight black brows. He had a square, rugged jaw that hinted at an obstinate streak, yet his mouth was a generous one and, she thought, much inclined to laughter. Intriguing contrasts in a face that also reflected intelligence and wit.

"And before that?" Miranda asked, curious as she pulled the pump handle down to draw a second tankard. "You're not from 'round these parts, I warrant?"

She could tell by the way he spoke that he'd

had more schooling than most in the Cove area could lay claim to. As much of an education, perhaps, as Squire Draker up at Windhaven House, five miles to the west, or the Rev. Boreham, say. The pleasant lilt to his voice hinted at roots deep in neighboring Devon, however.

What was his business, she wondered as she set the tankards on the bar before the pair? Was he a traveling squire? Another insurance investigator from Lloyds of London? The good Lord knew, there'd been more than enough of those about lately! Four of them had taken lodgings at the Gull last month while they were in the village. They'd spent an entire week poking about, asking questions about the *Lady Anne*.

Was this man another investigator, or a member of the gentry, turned artist?

She swallowed a snort of laughter at the thought of the tall, broad-shouldered rogue with the laughing green eyes donning beret and smock. Lord, no! Not this one! He was no artist. He'd never be caught dabbling in watercolors!

"You have a keen ear, my lass," the stranger acknowledged with an amused grin and a wink that brought a blush to Miranda's cheeks. "I hail from Plymouth."

"I guessed as much, sir. And what brings you here to Lizard Cove?" she murmured, ringing a small hand bell to summon Maisie from the kitchen. "Are you an artist, perhaps?"

She looked up at him innocently through a sweep of dark tawny lashes, trying not to smile.

"We have more than our share of them 'round here. They come down from London in droves to capture our Cornish light and the changing moods of the sea. Or so they claim," she amended, suddenly embarrassed to be chattering away like a magpie.

"Do they, now? Well, I doubt Mr. Longfield or myself have an artistic bone in our bodies between us, do we, Simon?" he declared, looking her over in a bold, assessing way that made her stomach flutter in a silly, yet wholly feminine response. "We were sent by Trinity House—the office that runs the lighthouses, aye? I'm to be the Lizard's keeper, once Mr. Longfield here has properly taught me my duties."

"A lighthouse keeper? You?" *Him?* she echoed silently. Was he teasing her? She'd never seen anyone who looked less like a lighthouse keeper than this tall, devilishly handsome man!

"As I said, I'm Keeper Morgan St. James. Your obedient servant, ma'am." He inclined his head, an amused smile drawing up the corners of his mouth.

"And yours, Keeper St. James," she murmured, bobbing a curtsey and hiding a smile of her own as she politely inclined her head.

So. She had been right about Billy Ashe not coming back. Good riddance to him, too, the idle wretch! The cove was better off without a lighthouse keeper who abandoned his post and neglected the light he was sworn to tend. His fondness for rum had cost good men their lives.

"I take it you'll be needing lodgings here for the next few nights, then?"

"How so?" the stranger asked, frowning now. "I was told there was a keeper's cottage attached to the lighthouse."

Dark green. His eyes were dark green, she noticed suddenly. Green flecked with gold and hazel and sparkling with life, as if sunlight had been trapped in their shining depths. Looking into them was like gazing into a deep woodland pool, with sunshine slanting across its surface.

"There . . . er . . . there is." Embarrassed by her fanciful thoughts, she quickly looked down at the bar top and pretended an interest in wiping its spotless if scarred surface, though only the good Lord knew what she was cleaning! "But the last keeper left it in a sorry state. It'll need a thorough cleaning before it's fit to live in," she mumbled.

"Perhaps a girl from the village might be willing to clean it up a bit? For a price, of course?"

She laughed. "I doubt you'll find anyone, Mr.

St. James. The good people of Lizard Cove would sooner let their daughters keep house for the devil than a stranger, good coin or no!"

"Is that so?" He looked more amused than annoyed by her careless comment—one that had slipped out before she thought to curb her tongue. "Then we'll have to shift for ourselves, won't we?"

Miranda turned bright pink. "Perhaps not. I'll see what I can do for you. Our Maisie might be willing."

"Maisie?"

"Maisie Pettit. The serving girl."

"Yes. We would appreciate it. Meanwhile, has your master any rooms available?"

Miranda hid a smile. "We have ten rooms at the Gull, sir. At present, only three are occupied. I'm sure those that are vacant are more than adequate for your needs."

"Thank you, ma'am," he murmured, inclining his head in a cordial, if teasing fashion, and tipping his tricorn hat.

His gallantry brought a smile to Miranda's lips. It also confirmed her first impression that the tall, handsome stranger was of the gentry. The black-sheep scion of some well-placed family, perhaps? Or a prodigal son, driven from the family nest for some misdeed or other, now forced to make his own way in the world?

But even so, as a lighthouse keeper? . . .

"Summon the landlord for me, there's a good lass," the dark one ordered, breaking into her idle thoughts. "Then bring hot water up to our rooms. The track across Bodmin is a damned dusty one this time of year."

"Very good, sir. Is that all you'll be wanting, *sir*?" she shot back, riled by his tone. As men were wont to do, he had simply assumed she was a serving wench, rather than the innkeeper. His tone said as much.

He frowned, clearly wondering what he'd said to put the fire in her eyes and the frost in her tone. "For now, aye. Thank you, ma'am."

She nodded, her anger fizzling. It wasn't his fault, after all, if she was young enough to be a serving girl, and a woman where he'd expected a man.

"You're quite welcome, sir. Now. If you'll have a seat and enjoy your ales, I'll see that your rooms are readied and hot water is brought up for you. Big Jan will be here shortly with your victuals. Enjoy your stay, Mr. St. James. Mr. Longfield."

Green eyes twinkled in his striking face as he looked down at her. It was a strong face, she noticed, one filled with intelligence, character, experience and, she fancied, more than its fair

45

share of sadness, despite the glint of laughter in his eyes.

"I'm sure we shall find our accommodations most satisfactory, lass," he said softly, "if they are half as fetching as the barmaid."

Barmaid, indeed! She'd give him "barmaid!" But when he looked at her that way, what he called her didn't matter anymore. What mattered was that her hair was windblown, her lace cap lost, and her simple draw-necked shift and worn green skirts too wretched for words. How rustic she must look to an educated man like him. He probably thought her a proper country bumpkin!

Annoyed that she'd not given more thought to her appearance before greeting her guests, she turned smartly on her heel and went down the passageway to the inn's kitchen, calling for Maisie as she went.

Carrying both tankards of ale, the man St. James had introduced as Simon Longfield led the way across the taproom to a worn wooden settle, one of a pair placed on either side of an equally worn trestle table.

"Very fetching, eh, Simon?" Morgan St. James observed, following him. He nodded in the direction the young woman had taken. "Very fetching, indeed! Cornwall's scenic properties impress me more with every moment!"

"Hhrrumph," Longfield snorted. "So you said."

With a shrug and a grin, Morgan followed his taciturn companion to a seat at the settle the young woman had indicated. A confirmed bachelor, Simon Longfield struck Morgan as a man too much in awe of women. The fresh, vivid beauty of the young serving woman, the sheer vitality that surrounded her, had clearly rendered the older man speechless!

Although it was late August, a peat fire burned on the wide stone hearth. Its warmth and cheery glow were welcome, for chill winds off the Atlantic Ocean blew unobstructed across coast and moor in these parts. And, once inside, out of the sunshine, it was chilly, late summer or no.

Despite the bleakness of the moors, the Gull's landlord had taken pains to make his rustic inn a warm, welcoming place, Morgan observed. It was a fine hostelry where patrons could enjoy an ale and whatever tasty fare his wife had prepared in comfort.

He would wager the rooms were as clean as the radiant young serving woman had been, the bed linens likewise fresh-laundered, the fare tasty and well-prepared. Although a rural inn, set in an all but isolated spot, the Gull had a well-tended air to it.

"When we're settled, let's take a stroll up t' the

47

lighthouse, shall we, sir?" Simon suggested, stuffing the corner of a snowy linen napkin into his collar. He took up knife and fork, anxious to be fed. "See for ourselves what needs doin'?"

Morgan nodded as he drank, his mind only half on what the older man was saying. Instead, his thoughts were taken up by a far more pleasing subject. That of the Black Gull's lovely barmaid.

Now, there was a lass for a man to dream of in his lonely bunk! A beautiful woman like that could make a man forget his real reason for coming to Lizard Cove.

Almost.

Chapter Three

The Lizard Lighthouse had been built upon a craggy granite point that jutted out into the fierce Atlantic some fifty feet below. A pointed, black witch's hat crowned the whitewashed tower's glass eye, and a short passageway joined the lighthouse proper to the keeper's two-room cottage.

A shingled path, on either side of which bloomed scraggly rose bushes, led up to its front door. With the exception of a single bud, however, the delicate pink blooms had been battered to bits by the onshore winds. Such a location called for hardier inhabitants than those delicate blossoms.

Morgan whistled as he ducked his head to go inside the little dwelling. The place was in shambles, exactly as the young woman at the Gull had warned him.

"Not exactly what you're used to, I dare say, sir?" Simon observed, looking about him.

"I've stayed in worse places. From the look of things, the last keeper left in some haste. Do you agree?"

"I do, indeed, sir."

Morgan sighed. "The name is Morgan, Simon. Or St. James. You can drop the 'sir.' Remember? The plan, man! You're supposed to be my senior."

"Very good, s . . . Morgan," Simon agreed unhappily.

The first room was large by cottage standards, yet the single small window let in little light. The hearth was obviously used for heating the cottage as well as for cooking, but with its earthen floor, it would still be a bleak, cold place to live come winter.

If all went well, he'd be gone long before then.

The furniture had been overturned and broken, as if hurled against the wall and left where it chanced to fall. A wooden stool lay half in and half out of the ashes in the hearth.

Morgan crouched down for a closer look. One leg was badly charred. Fragments of white ash

50

crumbled away when he touched the stump. In fact, everything he'd seen so far supported Ashe's account of events the night the *Lady Anne* ran aground.

After being surprised by his attackers while filling the Argand, he'd been dragged down the iron stairs to the keeper's cottage. There, he'd been beaten to within an inch of his life. He had come around to find himself alone, apparently left for dead. Battered and bleeding, he had crawled outside to find help.

Instead, he had looked on in horror as those poor devils who survived the wreck of the *Lady Anne* struggled to shore, only to be clubbed to death there.

Ashe had become, in effect, a reluctant witness to their murders.

Spotted by one of the wreckers, he'd quickly realized his own life was in jeopardy and had fled with only the clothes on his back.

Battered and bleeding, Ashe, now a fugitive and uncertain whom he could call friend or foe, had passed that dreadful night hidden under a leaky rowboat pulled up onto the beach.

At first light, he'd managed to stumble up onto Bodmin Road, where a farmer driving a cart piled high with seaweed had found him and taken him as far as Bodmin.

From there, Ashe had managed to make his

way to Plymouth, and thence to London, and the Dorchester Square townhouse of sirs Robert and Morgan St. James, who owned the St. James' Shipping Line.

Everything about the condition of the cottage supported rather than contradicted the lighthouse keeper's story.

Enamelled tin pans were scattered about on the stone-flagged floor, along with a dented enamel plate or two. Several wooden shelves stood empty, except for a thick layer of dust and grit. One shelf hung by a solitary nail.

In another corner, a sack of flour and another of potatoes had burst and spilled their contents into the room. The foul stench of rotted potatoes made him gag.

"Either Billy Ashe was a bloody poor housewife, or this is where they beat him," Morgan observed, stepping around the debris to the far room, which proved in no better condition than the first.

A narrow bed stood against the whitewashed wall. It was spread with a thin pallet of striped ticking on which ominous rusty stains had spread and dried. The keeper's blood? He thought so.

A blanket lay in a gray puddle of wool upon the floor. All other bed linens, if there had been others, were gone now.

But nowhere did he find any evidence of bottles, jugs, or liquor of any kind. An odd occurrence, surely, in the cottage of a man reputed to be a drunkard?

A peg upon one wall held a few dark, threadbare garments, heavily yet tidily darned in the sailor's methodical fashion. A wooden sea chest at the foot of the bed, carved with the initials W. A., and a sailor's canvas duffle bag held other equally worn garments, sewing and darning kits, and so on. There was nothing more, except for the cobwebs in every corner, and the layer of gritty sand underfoot that had blown in through the open door.

"The Gull has much to recommend it, compared to this grimy hovel, aye?" Morgan observed softly.

"I'm not surprised you'd think so, s . . . Morgan," Simon agreed, removing his reefer jacket and rolling up the sleeves of his collarless shirt. "I'll get to work burning the pallets."

It wasn't so much a statement as a challenge, Morgan thought, nodding and following suit. He grinned. Longfield was a feisty old devil, not afraid of hard work, nor too proud to bend his back to any worthy task.

But then, neither was Morgan. If nothing else, being at sea for several years had taught him the value of neatness and order.

"Add a cat to the list of things we need," Simon told Morgan with a look of distaste as he stripped the ticking pallet from the bed frame. Nestled snugly in its worn cover were several nests of squirming baby mice.

"I'll run these little 'uns off, then I'll burn the pallet, aye? Cats and dogs I can stomach. But I don't fancy these little blighters in my mattress."

"No?" Morgan grinned. "They're an improvement over some I've shared mine with." He shook his head as Longfield, clearly a pious sort, shot him a reproving glance. "I meant *vermin*, Longfield. Not women. You've not seen rats till you've been to the Orient. Big as dogs, the water rats are there, and vicious besides."

"Happen they are, sir. But we'll get that mouser anyway, aye?" Longfield suggested, tossing Morgan the broom. "Here you go, sir. If you'll get started with the sweeping, I'll cart this lot outside and burn t' worst of it, aye? And while you're at it, open the doors and windows, would ye, sir? A bit o' sunshine and some fresh sea air will improve the smell of the place no end, I'm thinking. By the time we're done, we'll have ourselves a roaring appetite for the inn's roast lamb."

"Roasted lamb, was it? I didn't notice. My mind was on other matters." He winked.

Simon snorted his disapproval. "If you ask

me, Mr. St. James, you already have a substantial appetite, sir, and not only for the innkeeper's lamb," he said without smiling.

"*Information*, Simon. That's all I'm after there," he insisted with a patently evil grin. "Information, pure and simple. And serving girls do love to gossip, don't they?"

It was almost dusk before Morgan left the lighthouse again.

Casually clad in reefer jacket and sailor's canvas breeches, he headed down Gull Lane with an easy, loose-limbed stride, striking out for the village. He'd a mind to have a drink elsewhere before he ate his supper at the inn. The damned dust in the cottage had left him with a dry throat! He'd combine a bit of reconnoitering with slaking his thirst. . . .

Fishermen's cottages, each unique in design and color, clung to either side of the steep, twisting cobbled street that led down to the harbor, where there was a chandler's, a cooper's and a tavern, among other small shops.

Several fishing boats bobbed at their moorings along the stone quay, while a quarter-mile down the beach, he could see rowboats of various colors dragged up onto the golden shingle, beyond reach of the incoming tide.

It was beneath one of those that Ashe must

have hidden to escape the wreckers. . . .

A few hungry gulls, refusing to abandon their day's quest for stray pilchards, still wheeled overhead, screaming mournfully.

A disreputable-looking tavern stood close to the small stone quay. The painted sign read The Safe Harbor.

Several men, all fishermen, judging by their jerseys, canvas trousers and knitted caps, sat outside the tavern on a wooden bench.

Tankards in hand, they sipped their ale and enjoyed the gaudy display of a fiery sun as it slipped over the horizon.

One man was mending his nets, deftly weaving the shuttle in and out of the mesh. Another puffed dreamily on a clay pipe as he gazed out to sea.

Yet Morgan felt every eye fasten upon him as he approached. And to the last man, they were hostile, wary eyes, filled with suspicion and mistrust. Exactly as he'd expected.

The fishermen of Cornwall were not so very different from those of his native Devon, after all. Raised in small coastal villages where smuggling was rife and the Preventive or Excise men were sworn enemies, locals were invariably suspicious of outsiders.

"A good evening to you, gentlemen," Morgan

greeted them with a cordial nod. "A fine night, is it not?"

Without further ado, he stepped past them into the Harbor's taproom.

The public house was a dark hole that reeked of burning whale oil and fried fish. The light dispelled the gloom in smelly amber puddles. It was a far cry from the hospitable aromas of lavender and beeswax at the Black Gull.

In the murk, Morgan could make out several wooden figureheads, taken from sailing vessels of the last century. Bare-breasted mermaids, saucy goddesses, sea nymphs and heroines hung upon the taproom's smoke-blackened walls.

The proprietor was a massive fellow with a bald dome that shone pinkly in the lantern's light, and a huge belly. Swabbing the counter with a dirty rag, he was deep in conversation with a younger man as Morgan came in.

Both fell silent and glanced up as he entered, their uninterested expressions changing to ones of curious caution when they saw the newcomer.

"A pint, if you please, landlord." Morgan fished a few copper coins from his waistcoat pocket and tossed them onto the bar.

"A pint it is," the landlord said gruffly, manning the pump. "Not from around these parts, are ye, sir?" he observed as he drew the foaming ale. He cast Morgan an inquiring look.

"Nooo. I'm a Plymouth man, born and bred. The name's St. James. Morgan St. James. And yours would be? . . ." He offered his hand.

The landlord ignored it.

"Might I inquire what business ye have in Lizard Cove, Mr. St. James?"

"Not smuggling business, that's for sure. At least, not yet, it isn't," Morgan assured the man with a wink. "Put your hackles down, man. I'm no bloody Preventive, if that's what makes ye so surly. Trinity House sent me down to Cornwall. They administer the running of all the lighthouses in England, including the Lizard light."

"Oh, do they now?" The landlord leaned across the counter, and grinned nastily at Morgan. "And what if I told ye we don't give a damn who administers what? We don't want no bloody keepers here!"

Morgan gave a casual shrug. His features implacable, he responded softly, "Take the matter up with Trinity House, then. I have my orders. Now. That pint, if you please, landlord. I've a powerful thirst on me."

The landlord picked up the tankard he'd filled and emptied its foaming contents into a slop jar.

"Slake it elsewhere, St. James. The Safe Harbor's run dry for the likes of you," he sneered.

"Suit yourself," Morgan murmured. As the man reached out, intending to pocket Morgan's coin, Morgan neatly swept it off the bar and into his own hand. Turning, he nodded to the only other patron. "A good evening to you, sir."

The man, a lean, handsome fellow, quick and alert as a whippet, had thick golden-brown hair worn in an old-fashioned queue. In one ear, he sported a golden earring. His eyes were as blue and untrammeled as the summer sky.

There was something familiar about him, though Morgan could not think what it was. As far as he knew, he'd never laid eyes on the fellow until that moment.

Not unexpectedly, the louts who'd been piled on the bench outside were blocking his exit when he left. To a man, their expressions were ugly.

"Step aside, friends. Let me pass."

" 'Friend' is it? Hark at him, lads! Talks pretty, don't he—for someone about t'get his teeth loosened!"

"Coming from you, I'll take that as a compliment."

Morgan smiled thinly. "Father invested a pretty penny in my schooling, before he disowned me." He grinned. "Care to find out what I learned on the docks of Macau? Or perhaps in the brothels of Persia?" He cracked his knuckles, his mirthless smile more chilling than any verbal threat.

"This 'un says he's to keep the Lizard light, boys," a deep voice explained behind him.

Morgan knew without turning around that the tavern's landlord had followed him outside.

"Morgan St. James, he calls hisself," the fat, bald man added darkly.

One of the men sniffed at Morgan. "Lightkeeper, eh? Smells more like Preventive man t'me." He spat onto the cobbled quay.

"Aye, and me," muttered several of the others.

"Sorry to disappoint you, lads. In fact, if we're talking about smuggling—" he cocked a dark eyebrow at the disreputable looking lot—"I've indulged in the free trade myself, a time or two." He winked and tapped the side of his nose. "The gaming hells of London don't come cheap, if you take my meaning. And I, alas, have an appetite for games of chance!" He shrugged. "A man does what he must."

"We lads wouldn't know about that. Gambling's for rich men, not God-fearing, law-abiding fishermen like us. Be off with ye, St. James, if that's really yer name. And don't bother coming back!"

"Least, not if ye know what's good for ye!" another added, cracking his knuckles as Morgan had done. "We've learned a pretty trick or two ourselves, aye?"

"A warm welcome to you, too, my friends," Morgan muttered under his breath as he shrugged off the fishermen, and climbed back up the steeply cobbled street that met Gull Lane.

He could feel the louts watching him as he went, but it wasn't until he reached the lane that he realized he was not alone. The young man with the earring had followed him out of the Safe Harbor.

"I can find my own way, friend," he said in a deceptively mild tone. "You've no cause to follow me home."

"I'm not. We're both headed the same way, St. James. And I wanted to tell you, you can get yourself that pint at the Gull without bruising your knuckles. That is where you're staying, is it not?" the man called after Morgan.

"News travels fast 'round these past. Aye! I went down there hoping for a hand or two of cards, or a game of dice." He nodded in the direction of the Safe Harbor. "Your friends gave me the cold shoulder instead."

"You moved too fast. Made the lads wary of ye. The people of Lizard Cove need time to accept newcomers. They're afraid of strangers, aye? That's all there is to it."

Morgan grinned. "I know. I'm from Plymouth."

The younger man held out his hand. "Rob Killigrew. You met my sister Miranda this morning. Brandy-colored hair? Turquoise eyes?"

"Ah, yes, The comely serving wench."

"Serving wench!" He snorted with laughter. "She'll blister your ears, if she hears ye call her that. She's your landlady, aye, not a servant! Mistress Miranda Tallant."

Morgan only dimly heard what he'd said after supplying his name. Rob *Killigrew!* The same name Ashe had given him. And what else had the man said? That his sister was the serving woman at the Gull. He groaned silently. No, not the serving woman. His *landlady*—and a married woman, to boot! Small wonder the lady had bristled at his flirtatious banter!

"Well, well. Is she, now?" Morgan murmured, frowning as he rubbed his chin. "That would explain the lady's immediate dislike of me. I . . . er . . . I'm afraid I mistook your Miranda for a . . . er . . . a serving woman." Morgan grimaced.

"You never did?" Rob's grin deepened, setting the blue eyes to sparkling in his lean, wind-browned face. He snorted, hard put to control his laughter. "Flirted with her a bit, did ye?"

He laughed heartily when Morgan's unhappy expression confirmed that he had.

"Ho! Our 'Randa won't have liked that, I'm thinking. Very sensitive about such matters, she is. Gave you a taste of her tongue, did she? Aye, I thought as much. And a bloody sharp tongue it is, too, when she chooses, God love her!"

Morgan chuckled as they crossed the cobbled yard to the door of the Black Gull. "To give Mistress—?"

"Tallant. Miranda Tallant."

"To give Mistress Tallant her due, the lady practiced considerable restraint, despite having been deeply insulted by me. There was frost in her tone, yet in every other way, she was a most gracious hostess."

"Has a quick temper, Miranda does. Had it ever since she was a babby," Rob declared with some pride. "Takes after our Mam, Da' says. Spirited woman, our mam is. Have you met Da' yet?"

Morgan shook his head. "No."

"You will, soon enough." He grinned. "Go on in with you."

"Can I stand you a jar?"

Rob grinned. "Later, perhaps. I'll hold you to the offer, aye?"

With a nod, Morgan went inside.

This evening, the Gull's taproom was crowded with noisy patrons, he saw.

Pipe smoke clung to open rafters gone black

63

over the years, and the air was warm and full of smells. The savory aroma of lamb and onions. Ale and spirits. Sweat and damp wool.

The patrons seemed decent, simple folk, for the most part. Fishermen, farmers and shepherds drawn from their cottages or their isolated farms and flocks up on the moorlands by a common hunger to meet with others of their kind. Several shaggy sheepdogs sprawled at their masters' feet.

All eyes turned to Morgan as he stepped inside the door and shouldered his way to the bar. The buzz of conversation stilled momentarily. But the glances cast his way here were more curious than hostile, as they had been at the Safe Harbor. Or so he fancied.

"Mr. St. James! Over here, sir!"

Following Longfield's energetic wave, he wove his way between the press of drinkers to the same wooden settle at which they'd eaten their noon meal.

Simon was seated before a foaming tankard. Hovering at his elbow was a pretty serving girl with a neat lace cap pinned to her braided, dark-brown hair. Her sac and skirt were both neat as a pin under a snowy apron, he noted approvingly. The landlord ran a fine establishment, from what he'd seen of it so far. Or rather, he amended, his beautiful wife did. Where was the fortunate fellow who'd wed such a jewel, he wondered, looking around for someone who looked the part of Tallant, innkeeper and lucky dog.

His eye fell on a brace of stocky blond giants drinking in the corner, and lingered there.

The pair's height and girth dwarfed all other men in the taproom. The younger one's hair was the color of wheat, the older one's grayed yellow with age. Both faces were ruddy and flushed as farmers. Of Danish or German extract, by the looks of them, Morgan decided. Father and son, undoubtedly. Could the younger of the two be the lovely innkeeper's husband?

At that moment, the younger man chanced to look up. When his vivid blue eyes met Morgan's, they filled with hostility and challenge, like an enraged bull.

Morgan met that maddened glare head on, then casually looked elsewhere, coolly dismissing both the man, his size and the threat he presented, before taking his seat opposite Longfield. He'd made enough enemies for one day without courting more. Nevertheless, he did not intend to back down if it came to that.

"Simon, have you supped already?"

"Not yet, no. Mr. St. James, Maisie here has a cat for us."

The serving girl gave him a shy smile.

"Ah. And is this cat of yours a good mouser, Maisie?" he asked, lowering his long frame onto the settle and favoring Maisie with a slow, appreciative smile. "We've mice to spare at the keeper's cottage."

Miranda knew the very second the new keeper came in, despite the crowd in the taproom.

It wasn't surprising, really. Morgan St. James was hardly the sort of man to go unnoticed, even in a crowd. He was too tall, too dark, too ruggedly good-looking not to stand out in any gathering, and especially here!

There were few women in the taproom, but every one of them turned to gawk at her guest, openly admiring what she saw, the bold baggages.

By far the boldest in her appraisal was Lady Dinah Draker, Squire Draker's beautiful and much younger wife. The pair and their coterie of friends had stopped off at the Gull on their way home from the Bodmin Horse Fair. They had come, they declared noisily, to celebrate the squire's purchase of a fine new hunter and a team of matched carriage horses by dining on the Gull's famous lamb pie, washed down by the inn's finest ales and spirits.

Dinah Draker wore wine-red velvet from head to toe, Miranda noted with a tiny twinge of envy.

Her riding habit had been cut to display her striking hourglass figure to its greatest advantage.

Her skin was pale and luminous, her lustrous hair as black as a raven's wing, while her long-lashed eyes were a tawny amber that glittered as she stared covetously across at the handsome newcomer, now seated at the corner table.

Miranda sniffed in disgust. Look at her, the bold baggage, openly ogling another man—and her husband not three feet away! Still, the lady of Windhaven's reputation had always been less than lily-white.

Gossip claimed beautiful Dinah was the love child of a widow who had been the housekeeper of a bishop. They claimed Dinah had wed the widowed squire, who was besotted by her dark beauty, when her mama passed away, and her own father refused to acknowledge her as his own, or support her in any fashion.

In return, Draker had lavished his fortune on his sixteen-year-old bride, indulging her every whim in return for her virginity.

Now the lady in question had reached the jaded age of twenty-and-four, and there were those who claimed Draker's fortune had been bled dry by his wife's expensive tastes and love of luxury. It was also rumored that Lady Dinah took lovers behind her middle-aged husband's back: virile young farm lads and gardeners with muscle and stamina and certain other physical attributes, who were willing and able to indulge the whims her husband was unable—or unwilling—to satisfy.

Miranda's own face flamed. Was she any better than the bold Lady Dinah? She had been staring quite openly at Morgan St. James herself. Still, to be honest, she couldn't seem to help herself! He was, after all, a handsome devil, and a fine figure of a man, even if his looks were not really to her liking and his manner far too forward and saucy.

She liked men who were big, blond and gentle, not like the Coppingers, but as her Daniel had been. Men who looked like great, gruff bears, but were gentle as lambs at heart.

Feminine instinct warned her that Morgan St. James was no lamb. Quite the opposite! There was a certain wicked sparkle in the way those deep-green eyes looked a woman over that screamed big, bad wolf! Such dark, intense, good looks hinted at dark, intense emotions in the man, too. Fierce desires and passions that were as out-of-control as a runaway horse, or a raging storm.

Just the thought of being swept up in such a storm of desire made her shiver. . . .

Such a man would not suit her, no, indeed!

She had no wish to be swept off her feet, forced to feel things no decent woman should ever want to feel, she reminded herself sharply. She prided herself on being calm and collected, always in control of herself and of her emotions. She took pains to squelch the flights of fancy she had, sometimes, about leaving this sleepy little cove and sailing clear around the world to see the places she'd only dreamed about. Why, she pitied the poor woman who succumbed to St. James's roguish good looks, she told herself—if some poor woman had not already succumbed!

There might, of course, be a Mrs. Morgan St. James, and a handful of handsome little Morgans. . . .

It was, for some reason, a most unsettling thought.

Miranda's eyes narrowed when she noticed Maisie leading the wolf in question through the noisy, laughing crowd. They were headed for a side door that led out to the stables.

Why, that lecherous rogue, she thought indignantly. Not twenty-four hours beneath her roof, and he a married man with children, no less, yet there he was, trying to take advantage of a serving girl's sweet, good-natured innocence!

She'd see about that!

Angrily winding her way between her patrons, she followed the pair outside.

Sweet night air billowed all around her as she stepped down into the inn yard, warm and scented with geraniums, honeysuckle, phlox and sweet williams. The flower perfumes were underscored by the scents of kelp and brine off the sea. The heady fragrance was intoxicating in its sweetness.

"Maisie! Where are you off to?"

"I were just going to take Mr. St. James to the stable, mum."

"I think not. Run along inside, my girl. There are tankards waiting to be filled, aye? Our patrons don't like to be kept waiting, do they? Go on, now. I'll see to our new guest."

"Very well, mum," Maisie said sheepishly, the smile fading from her shy, pretty face. Darting a quick glance over her shoulder at St. James, who smiled and nodded, Maisie picked up her skirts and scuttled past her mistress, back to the taproom.

"Well, now. What business have you with my servants that warrants a visit to the horse sheds after dark, Mr. St. James?" Miranda demanded sharply when Maisie was gone. "Is something amiss with your horse?"

"Blame me, if you must, Mistress Tallant. Not the lass. She wanted only to show me a cat," St. James explained softly, an amused smile playing about his lips. Her tone was sharp, her expression annoyed, almost as if she was jealous.

Temper had given her cheeks a flush of high color, too, and made her stunning turquoise eyes as radiant as jewels. He could readily imagine her clothed in peacock velvet, edged with the finest Brussels lace, her brandywine hair caught up and intricately dressed with sapphire pins. Flicking his head to banish the delightful image, he pushed a dark lock of hair back from his brow.

"Simon feels we're in desperate need of a mouser up at the lighthouse. The keeper's cottage is overrun with mice, you see? Maisie says you have cats to spare?"

"Cats? Oh, yes, indeed we have, Mr. St. James," Miranda confirmed with a tight nod and a disbelieving little smile. "If you'll follow me, I'll show you them."

She led him into the stables, where the mail and stage teams rested in the soft amber glow of a single lantern. The scents of hay and horseflesh, saddle-soap and leather harness were pungent on the warm air.

"It's just me, Tommy!" she called to the bleary-eyed stableboy who peered at them from a heap of hay in one of the horse stalls. "Go back to sleep."

She stopped before an empty corner of the carriage house, where a huge ginger queen, her eyes half-closed in contentment, lay upon the straw.

Five half-grown kittens nursed at her swollen teats, their fat little paws rhythmically kneading her belly.

Even standing as she was, Miranda could hear their contented purring.

"These are Maisie's cats, Mr. St. James. Hardly old enough to be the mousers you're needing. Still, I'm sure Dolly wouldn't miss one or two, would you, Doll?" She crouched down. "They've been weaned for some time now, but they still love to nurse. And this silly old thing lets them, don't you, Doll?" she murmured, tickling the mother cat beneath the chin. "She's a wonderful mother."

The cat closed her golden eyes and purred in delight.

Morgan hid a smile. He'd purr, too, if she were to tickle him beneath the chin.

Crouching down, he inspected the kittens one by one, plucking the greedy little beasts from their mother's rosy, elongated nipples. They responded with sleepy meows of protest, dribbles of milk on their little chins.

He examined each kitten in turn, finally selecting two fat little females, one a smoky gray with white paws and a white bib, the other a fluffy calico of ginger and white.

"She-cats make the best hunters, they say. This pretty pair will do well, Mistress Tallant," he declared, to her obvious surprise. Her expression was priceless. His lovely landlord must have thought the quest for a mouser was merely a ruse to entice her Maisie into the stables for a quick romp!

"They're big enough to scare off the mice for now, aye?" he added, still amused. "And in a few weeks, they'll be big enough to eat them, won't you, girls?" he murmured, rubbing his face against the kittens' soft fur.

"I'm not surprised the keeper's cottage has mice. Mr. Ashe—he was the former lighthouse keeper—he left quite suddenly, and took nothing with him. They'll have been in the stores, I expect. The mice, I mean."

"Why was that?" he asked casually. "Why did he leave? Do you know?"

Miranda straightened, watching as he tucked the two squirming kittens into the front of his waistcoat, so that only their pointed little faces and ears showed. She was clearly wondering how best to answer him. Did her hesitation imply something? A knowledge of her family's doings?

He realized he was hoping desperately that it did not.

"I'm sure I don't know," she murmured at length, looking away.

Disappointment filled him. The woman was lying! He could see it in her face, as plain as day.

"No? I'm surprised. I would have thought the mistress of the only inn hereabouts would know all the goings on."

"Well, there was talk, of course. . . ." she allowed, plainly reluctant to gossip about Lizard Cove matters with an outsider. "But then, there's always talk in a place this size. Only . . . one never knows how much of it is true."

"Rest assured, ma'am, that you may trust me with your confidences." A slow, sensual smile curved his generous lips. "I am not a man to . . . kiss and tell, shall we say?"

She blushed. "Very well, then. They say that Keeper Ashe was a heavy drinker. That he fell into a stupor one night last month and allowed the Lizard light to go out. That same night, a terrible storm blew in from the ocean. Without light to guide her, a schooner ran aground on Lizard Point, and there was great loss of life. Naturally, the men in the village were angered by Ashe's negligence. Still are!"

"I see. But that doesn't explain Mr. . . . Ashe was it? Mr. Ashe's departure."

"He was to blame for the deaths, don't you see? His negligence caused them. To punish him for what he'd done, some of the men beat him, then ran him out of the village."

"Ah. I see. Well, if the wretch allowed the light to go out, I dare say he deserved what he got," Morgan said softly. "Your father and brother are to be commended."

She frowned. "Why them?"

"For seeing the guilty party held to account."

"My brothers and Da' had nothing to do with Ashe's whipping," she denied sharply. "That was . . . well, it was other men's doings."

"Would you happen to know their names? I'd like to reassure them."

"Of what?"

Meeting her slanted turquoise eyes, he murmured, "That it won't happen again. At least, not while I'm keeper." A chilling, mirthless smile hovered about his lips. "Mark my words, Mistress Tallant."

Miranda shivered. There was something in St. James's voice, some kindling in the depths of those deep-green eyes, that made her suddenly very much aware that they were alone, except for the animals in their stalls, and a young lad who was hard of hearing.

His crisp black hair shone in the lantern light. The same amber glow burnished his lean, rugged face, yet cast the rest of him in mystery and shadow. Some trick of light and shade gave him a dangerous look. He could have been a ruthless scoundrel, a dashing highwayman, a privateer, instead of a lighthouse keeper. . . . if that was truly what he was.

Again, she felt a tug of response to the man. An awareness, a sexual stirring, deep in her belly. He was not her sort at all, she reminded herself hastily. But Lord, he was handsome, for all that!

"As I recall, I was uncivil to you this morning, ma'am," he observed softly, his voice as smooth as cider. "I implore you to accept my apologies. I could claim I mistook you for a serving woman, and in so doing, attempt to excuse myself. But that would be a poor excuse on my part. Even a servant has the right to expect common courtesy, does she not?"

"Indeed she does, sir," Miranda admitted with a shy, pleased smile, surprised by his candor. "Please, consider your apology accepted, and the matter ended. We shall start afresh, you and I, and I shall do my best to ensure that your brief stay with us is an enjoyable one. Now, if you'll excuse me, I really must tend to my patrons."

"A truly gracious lady, as well as a lovely one, if you will excuse my boldness in complimenting you, ma'am. Your husband is a most fortunate man, Mistress Tallant," he called after her.

She pulled up short before the kitchen door,

but did not turn around to face him as she answered. "I appreciate your compliment, sir," she told him, staring hard at the door. "But 'tis I who am the fortunate one."

And with that tiny white lie, she hurried inside.

Rob was seated at the kitchen table when she went in. He was devouring a platter of the lamb pie she'd made for her guests' supper. The savory aroma of lamb, rosemary and onions baked in a crumbly pastry crust filled the kitchen, mixed with the yeasty aroma of the bread she'd baked to go with it.

"And where have you been, little sister, that you're so flushed? Has that Carl been bothering ye again?"

Rising, Rob strode quickly to the door she'd just entered, flung it open and stuck his head outside.

Over her brother's shoulders, Miranda saw Morgan, petting the kittens he had tucked inside his waistcoat as he crossed the yard.

Rob glanced at Morgan, then back to her. A knowing grin curved his lips. "Ah. So that's the way the wind's blowing, is it?"

"The wind blows nowhere," she insisted hotly, brushing past him to close the door. "You read too much into everything."

"Do I, little sister?" Rob asked sharply. "Do I really? Is that the only reason your cheeks are on fire?"

"Yes! So stop talking nonsense, do."

"I will. But what about you? And what about tonight?" he demanded in a far lower voice. "Your . . . gentleman admirer's a guest here! What if he takes it into his head to come sniffing after you tonight?"

Infuriated, she brought the bone handle of the bread-knife down across his fingers with a thwack.

"Ouch! What was that for?" he demanded, sucking his stinging knuckles.

"For making foolish assumptions! Tonight will go as it always goes," she said firmly. "Don't you fret about my part in it. Just eat your blessed supper and worry about your own doings, Rob Killigrew. You may be my brother, but you're not my keeper—any more than he's my admirer, gentleman or otherwise," she added with a hiss.

"I'll hold my tongue when I'm convinced you have our safety at heart. We know nothing about St. James, Miranda. Nothing at all! Despite that pretty face of his, he could be a Preventive man. Remember that. Or . . . he could be just what he claims, despite his gentrified ways. The new lighthouse keeper. Until we know for sure, be on

78

your guard, aye? Don't let him sweet-talk ye into betraying us."

"Haven't I always been careful?" she flared, rounding on her brother. "I told you, the man's a guest here. No more, no less. Why, I don't even care for the looks of him!"

But as she flounced back into the taproom, guilt lent a fiery color to her cheeks and sparked a glitter in her turquoise eyes. Despite what she insisted, it was a lie.

She liked his dark and dangerous looks *too* well!

Chapter Four

The ormolu clock that sat upon the marble mantel showed a quarter past midnight when he heard the noises below his window.

The sounds were quickly followed by a low voice, telling someone to "hush."

Stepping around the basket in which the kittens slept soundly, he pinched out the candle-flame and padded to the window in his stockinged feet.

Drawing the lace curtains aside, he peered down into the cobbled inn yard below.

It was the dark of the moon. He could make out the looming bulk of the stables and the

Penelope Neri

carriage-houses, set at a right-angle to the inn proper, but little else.

No lantern pricked the darkness. Neither moon nor starlight illuminated the night. The inn yard and the rolling moors beyond were black as pitch.

Still, those muffled sounds: What had they been? And who—or what—had made them?

Picking up a sleepy kitten, and avoiding a floorboard that creaked, he went to the door and pressed his ear to the jamb.

There! A furtive footfall. The telltale creak of a door opening or closing! Someone was up and moving about down below. But who would be abroad at this hour of the night? A traveller who'd arrived late at the inn, and was in need of a bed? Or . . . someone less respectable?

Moments later, he slipped down the landing as silently as a thief. Pausing at the top of the stairs with one hand on the bannister, he put down the kitten and cocked his head to listen for tell-tale sounds.

There was none.

He'd crept half-way down the staircase when the innkeeper's wife appeared in the hallway below, so suddenly, he jumped in surprise.

"Mistress Tallant!"

The woman wore a pale wrapper over a gathered bedrobe. Long coppery hair spilled about her shoulders, unbraided and glorious. Her slanted turquoise eyes were almost feline in the gloom. They added to the illusion of otherworldliness created by the halo of light cast by her candle. It made her seem ethereal, luminous as a lovely ghost. . . .

"Trouble sleeping, Mr. St. James?" she asked, staring up at him.

The husky, almost challenging quality of her voice made his innards clench.

Another face swam out of the blackness, appearing as a pale, blunter oval beside the woman's.

Rob Killigrew, Morgan realized, catching the gleam of the man's gold earring as brother and sister stared up at him.

Feeling the brush of a furry head against his feet, he bent and scooped up the kitten that he'd brought from his room.

"On the contrary, ma'am," he explained, making a show of scratching the little beast's tufted ears. "I was fast asleep when a noise below my window woke me. Then I heard this little beast scampering up and down the landing. How she escaped from my room is a mystery to me!" He shook his head, all innocence.

"And to me," the innkeeper's wife observed drily. "I wonder what it was you heard, sir?"

Her lilting voice was smooth as silk. If it bothered her that a guest was up and snooping about her inn at this unlikely hour, she gave no sign of it. He had to admire her sangfroid.

"I thought perhaps you might be able to tell me?"

"Hmm. 'Tis difficult to say. Perhaps it was the Gull's old timbers settling, sir? Or mice, perhaps? Or . . . could it have been my brother and me?"

"Perhaps. But . . . I'm almost certain it was a horse?" he suggested, one black brow cocked in inquiry. "I could have sworn I caught the jingle of a bridle. The scrape of a horseshoe against the cobblestones. . . . Though I doubt it was the mail coach I heard, don't you?" He grinned.

"At a quarter after midnight?" Miranda Tallant's laughter tinkled, liquid silver. "Indeed I do, Mr. St James. You are quite right about the horse, though," she confirmed, smooth as silk. "It was Rob's. He came here to fetch me home. My mother has been taken ill, you see."

"Has she, indeed? I'm most sorry to hear it, ma'am. I trust the poor lady will soon recover."

She nodded. "As do we all, sir, thank you kindly. Now. If you'll go on back up to your room, sir, I'll bring you some brandied milk to help you sleep."

"Oh, don't trouble yourself on my account, ma'am." A smile curved his mouth as he scratched

84

the kitten beneath its tiny chin. Her 'suggestion' was actually an order, despite her honeyed tones. His eyes met hers and held. "I'll have no trouble nodding off now that I've satisfied my . . . curiosity. Goodnight, Robert." He nodded at Rob. "And a very goodnight to you, too, Mistress Tallant. Be sure to extend my good wishes to your husband, aye?"

"Oh, I certainly shall," Miranda promised, jabbing her elbow into Rob's ribs when he tried to speak. She bobbed Morgan a curtsey, then darted a quick, searching look at Rob, who returned her guest's nod. "Goodnight, Mr. St. James."

"Phew. That was a bloody close call. I warned you he'd be trouble," Rob said when the lighthouse keeper was gone.

"*You* warned *me?* You heard what he said. A sound woke him. A sound *you* made! I told ye to muffle the blasted bridles."

"They were muffled, my girl," Thaddeus Killigrew corrected his daughter gruffly, ducking through the secret opening at the rear of the old brick fireplace.

He was an older, slightly stooped version of Rob, his youngest son, but wore no earring. And, where Rob's hair was a golden shade of brown, his own hair was a shock of silver in the shad-

85

ows, gleaming palely against his weathered complexion.

"Took care of it myself, I did," he added.

"Still, you were heard, Da'!"

Her tone caused Thad Killigrew's head to snap up, eyes wide, alarm in every line of his face.

"Were we, by God? By whom?"

"One of the guests. A Mr. Morgan St. James of Plymouth, Devon."

"Another bloody artist, no doubt. Full of pretty fancies!" Thaddeus snorted in disgust.

"Not this one. Says he's come t' keep the Lizard light."

"Well, God help him, then!" Thad said grimly. "I'll say this for him, though. He has sharp ears, your lodger, Miranda."

Rob nodded. "Sharp as a bloody cat's."

"Or a Preventive's." Thad's silvery brows lifted inquiringly.

"Aye, could be. And from what I've seen of him, I'll wager his wits are just as sharp."

Father and son's eyes met.

"Would you now? Hmmm. I wonder. Why else would he be up and about at this hour? Tell me that?" Thad said aloud.

Rob turned his head and cast Miranda a knowing look. "There might be another reason."

"Oh ho. Smitten with our 'Randa, is he, the rogue?" Thad exclaimed softly, missing none of the silent exchange between his two youngest children. "Well, I'm not surprised, a lovely young thing like her. Aye, and a widow of no small property, to boot. He'd not be the first t'set his cap for your sister, since her Daniel passed on, would he, my lovie?" He hugged Miranda about the waist.

Angrily, she pushed him away, scowling in the gloom.

Rob grinned. "Aye. And this one's a sight prettier than Carl Coppinger, is he not, Miranda? Still, I doubt 'tis her property Mr. St. James is after." He winked. "Talks like gentry, this one does."

"Do you consider your sister too common to attract a gentleman, then?" Thad demanded angrily.

"Oh, have done, both of you. And stop talking about me as if I'm not here," Miranda snapped. "As far as St. James knows, I'm a married woman. I'm not about to enlighten him."

"Enlighten, you say. Clever lass. Words are like gold, are they not? A wise man—or woman—spends them thriftily, and where they will do the most good!"

Dropping to her knees, Miranda shook her head in exasperation as she set about laying a new fire. They'd had to extinguish the old one in order to remove the newest shipment of smug-

gled contraband from its hiding place in the
cache behind the kitchen fire. A tunnel led from
there to a sea cave on the shore below the cliffs.
Even now, a string of ponies, their hooves and
bridles muffled by sackcloth, were slipping
through the dark night, carrying the smuggled
goods across the moors and down country lanes
to their ultimate destinations.

Her hands shaking with annoyance, she
ducked her head to hide her flaming cheeks,
though it was doubtful the pair of them could
see her furious color in the murky light.

Lighting the new fire with embers saved from
the old, she lifted the soup kettle back onto its
iron hook over the coals. A kettle filled with savory broth, made rich with meat and vegetables,
was kept simmering day and night, ready for
even the latest hungry traveller. It was also the
perfect disguise for the tunnel's entrance.

"Did the others get safely away?" Thad inquired.

"Aye. It was their leave-taking St. James
heard. That new pony's too flighty. I warned Gil
not t' use him."

"I'll talk to him about it. We'd best be off ourselves now. Keep an eye on that lodger of yours,
my lass. If he wants t' flirt with ye, give the man
a chance, aye? Pretend you're interested."

"Pretend I'm *interested!* But . . . he thinks I'm married! How will it look?"

"Whist, Miranda, I'm not telling ye t' bed the man! Just t' be . . . hospitable. Smile. Draw him a pint or two, on the house. Ask him about himself and mark what he says. Then ask again, and see if he tells ye the same. I'll not sleep sound till we know more about the new keeper."

Miranda sighed. "Oh, very well. I don't even like the wretched man, but . . . I'll do what I can."

"Good lass." Her father kissed her cheek and hugged her.

"How is Mam, really?" she asked before he released her.

Thaddeus's grin faded. "Not good, lovie. Didn't recognize Gil today, she didn't. Gil, her pet! She chased him with her broom and called him a Gypsy, to boot! I've not seen him weep since he was a wee lad, but he wept like a babby today."

Miranda blinked back tears. Poor Gil. The oldest of her two brothers, he had always been Mam's favorite. This latest incident proved Mam's wits were going as nothing else had. As if they needed more proof. . . .

Remembering the caring, intelligent woman Catherine Killigrew had once been broke Miranda's heart. But since the beginning of summer, Mam had grown confused, prone to violent, often irrational outbursts. Her occasional brief returns to normalcy were torture for her family now, for they did not last. They only served to remind them of what they had lost.

"I'll come by t' see her in the morning," she promised, squeezing her father's hands. "Maisie and Big Jan can watch the inn for an hour or two. My visit will give Kitty and Juliet a bit of a rest." Kitty was Gil's wife. Juliet, Miranda's younger sister.

Thad Killigrew nodded. "You're a good lass." He kissed her cheek again. "Sleep well, my lovie . . . and mind ye, lock your door."

"Take care, Da'. A goodnight to you." His jaw was raspy with stubble beneath her lips as she rose on tiptoe to kiss him in return.

"Let's go, lad," Thaddeus told Rob.

The pair left as quietly as their half-dozen companions had done. Soon Miranda was quite alone, except for Betsy. The great black-and-white cat curled in the chimney-nook, watching Miranda with unblinking golden eyes.

She filled a saucer from the cream jug in the cold pantry, set it down before Betsy, then climbed the stairs to her chamber at the end of the landing.

His ear pressed to the wooden jamb, Morgan heard her light footfalls pass his door, then the click of the key turning as she locked the door behind her.

So. Her brother had come to fetch her to her ailing mother, had he? Morgan thought with a mirthless smile. If that were truly so, he had forgotten to take her with him when he left!

Why would the lovely witch lie about such a thing?

Why, indeed?

Unfortunately, he believed he knew, only too well. . . .

He was still thinking about Miranda Tallant the following morning, as he leaned over the iron railing of the narrow catwalk that surrounded the Lizard light's viewing room.

Enjoying what was fast becoming his favorite pastime, he gazed out at the wild, beautiful land of Cornwall, which spread in undulating green folds to east, west and north of Lizard Head. King Arthur's country, or so he'd always thought of it. The land of Camelot and Guinevere, and the irascible Merlin.

Below his vantage point, small islands of wet black rock jutted up from the gray-green Atlantic on which the lighthouse stood. On some of the bigger granite slabs basked sea lions, their chocolate eyes closed, their sleek black bellies offered in sacrifice to the warm sun of late August.

To the east, the coastline unravelled, a dramatic vista of plunging cliffs, picturesque fishing villages, mysterious coves, inlets, bays and rivers. Places that had served as home to more than one pirate.

And to the north rose the six chimneys of the Black Gull Inn, and beyond it, the rolling moors of Bodmin.

There, scattered amongst the ruins of Cornish tin mines, china clay pits and isolated thatched cottages, flocks of sheep grazed the coarse turf, and shaggy wild ponies drank from singing brooks that tumbled down into sparkling brown pools flavored with peat moss.

If he closed his eyes, he could remember exactly how that water had tasted, for he and Simon had stopped to drink from those streams several times on their trek across the moors to Lizard Head. It had been dark to the tongue, somehow. Dark and grassy.

On Bodmin's windswept tors, the wind moaned between circles of pitted gray stone: henges that loomed in silent guardianship over this wild and beautiful land. They were reminders of the ancient Celtic tribes who had once roamed these parts, and worshipped pagan gods at their stone temples. Perhaps they were the temples of the Druids, from whom the sorcerer Merlin was said to have come?

It was not something he talked about, but when he pressed his fingertips and palms to the hefty slabs, he felt vibrations against his skin. A slight humming, almost as if the stones were singing. Aye, *singing!*

Their secret music seemed, in some strange way, attuned to something inside himself. A chord, a note—something wild and just waiting to burst free. It was a feeling he'd had before, standing on the decks of a clipper, his face thrust into a howling gale. He had rarely felt it since becoming a landlubber again, and had not expected to experience it here, until he'd touched the circle of stones.

But when, astonished, he'd asked Simon to confirm what he had felt, the older man could not feel the vibrations. In fact, he'd shot Morgan a doubtful look, clearly wondering if he was "tetched" in the head!

" 'Tis cold hard stone, sir, and that's all it is," Simon had muttered firmly, his expression daring Morgan to say otherwise.

Simon's reaction had not altered Morgan's feelings that this place, so close to Land's End and the western-most point of Great Britain, was not only breathtaking, but magical. It was as wild and glorious as the sea that had bewitched him utterly and seduced him with her promise of adventure when he was thirteen.

When his mother had passed on after a lengthy illness, he had responded to his grief by running away from home, and into the comforting arms of another female—the sea.

Filled with the hot blood of youth and eager to drown his sorrow in new adventures, he'd given no thought to what his departure might do to his father, left behind to grieve alone for his beloved Anne.

He had not returned until seven years later. And when he had, it had been as a man made sadder and wiser himself by the loss of the woman he had loved. A hard, athletic man who, thanks to more wild adventures in seven years than most men could lay claim to in their entire lives, seemed older than his years.

He had traveled the world over countless times. He had seen the fabled mysteries of the Orient, the beauty of far-flung Macau, Tahiti and the Sandwich Isles; the breathtaking wilderness of the Yukon, where snow blanketed the ground like luxurious furs; as well as the rowdy mining camps of Yerba Buena.

Long, isolated sea voyages between landfalls had left him with a love for adventure in literature, too, and the new worlds that awaited discovery between the pages of a book. In fact, his small collection had often proven a better companion than any crew member during the longest sea voyages, or in those times when his vessel lay becalmed in foreign waters.

A box of his favorite classics, leather-bound, gold-leafed first editions that Geoff and Nanon had given him one Christmas, were stowed in his room at the Gull, awaiting carting to the lighthouse.

With his books, the panorama of the glorious countryside around him, and his memories, the solitary post of lighthouse keeper was one he fancied he would enjoy for its duration—perhaps as much as he enjoyed running the shipping line he and his father had started.

They'd begun the business when he returned from his travels ten years ago, at the age of twenty. The schooner *Lady Anne*, named for Morgan's late mother, had been the first vessel of the St. James line. The *Lady Nanon*, named for his father's young ward, Morgan's cousin, Nanon Dubois, had been their second. A third had been christened the *Lady Jade Moon*, after the Chinese beauty Morgan had loved and lost to an epidemic of yellow fever in Hong Kong eleven years ago.

Nan's husband, Captain Geoffrey Christopher, Morgan's oldest and dearest friend, had also enjoyed a love affair with the sea. Unfortunately, Geoff's volatile "mistress" had cost him his life.

After a memorial service for Geoff and his crew at a Plymouth church overlooking the picturesque harbor, Morgan had promised Nanon that the death of her husband and his men would be thoroughly investigated. If there was any truth to William Ashe's claims that several of the *Anne's* crew had not been drowned, but clubbed to death by wreckers for the cargo in the *Anne's* hold, their murderers would not go unpunished, he swore.

Ashe had given him more than enough information to conduct his own investigation into the matter, quite independent of Lloyds. He had also provided Morgan with a name, which, in turn, had given him a direction in which to look. A starting point.

Killigrew.

With Ashe well on the road to a full recovery, Morgan had gone to Trinity House in London, and there enlisted the lighthouse administration's aid in finding the unscrupulous wreckers who had resorted to murder for gain.

The officials at Trinity House had welcomed his suggestion that he assume the role of the Lizard's new lighthouse keeper in order to pursue the investigation.

To that end, they had chosen Simon Longfield, one of their travelling agents—men who went from port to port, collecting the lighthouse dues—to teach him what he needed to know, in order to keep the Lizard Light safely lit for shipping while he conducted his inquiries.

"Sir? Did you hear me, sir?" Simon's voice broke into his reverie.

Judging by his tone, it was clearly not the first time the man had spoken.

"Noo, I'm afraid not," Morgan admitted sheepishly. "You . . . er . . . you caught me woolgathering."

"Hrrumph," Simon said, hanging on to his lapels. He managed to load the cough with disapproval.

Not unlike his butler, Phillips, Morgan thought, trying hard not to smile.

"As I was saying, Mr. St. James, sir, seasoned mariners know each lighthouse by her characteristic, as do her keepers."

"By appearance, you say?"

"No, sir, not by looks." Simon appeared pained. " 'Tis as I said. By her *characteristic*. Or, by how often her light flashes. Take the Eddystone Lighthouse, for example. The Eddy flashes twice, very quick like, every ten seconds. Then there's the light at Plymouth Hoe. . . .

Of course, the light didn't really flash, Morgan corrected silently as Simon rambled on, naming the characteristics of several lighthouses Morgan would never set eyes upon. The warning beacons themselves remained steadily lit, while the apparatus, or the optic that created the beam of light, rotated, giving the illusion the light itself was flashing.

"I see," Morgan said, genuinely interested. "And what is the Lizard's characteristic?"

"One brief flash, sir, every three seconds."

"And do all captains know these characteristics?"

"Aye. Or should, for those coasts they sail. When the light remains shining for longer than it's off, 'tis known as 'occulting.'"

"Occulting. All right. I've got it. And when she's off for longer than she's on?"

"That's called flashing."

His lesson lasted for another few minutes, then Morgan begged off, telling Longfield he wanted to bring his trunk of books and their horses up from the inn before dark. Why he felt the need to make an excuse was a mystery to him, but for some reason, he did.

"Seems foolish to board them, since you've repaired the fence and the horseshed here, don't you think?" he continued, trying to justify his intentions. "The . . . er . . . the horses, I mean?"

"It does, aye. Go on with you, then, sir," Simon urged with a long-suffering sigh and a look that said he knew exactly what Morgan was up to. "I'll fill the Argand while you're gone."

The Argand. The great lamp in the tower, Morgan recalled. It burned whale oil, which was stored in huge barrels in a stone storehouse behind the keeper's cottage.

Morgan shot Simon a grin, knowing he'd guessed his ulterior motive for returning to the inn. "Good man!"

He was half way down the lane leading to the inn, whistling a merry tune as he strolled along, when he spotted some clumps of sea pinks and blue campions growing between stalks of blond grass. The wildflowers were tossing their pretty heads on the salty breeze.

Impulsively, he bent and gathered a small posy. The petals were the same dewy pink as Miranda Tallant's blushing cheeks. . . .

Keep this up, and you're half-way to committing adultery with the woman, lad. Or earning yourself a black eye from her husband, he reminded himself. Either way, that little beauty's spoken for. . . .

But, spoken for or otherwise, Mistress Tallant was not at her inn, he learned. The discovery left him as deflated as a pricked balloon.

"Gone home t'the family farm for a while, she has, sir," Big Jan, the lofty fellow behind the bar told him as he buffed heavy glass tankards on a snowy linen cloth. Behind him squatted a row of barrels, each outfitted with a spigot.

"Farm?"

"Aye. The Eastmoor Farm." The man gestured vaguely. " 'Tis a ways t'the east, aye? Two mile, or thereabouts."

"And what of the landlord?" Morgan asked casually. "Did he accompany his lady there? Or is Mr. Tallant still away?"

"Mr. Tallant? Ye mean, Mr. Daniel? Oh, ah. That he is, sir. That he is," the man agreed solemnly. "Still away—and likely to remain so, too."

One of the man's beetling dark brows lifted. Was that a flicker of merriment in those black eyes? No, surely not. The gloomy, bony fellow did not appear to have a merry bone in his body!

"I see. Then there is . . . some . . . some rift between your mistress and her husband?" Did he sound too hopeful?

"In a manner of speaking, aye, sir," the man confirmed in his stoic West-country manner.

"I see," Morgan murmured, inordinately pleased by this tidbit of information. "And is this rift likely to become . . . permanent?"

"Indeed it is, sir," the man confirmed. "Very permanent."

Thanking the man, he went out, and had the stableboy, Tommy, saddle his horse.

Moments later, he was cantering the glossy chestnut eastward, in the direction of the farm Jan had indicated, filled with an eagerness that had little to do with his investigation—and a great deal to do with the innkeeper's lovely wife.

Visions of her bright hair tumbling like skeins of copper floss over his chest had danced in and out of his dreams last night. And her eyes, teal-blue with desire, had been inviting as she huskily whispered, "Trouble sleeping, Mr. St. James? . . ."

Sweet Lord! Any normal, red-blooded man would have trouble sleeping after such a vision!

Chapter Five

"Who is he? Get him out of my house! Juliet! *Juliet!* Where's my baby? She's gone! The pond, Thad! Go quickly and find her! The poor mite will drown herself, fast as winking, I know it!"

"Juliet's here, Mam. She's all grown up now, remember?" Gil Killigrew soothed, gently restraining his wild-eyed, agitated mother.

Yet Catherine Killigrew shook her broom at him and shrieked, "What would a Gypsy know about minding children? Your poor little ones are half-starved and dirty! Be off with you, you wretch! Go on! Oh, Julie, dearling, where have you gone?" she mumbled darkly, wringing her hands. "Come to mam! She'll tumble into the pool, sure, and there's an end to her," she wailed, shoving faded auburn hair from her eyes. The expression on her gaunt face was confused, suspicious; her movements restless. "Find her, Thad. Please?" she begged Rob. "Don't let our baby drown!"

"I won't Mam. I promise. Go on with Miranda, and I'll find her. See? 'Randa's waiting t'comb your pretty hair."

"That's right. Come along, Mam," Miranda told her gently, taking her mother by the elbow and leading her to a stool by the hearth.

"Just you sit here. We'll braid your hair, shall we? You'll look prettier than Jan Van Dyke's mama at St. Breoch's on Sunday mornings when I'm done. You like it when I comb your hair, aye, mam?"

"But the baby? . . ." Catherine's haunted dark eyes lifted to Miranda's. Her lean fingers plucked at her daughter's delicate wrist, suddenly tightening until Miranda yelped.

"Never mind my blasted hair!" Catherine exploded suddenly, violently, kicking the stool aside. "What about my babby? What about Juliet? Why are you keeping me from her?"

"Gil will find her, mama," Miranda crooned, righting the stool and pressing her mother down onto it again. "I promise."

She began deftly combing the older woman's

hair, then plaiting the long, faded red strands into two neat braids. She talked while she worked in a low, soothing voice, or hummed some melody or other as if quieting a frightened child or animal. Her soothing stream of words, her gentle rhythmic movements slowly lulled the sick woman into stillness.

"Juliet, dear?" Miranda said over her shoulder at length.

"Yes?" The younger girl looked up from her darning. She appeared pale and close to tears. Her lower lip was quivering, Miranda saw, her heart going out to her younger sister.

"Warm some milk for Mam, would you, love? When it's ready, add a few drops of laudanum to the cup, aye?"

"Already?" Juliet glanced at the grandfather clock that ticked in one corner of the large farmhouse kitchen. The golden Labrador, Tess, and her mate, Black Jack, slept beside it in a tangle of paws and tails. "Isn't it too soon?"

"I don't see that we've much choice. Do you? She'll be up the moment I stop fussing with her hair."

"I know," Juliet agreed. Moving about pantry and kitchen, she poured milk into a pot, then set it to heat. "Every day, she's a little worse. And every day, she needs more laudanum t'settle her! Poor Kitty's half out of her mind, you know, and

105

her so heavy with the coming babe. She and Gil are desperate. So's Rob, although he claims he's not."

"I know," Miranda acknowledged as she tied the ends of the cream shawl she'd knitted over her mother's chest. She fondly stroked the older woman's head, smoothing a stray lock of hair neatly behind her ear.

Drawing a small bottle from the pocket of her gown, she splashed eau de cologne into her palms, rubbed them together, then soothed her cool hands over her mother's brow.

The hems of mam's nightgown were splashed with mud, she noticed, proof that Catherine's search for "baby" Juliet had taken her outdoors, to the barnyard—or perhaps even further afield—before Miranda's arrival.

One of the men must have found her outside and brought her back in. But how long could this go on? How long before they found her floating in the pool, Miranda wondered, bleak-faced with worry? They were only human, after all. It took but a moment's lapse, a half-minute's inattention, and Mama would be gone, fleeing blindly like some small frightened animal across the moors, terrified of the keepers who tried to keep her safe.

"What if someone finds out?"

"Shush, now. No one knows anything, and

precious few people come to Eastmoor. Don't worry, love. No one's going to take her from us! Besides, Da's already written to that physician in Bodmin, remember? God willing, she'll be better soon. Dad says he'll take her to Bodmin himself, if worse comes to worst," Miranda soothed.

"And now it has," Juliet said softly. The tears she'd held back brimmed over, splashing onto her lap from cornflower-blue eyes. Her dark blonde lashes were spiked and wet in her round, pretty face. "She's no better, is she? No better at all. Oh, 'Randa, she doesn't even recognize me anymore. She thinks I'm a baby still!"

"Hush, now. You'll always be a baby to our Mam. Count yourself lucky she still remembers your name," Miranda urged briskly. "The Good Lord knows, she hasn't known mine this past two months. Aye, and she thinks our Gil's a Gypsy, the poor love! But never mind all that. Warm the milk, do, there's a dear."

Soon after, the two young women coaxed Catherine Killigrew to drink it, then helped her up the stairs to the biggest of the farmhouse's three bedchambers, tucked snugly under the eaves.

After they'd changed her muddied nightgown, they tucked her into the wide poster bed she'd shared with her husband for thirty-one years.

The same bed in which she'd delivered four robust babes.

Within moments, Catherine drifted into a deep, laudanum-induced sleep. They gently bound her wrists to the bedposts with silk kerchiefs, to keep her from running off when she awoke, then went back downstairs.

"Now, then. The laudanum will hold her for a bit, at least until we're done with our work. I don't know about you, but I'd say we've earned a nice dish of tea, aye?" Miranda said. The pale lilac shadows beneath her younger sister's eyes had not gone unnoticed. She squeezed Juliet's shoulder. "Put your feet up, lovie. I'll put the kettle on."

"All right," Juliet agreed, flashing her older sister a grateful smile. But instead of resting, the girl carried a wooden basket of peas to the kitchen table and began to shell them. "I may as well do these, before she wakes up."

With her red-gold head bowed, her long, capable fingers popping the fat green peas from their pods, Juliet reminded Miranda of their mother in happier times, sitting at the table in a ray of sunshine, and shelling peas the same way.

"I hear you have a handsome gentleman staying at the inn?" Juliet observed, breaking into her thoughts.

"Hmm? Oh, yes. We have several very fine-looking gentlemen," Miranda said with a dismissing shrug. She was careful not to glance in Juliet's direction. "A couple of artists from London among them."

"Indeed? And are all of your guests prone to sleepwalking? And to eyeing their landlord like a 'tasty morsel of cream cake?' I think that was how Rob described it?"

"*Cream cake!* Oh, what nonsense he talks!" Miranda exclaimed, rolling her eyes and pursing her lips in a great show of disgust. "He had no right to say any such thing. Besides, Mr. St. James isn't really a guest at all. He's the Lizard's new lighthouse keeper."

"Oh? Then why's he staying at the Gull?"

"Because the keeper's cottage needs to be cleaned and put to rights. It was a terrible mess, and you know how the villagers are about letting their women clean for strangers. To be honest, I felt sorry for the man." She tossed her head defiantly.

"Oh, did you now?" Juliet asked, her blue eyes sparkling. Her mouth twitched at the corners with mischievous laughter. "Miranda Killigrew Tallant, you've never felt sorry for a man in your life!"

"Well, I did this one, so I've been kind to him, you see. And he's been very . . . cordial in return," Miranda said, choosing her words carefully.

Remembering the way Morgan St. James had looked down at her from the top of the stairs—as if she was a "morsel of cream cake"—she could not help the faint pink blush that rose up her cheeks. "Cordial" had not made her face burn under the scrutiny of the man's willow-green eyes. Nor had cordiality set the butterflies swarming in her belly.

Sweet Lord, no!

"Is that all? Then I wonder why Da' and Rob would think he's other than he claims?" Juliet asked.

"I wouldn't know. Perhaps because his looks don't match the way he speaks. Or because he walks like a sea-faring man, yet sounds well read. As educated as Squire Draker or Rev. Boreham."

"Comparing him to Draker does little to commend him! I loathe and detest Squire Draker and his silly daughters," Juliet said heatedly, wrinkling her nose in displeasure. "And as for his lady! By all accounts, she is no better than a—"

"Juliet, really," Miranda scolded mildly, hiding her smile. Had she not thought the very same thing the evening before?

"Da' and Robbie don't believe your guest is a

lighthouse keeper, either," her younger sister continued. "I heard them say so last night, when they came in. Da' said . . . why, I do believe you're blushing, sister dear!" Juliet exclaimed, laughter dancing in her blue eyes. "Do those pink cheeks have something to do with a pair of broad masculine shoulders, perchance? Or a certain devil-may-care smile?"

Juliet popped a pea-pod into her mouth.

"Or does the thought of running your fingers through the keeper's bonny gold hair bring color to your cheeks?"

"For your information, his hair is black!" Miranda shot back, scowling as she splashed hot water into the sturdy old brown teapot. "Black as sin." She swirled the hot water to scald the pot, then discarded it on the fire, making the flames hiss. "Perhaps," she added, "even *blacker!*"

Measuring two heaping spoonfuls of black Bohea into the teapot from an enamelled tin caddy, she added boiling water, stirred briskly, then replaced the lid with far more force than was necessary.

The fragrant aroma of tea filled the whitewashed kitchen. Miranda inhaled, sighing with appreciation, her moment's annoyance gone.

Thanks to the efforts of the "gentlemen" who plied the "free trade" and smuggled luxury items into England from the Continent, the tea they enjoyed was of a quality not found in many farmhouses. In fact, Bohea or Hyson were the favorites of England's most discerning host-esses, Miranda reflected, hiding a smile as she filled a Spode Blue Italian dish for herself, and another for Juliet, and set them on matching saucers. Aye, and every blessed drop was made all the tastier for its illicit origins.

"Did you collect the eggs this morning?" she asked Juliet, after they'd finished their first dish and were half way into a second.

Her sister made a face. "No, not yet. I wanted to finish this bit of darning before I went out to the henhouse. Rob has holes as big as my fists in his stockings. I'll go and do it now, shall I?" Flustered, she cast her sewing aside.

"No, silly. Sit down. Drink your tea and finish what you're doing," Miranda urged, taking the egg basket down from its peg in the chimney nook, where her father and brothers' long-barrelled guns were propped. "I'll gather them. I always had the knack for egg-collecting, even from Mam's spiteful hens. Remember?"

Juliet laughed. "Do I! Even that evil Rebecca would let you take the eggs right from under her without a cluck, but she pecked me black and blue!"

"Some of us have the charm, and some don't,

aye?" Miranda teased. "Enjoy your tea, love. I'll be back soon."

After she'd gathered the eggs, she would talk to Gil about Mam's care, she promised herself as she went out into the barnyard. Something would have to be done. Things couldn't go on this way, that much was certain.

Although she had been born and raised at Eastmoor Farm, and had missed her childhood home and her family dearly after she and Daniel were wed, it was a blessed relief to leave lately, Miranda thought guiltily as she left the farm with a farewell wave for Kitty and Juliet.

The two young women hung over the farmyard gate, their expressions wistful as, waving, they watched her go. Tess and Black Jack followed her out, then waited by the gate, their long tails wagging.

Miranda's sturdy shoes fairly flew over the springy turf as she trod home across the sun-drenched moors. She was so deep in thought she was deaf to the curlews that wheeled and called overheard, completely unaware of the rabbits that dived into their burrows as she drew near.

The strain of caring for Mam, coupled with the need to keep her deteriorating condition a secret from those who might want to have her

113

put away in a horrid institution, had told on poor Juliet, Kitty and the men.

When her sister-in-law returned from the village, her belly swollen with Gil's first babe, due in late November, Miranda had been shocked to see how pale and tired Kitty looked. Much of her fresh prettiness had faded, her looks fallen victim to too much work and the strain of caring for her ailing mother-in-law, coupled with her condition.

I'm the lucky one, Miranda thought guiltily. I can get away from it all. I have the inn to escape to, whenever Mam's too much to bear. The Black Gull, my guests, my servants give me ample excuse to leave. While they . . . ! The poor dears have nothing but their love and their duty to keep them there, day in and day out, bless them, with precious little respite. What will they do when the baby comes? What then?

Perhaps, in some ways, the unthinkable was the best solution. Maybe committing Catherine Killigrew to an asylum was the answer. Yet everything within her revolted at the thought. You didn't put someone you loved in such a place.

Before she knew it, she'd climbed a windswept tor to the circle of ancient standing stones at its crest. She blinked, surprised as always by the sweep of rolling green moors that spread away from her lofty look-out point for as far as the eye could see. Her feet had surely taken wings as her thoughts raced on, to have come so far so quickly!

Time to catch her breath, she decided, before going on.

Dropping down to the coarse turf, she leaned against one of the standing stones and drew a chilled earthenware bottle from her basket. Uncorking it, she gulped down the apple cider it held. It was delicious, cool, tangy and refreshing to her dry throat. She unknotted her Spanish shawl and let it fall about her hips in a bright poppy-colored puddle of silk.

Head propped against the cool stone, she closed her eyes and pressed her palms to the rough slab behind her. At once, the wild music of the henges poured through her fingertips, surged into her veins. A deeply buried part of her responded, bursting into blazing, vibrant, wonderful *life*! With the sensation came a heightened awareness of the world around her—its sights, its smells, its colors—that she could not explain.

Daniel was dead and buried, and she! . . . Why, in a very real sense, she was buried, too.

Buried alive.

Springing to her feet, she grabbed a corner of the shawl in one hand, the handle of the basket in the other. Arms trailing the shawl above her head like a banner, she ran down the steep hillside, gaining momentum near the gleaming lake at the bottom.

From here, it looked like a mirror of smoky crystal. Still and silent, full of mystery, it reflected the clouds in its surface.

Ancient legend claimed it had once belonged to the legendary Lady of the Lake, in whose lilywhite hands the mighty sword, Excalibur, had once been brandished; a mythical weapon fit for Arthur, high king of Britain.

From the shade of a twisted oak, Morgan watched the innkeeper's wife careen down the slope toward him like a wild woman, yelling some strange battlecry at the top of her lungs.

He strained his ears to catch the words she was yelling.

"Aliiiiive, do you hear me?" she was screaming to the canopy of blue above her.

Skylarks who had made their nests in the turf about her feet took sudden, soaring flight in a frantic effort to lead her away from their nests.

But only the wheeling curlews answered her cries. The wind snatched her words away, aided, perhaps, by the speed of her downhill rush.

Still, he could make out the most important ones.

"I'm aliiiiiiive!" she was yelling, over and over. "Aliiiiiiiive!"

When she reached the bottom of the hill, she could not have stopped, even had she wanted to. She was going much too fast for that. In another second or two, she'd pitch headfirst into the drink.

Leaving his horse, Morgan dashed across the muddy turf toward her, shot out his arms and linked them about her slender waist in a tackle. Quickly, he swung her back and around, onto the lake's grassy banks.

It was her safety he was worried about, he told himself, inhaling and filling his nostrils with the grassy scent of her hair, and the alluring fragrance of sun-warmed female skin. That was the reason he'd grabbed her. The only reason. Simple concern for another's safety.

It had nothing to do with the way her rounded bottom squirmed frantically against his middle. Nor—Sweet Lord!—with the arousing way she wriggled to escape his arms.

"What the devil are you doing, you blasted idiot?" she demanded furiously, trying to pluck his hands from her waist. "Take your bloody hands off me!"

"Idiot! *Me?* You might thank me for saving you instead of cursing me, you ungrateful harpy!" he growled when she leaped away from

117

him as if scalded the very instant he freed her.

"I might fly, too, but I don't, do I?" she shot back. "And as for you saving my life! . . . Ha! The devil you did anything of the sort, you . . . you dolt!" she sputtered again, fighting for her balance.

"Another step, and you would have toppled into the lake!" he growled. His eyes, narrowed now, were a crackling green in his anger. "What would you have done then, woman? Answer me that, aye?"

"What do you think I'd have done, you . . . you lunatic? I would have *swum* out. Or waded out, more likely. From this bank, the wretched pool's only a yard deep, at most!"

"You would still have been soaked to the skin for your trouble," he shot back, surprised—and intrigued—to hear that she could swim. Few Englishwomen could.

The sudden, tantalizing image of the lovely innkeeper's wife as a mermaid with a scaly tail and pink scallop shells covering what were surely delectable breasts, swam into his imagination. He had to blink several times to rid himself of the provocative image. . . .

"That's my business, St. James. Not yours," she shot back rudely.

"Aye. I suppose it is," he agreed, once again sounding like Phillips, his crusty butler. "I wonder. What would your husband have said, had you returned home soaked to the skin, hmmm?" he crowed.

In that moment, he could cheerfully have murdered her absent husband, rift or no rift between them.

"That's my business. Not yours!" she retorted, retreating from him.

She seemed about to say something more, but then snapped her jaws shut instead. Cocking her head to one side, she eyed him like an inquisitive kitten through a curtain of silky copper hair that fell to her elbows.

"Is it really only a yard deep?" he asked after several moments of silence.

"Probably less than that." A tiny smile tugged at the corners of her delectable mouth. "It'd be devilish hard to drown in such shallow water, unless I was drunk."

"You're not, are you? Drunk, I mean?" he asked seriously, but his eyes twinkled now.

"Drunk!" She giggled. "Why on earth would you think I was drunk?" she demanded, sitting down on the grass with her back against a tree trunk.

He dropped down beside her.

"Well, there was all that yelling. . . . What the devil was I supposed to think? And the way you were running down the hillside, like some sort

119

of madwoman!" He caught her eye, and realized she was laughing. He laughed too.

"I suppose I did look drunk," she admitted. "But I'm not. All I've had to drink is the cider in this jug—and it isn't even hard cider. Would you like some?" she offered, holding the jug out to him. " 'Tis a warm day, aye?"

"Thank you." With a nod, he took the earthenware jug from her, uncorked it and tilted it to his lips.

As he took a long, thirsty swig, she stared at his throat, and at the way his Adam's apple bobbed beneath the smooth skin, wondering how it would feel to press her lips to that spot, just so. . . .

"Why were you running?"

She shrugged. "Just because I felt like it! I . . . well . . . sometimes, I feel as if I'm bursting, you know? As if a. . . . a part of me has grown too big for my skin. It's as if another me is trying to get out, to journey all over the world. When such moods come over me, I'm afraid Lizard Cove and my life here are far too narrow to contain me!"

She broke off, embarrassed to have spoken so freely. Why, he was little more than a stranger, yet she had shared some of her deepest, darkest secrets with him. Unless she got away from him—and soon—she'd be telling him all about

Mam's condition, and God only knew what else. . . .

"I know how you feel."

"You do, sir? Really?"

"Really," he said firmly. "In fact, I fancy we are kindred spirits, you and I. We share a love of adventure and new places. That is what took me around the world more times than I care to count. Cornwall's a beautiful place, Mistress Tallant, but there are many other beautiful places in the world. You should see them all!"

"They say it's magic. Did you know that?" she told him suddenly. "This lake, I mean. So are all the standing stones hereabouts. *Men-hir*, we call them in Cornwall. Long stones. And the henges up there?" She nodded toward the circle of standing stones that stood in an endless dance upon the crest of the tor. "Sometimes, when I touch them, I . . . well, I can feel them humming."

"You can, *what*?" he demanded sharply. His dark head came up. His eyes narrowed.

She regarded him for several seconds, perhaps debating whether to repeat her words or share some confidence or other. Then her shoulders slumped. "I know. You're right. It's just foolishness. The result of an overactive imagination. Mam's right. I talk too much. Don't mind me."

"No, please. Tell me."

"No," she said gently. "For you'll only think me tetched. Did you know young people from nearby villages used to bring offerings here?" she went on in a brighter voice. "They came to ask the Lady of the Lake to help them find their true love."

"And? Do they still make offerings here?"

"Some do, aye."

"Is that the real reason you came here today? To ask the lady for a favor?" he wondered suddenly.

Their eyes met.

She looked away first, and laughed. "Not this time. I did once, though, many years ago." She shrugged. "It seems a lifetime ago now."

"And?"

"And what?" She frowned.

"You must tell me the end of your story, ma'am. Did the Lady of the Lake ever grant your wish?" For some reason, his mouth was dry, his body tense as he awaited her answer. "Were you granted your heart's desire?"

She shook her head. Sadly, he thought.

"No. No, I was not. But then, who is in this life? Most of us get exactly what we deserve, and no more, aye? We should be grateful for small mercies, don't you think, and not expect our wishes to be granted."

"I disagree, Mistress Tallant. The way I see it, life is too damned short to settle for less than what we want from it. So, as long as no one is hurt by our actions, I believe we should reach out for what makes us happy. Grasp it in both hands, and hang on tight."

"I think perhaps you've felt the stones' singing, too, have you not, sir?" she said, smiling mysteriously, her exotic eyes more cat-like than ever. Flustered, she quickly looked about her for her things. "I really have to be getting back now, Mr. St. James. My guests won't be happy if there's no supper this evening. That Mr. Forbes and Mr. Archer come back starving every night. It must be the sea air and all that painting they're doing, I expect."

He nodded. "Your shawl, ma'am."

Standing behind her, he draped the fringed shawl about her shoulders, letting his hands linger on her upper arms far longer than was proper. The faint herbal scent of her skin made him giddy. When the wind tossed her hair again, an inch or two of her pale downy neck was exposed. He ached to nuzzle it. Aye, and to kiss it. It had been a long time since he'd wanted a woman this way. Not since Jade Moon.

The image of her pale, oval face suddenly filled his head.

Hardening his jaw, he let his hands fall to his

sides instead of taking Miranda Tallant in his arms as he wanted to do. She was another man's wife, after all. Off limits. Forbidden fruit.

As if reading his thoughts, she grasped the shawl's ends and knotted them over her breasts with a murmured, "Thank you."

Her whispered words broke the moment's spell. She could not meet his eyes, he realized.

"My pleasure, ma'am."

Catching his grazing horse, he swung himself astride it. Harness creaked and bridle jingled as he settled himself into the saddle.

"Ride behind me, Mistress Tallant," he urged. "We're both going to the inn, after all."

"Thank you, sir, but no," she refused shyly, shading her eyes as she looked up at him. " 'Tis a fine day, and I like to walk." A half-smile played at the corners of her lush mouth. "The wind blows the cobwebs from my head and lifts my spirits, you see? My mother claims I'm fey. Perhaps she's right."

"Ah, yes. The poor lady. How is she today? Much recovered, I trust?"

"Better, yes, thank you kindly."

"It's a wonder she's recovered so soon! I had thought, from the late hour of your brother's summons, that Mistress Killigrew's condition was urgent."

She flushed. "My brother was mistaken, sir.

124

Mam was not as poorly as he'd thought. Now, if you'll excuse me? A very good day to you, Mr. St. James."

"Please. You must call me Morgan, now that we have shared our hearts' desires." She seemed very anxious to be gone, he thought. Why? Did his questions about her family unnerve her? And if that was so, what had she to be nervous about—unless she had something to hide? . . .

"I think not. Good day, Mr. St. James." With a pointed nod and a toss of her fine copper mane, she cast him a last look, picked up her basket and marched off across the turf, headed once more for Lizard Cove with her bright hair streaming behind her on the breeze.

He watched the lithe play of her hips beneath dark skirts that lifted and fell, lifted and fell, allowing him teasing glimpses of petticoats and trim ankles until she vanished over the next hill.

It was not until the horse shifted restlessly beneath him that Morgan realized the full extent of his response to her. He had not so much as kissed the blasted woman, and yet he was hard with lust!

And so, rather than riding directly back to the inn, as he'd intended, he turned his horse eastward, and rode instead to St. Breoch's church.

Looping his mount's reins over the wrought-iron palings that surrounded the churchyard, he wandered beneath the lych-gate and into the little cemetery.

The communal grave in which his friend, Captain Geoffrey J. Christopher, lay buried alongside his crew, was here somewhere. He would recover his . . . composure and find the grave at one and the same time.

Personal belongings of sentimental, but little monetary, value had been sent home to the drowned men's families. Even those had been pitifully few in number. Several bits of scrimshaw for mothers or sweethearts. A few waterlogged prayer books and letters. A nicely carved pipe or two.

What, Morgan wondered, had become of the musical gold pocket watch and chain that Nanon, Geoff's wife, had given his friend on his last birthday? Did it lie at the bottom of the sea, consigned to a watery grave? Or . . . did its tinkling melody mark the hours and delight the ears of its owner's murderer?

If the latter were true, he would find it, someday, he swore, his jaw hard and set.

A narrow pathway of golden shingle and broken sea shells meandered between the graves, the oldest overgrown with stalks of long blond grass. Lichened tombstones, some erected centuries before, reeled drunkenly, while angels soared at unlikely angles over the settling mounds.

Across one of the more recent graves lay a posy of withered sea-pinks. His attention was snared by the name chiseled into the stone. Morgan paused and tipped back his tricorn.

"Well, I'll be damned!" he exclaimed, reading the name and dates of the deceased.

A slow grin curved his lips. "Rift" be blowed. The rift between Mistress Tallant and her "Beloved Husband, Daniel John Tallant" was the final one, made by God.

Perhaps it was unchristian to feel such glee where the loss of a good man's life was concerned, but damned if he could help it this time, he thought, grinning from ear to ear.

The lovely Miranda was a widow!

Chapter Six

"Well, well! Another fine day for your painting, aye, sirs?" Miranda observed, trying to make polite conversation with her guests as they sat at breakfast the following morning.

Several slices of smoked ham, warm bread, cheese and freshly churned butter already had disappeared into the pair's busy mouths, washed down with fragrant coffee or hard cider brought up from the Gull's cellars.

There was much noisy lip-smacking as the pair ate, using fingers rather than forks or knives. Artists they might be, but Forbes and Archer ate like trenchermen, Miranda thought. Regardless of manners, however, she made a point

of exchanging pleasantries with her guests for a
few moments each day. Such small attentions
encouraged travellers to return to the Black Gull
time and time again, she had discovered.

Nevertheless, this odd pair who had paid for
their lodgings in advance were unlike her usual
patrons.

Mr. Forbes and Mr. Archer had arrived together by public coach two days before the arrival of Mr. St. James and Mr. Longfield. They
had brought with them a number of bulky
trunks, and had announced as they made their
marks in the guest register that they were artists,
seeking to take advantage of the marvelous Cornish light they had heard so much about.

Each morning, the pair left the inn, lugging
along folding stools, portable easels, canvases
and a picnic lunch prepared for them by the
Gull's kitchen. They headed—or so they
claimed—for the beach, not returning until late
afternoon.

The pair were unlike any of the other artists
who had stayed at her inn. Men who had been
very intense and often somewhat effeminate in
manner.

Albert Forbes, for instance, stood six feet tall,
was broad-shouldered and sandy-haired, and
looked less like an artist than a blacksmith, or a
pugilist, with his large, misshapen nose red-

dened by broken veins, and gray eyes that lacked luster. Despite his considerable size, he carried himself erect as any military man, and seemed uncomfortable in his artist's smock and beret.

Percy Archer, on the other hand, was a slim, quick fellow with very straight, oily brown hair and a wispy moustache. He had a sharp-featured face that reminded Miranda of a bird, and was forever darting about, rarely settling in any one place for more than a second or two. His black eyes were bright and inquisitive as a magpie's, in sharp contrast to his companion's.

"May I see?" Miranda asked curiously, reaching for the canvases stacked against the taproom's whitewashed brick wall.

"Don't!" Archer said sharply, standing and placing himself protectively between her and the canvases. The face reflected in the polished brasses on the walls was red and furious. "They . . . ah . . . they are not nearly ready for . . . er . . . viewing yet, ma'am."

"No," his companion echoed loudly. "Not nearly ready."

Her hand hovered above the canvases, then dropped lamely to her side. "Then you must excuse me, sirs. I should never have presumed. . . ."

"No, Mistress Tallant," Percy Archer agreed,

impaling her with his snapping black eyes, "you should not."

She bristled at his tone. "My apologies for the intrusion, sirs. Enjoy your meal." With that, she retreated to the kitchen.

Maisie was taking loaves from the brick oven with a long-handled bread board when she went in. The yeasty aroma made her mouth water. High time she gave thought to her own hunger, she decided ruefully. Never mind her wretched guests!

"Sit, Maisie. Let's have a bite before we start the heavy work. I don't know about you, but I'm starved."

Maisie grinned. " 'A filled belly works harder than an empty one.' That's what my mother always says."

"Speaking of your mother, did you ask her if you could clean the cottage for the new keeper? I'm sure Mr. St. James would pay you well for your trouble," Miranda said, sawing through a warm loaf with a knife.

The livelihood of Maisie and her mother, a widow in poor health, depended upon Maisie's modest wage and what Mrs. Pettit could make herself by taking in plain sewing. But nowadays, with her sight going, such work rarely came the old woman's way.

Miranda tried to help by sending Mrs. Pettit

the Gull's sheets or curtains to be darned, or a basket of whatever food could be spared from the kitchen, with the excuse that it would only go to waste if they didn't take it.

Maisie shook her head unhappily. "No, mum. Me mam won't allow it. Says she'll go on the parish before she'll let any daughter of hers clean for a single man. Aye, and one who's a stranger t'the Cove, at that."

"Oh? And what does she think you do here, pray?" Miranda asked sharply as she buttered the bread, annoyed by the old woman's narrow-mindedness. "Clean only the rooms of the married guests? No, no, never mind answering me! I was just wondering aloud."

"Beg pardon, mum," Maisie apologized, hanging her head.

She was a pretty little thing in her snowy mob-cap and bibbed apron, her golden-brown curls framing her fresh, pretty face. But, pretty or no, she was destined to end up an old maid unless her mother died and freed the girl to marry.

"I know. Oh, well, don't fret, pet. It's all right. We can't help our mothers, can we now?" she murmured, giving Maisie a quick hug. She slid a plate of buttered bread, ham and cheese in front of her. "Come. Eat your breakfast, then we'll get on with the laundry. Perhaps I'll see to

133

Mr. St. James's cottage myself." She'd been toying with the idea all morning.

"You? Clean the keeper's cottage, mum?" Maisie's impish grin resurfaced. "Oh, go on with you, mum. You wouldn't . . . would you?"

"I don't see why not. I'm a respectable widow, after all." She grinned. "That should count for something. When you've eaten, fill the washcopper, Maisie. I told Jan to carry it outside for you earlier."

"Right you are, mum." Maisie smiled happily. "I don't mind doing them artists' laundry. Not a bit. Easy, it is. Not like that Mr. Clovelly's what was here last summer! Paint all over his clothes, he had. Red as blood, it were!" She shuddered and rolled her eyes. "Almost wore my fingers t'the bone, trying to scrub it off. Never a drop o'paint on theirs, there isn't."

Miranda licked a smear of creamy butter from her finger and laughed. "Blood, indeed. You and your imagination. Go on with you!"

It was early afternoon before the inn's ten guest rooms were sparkling.

Last week's linens had been stripped and the beds remade using freshly pressed, lavender-scented sheets. The floorboards had been swept and damp-mopped, the rugs taken out and beaten, the furnishings dusted and polished with lavender wax. The hearths were swept free of old ashes, and a fresh log fire set but not lit within each one. There was really no call for a fire until evening in the summer.

The delightful scent of lemon oil, beeswax and lavender polish filled the inn's hallways.

Leaving Maisie to mind the rabbit stew that simmered over the fire, and Jan and his lads to see to the posting coaches that came and went with their teams, Miranda washed her face and hands, took up her shawl and went out.

Armed with cleaning utensils, a bucket and a pair of faded rag rugs, she set off down the lane at a brisk clip, the blustery wind flapping her hair and skirts about.

The wind carried the smells of sea and shore on its breath: the iodine tang of sea-weed, the smells of saltwater, sunshine and fresh fish.

The lighthouse had been given a fresh coat of whitewash since she'd seen it last, she noticed, shading her eyes with her hand. The witch's hat that topped it likewise boasted a new coat of black paint.

Someone had mended the rail fence that enclosed the small pasture, too, she saw as she walked up the shingled path to the keeper's cottage. Aye, and pressed a half-barrel into service as a watering trough.

A lone horse was nibbling at a bale of hay as she passed by. There was no sign of the glossy chestnut Morgan had been riding up on the high moors yesterday, however. Aye, and a dashing sight he'd cut, too, mounted on it.

Did that mean he was not at home? Probably, she realized, furious at the depth of her disappointment.

What on earth was she doing, mooning about after a man like St. James? Didn't she have problems enough, with her Mam and all, without borrowing more from a man who could only mean trouble?

Still, her father had asked her to find out all she could about him. How could she do that unless she bumped into him now and again?

Receiving no answer to her knock upon the cottage door, Miranda lifted the latch and went inside, wrinkling her nose at the musty, unpleasant smells of mildew and mouse droppings that greeted her.

Someone had removed the damaged furnishings and mouse-infested bedding that had been there. But, unlike the lighthouse, nothing more had been done to make the cottage fit to live in.

Men! Most of them would wallow like pigs in a sty, if women let them!

Shaking her head, Miranda rolled up her sleeves, tucked her long hair under a mobcap, and got to work.

*   *   *

"Squire Draker. It's a pleasure to meet you, sir," Morgan said after the butler had ushered him into the study of Windhaven House. The small yet elegant mansion of weathered red brick and leaded windows, set in manicured grounds, was the residence of Squire Alan Draker, and was situated some three miles to the northwest of Lizard Cove.

"And to meet you, St. James. I believe I had the pleasure of meeting your father once, in Plymouth. Sir Robert is the local magistrate, is he not?"

"Was, yes. He retired from the bench quite recently. We've become partners in the shipping line that bears our name."

"Have you now? Splendid! He's a fine gentleman, your father, my boy. Very fine. You must be proud of him."

"I am, Squire."

Draker smiled as he went over to the oak sideboard where several crystal decanters set on a silver tray gleamed in the afternoon sunshine that fell through the leaded windows. "Sit, Morgan, sit! You'd welcome a drink, I shouldn't wonder, after the ride over? What will it be?" He cocked a steely brow in Morgan's direction.

"I'll have what you're having, sir."

"Splendid! I was about to have a brandy."

"A brandy would be most welcome, sir."

Morgan undid the button of his seaman's reefer jacket and took his seat in a leather wing-chair beside the fireplace, while his host poured their drinks.

Draker was younger by daylight than he'd appeared the other evening at the Gull. A robust country squire, he was perhaps fifty or so, with iron-gray hair worn in an old-fashioned queue, bushy mutton-chop whiskers, flinty eyes and a hard jaw that belied his hearty manner. His florid complexion was that of a man who freely indulged his appetites for both liquor and rich foods, though as yet he had none of the crippling signs of gout.

"Splendid. Splendid," Draker declared. "Here you are."

He handed Morgan a balloon glass, partly filled with red-gold liquid. The brandy was, Morgan observed fancifully, the same rich color as Miranda Tallant's hair. He had thought of her many times since yesterday, up on the moors.

"Your health, sir!" Draker declared.

"Hmmm? Yes, indeed. And yours, Squire," Morgan murmured, raising his glass in silent toast to the beautiful innkeeper.

"And now to the matter that has brought you here, sir," Draker continued. "Mince no words, St. James. I'm a busy man, and not one to beat about the bush."

138

"Nor I, Squire. You're a man after my own heart. This is for you," he added, handing Draker a letter of introduction. "It will clarify matters somewhat."

While Draker perused the elegant handwriting, Morgan cupped the brandy snifter, swirling the brandy inside so that the heat of his hands infused the spirit with warmth, before taking a sip.

It was a very fine French cognac, even for a connoisseur of Draker's obviously expensive palate, and Morgan's own. He wondered idly how the man had come by it. Legally, from a licensed public house—or had the cask been unloaded from a ship that hovered offshore by dark of the moon, then quickly smuggled inland on the backs of ponies with muffled bridles and hooves?

"This letter is signed by Lord Roundwood of Trinity House. I take it you're in Cornwall at the request of the lighthouse administrators, then?" Draker observed when he had read the letter of introduction.

"On the contrary. This investigation was my own idea."

"Hrrmph. His lordship implies that you've assumed the post of lighthouse keeper. I take it from your attire that this is also correct?"

"Indeed it is." Briefly, Morgan explained that

139

the schooner *Lady Anne*, which had sunk in August with all hands, had been a vessel of his family's shipping line. He added that he had reason to believe there had been survivors of the wrecking, but that these men had been murdered by those seeking to take possession of her cargo. He did not, however, confide his personal interest in finding the killers. He had told Draker only what he needed to know, in the event he was forced to call on the country squire for reinforcements, or in his capacity as the local magistrate.

"That explains your attire," the squire said disparagingly, scowling at Morgan's reefer jacket, canvas breeches and seaboots. "Damned nasty business, all this! Oh, don't get me wrong, St. James. I'm a Cornishman, born and bred to the bone. I find nothing amiss with the old custom of wrecking, in itself. For centuries, the good people of our coastal villages have had their royal charter, which grants them the right of salvage," Draker observed. " 'Tis a means for the wretches to make a better living, after all, is it not?

"But if what you say is true, then wrecking has gone beyond the pale! Only pitiless butchers would kill innocent sailors as they crawled ashore, in order to salvage the cargoes their vessels hold." He shook his head in obvious dismay.

"Unmasking these men will require considerable patience and the utmost secrecy, sir. I know it goes without saying, but I must have your sworn word that my true purpose in Lizard's Cove will not be revealed to anyone outside this room."

"You have it, St. James. Upon my honor as a man. But if you need me, you have only to send word to Windhaven House, sir. Every able-bodied man in my employ will ride posthaste to Lizard's Cove, to help you apprehend these blackguards."

"Thank you, sir."

Draker nodded. "Don't mention it. Now, enough of this sorry business. You must meet Dinah and my gels." He cocked an iron-gray brow in Morgan's direction. "Not married, are you, St. James?"

"Alas, no, sir. I have yet to attain that happy state," Morgan admitted with a grin.

"Splendid. Betrothed?"

"Regrettably no, sir."

"Even better!" Draker declared, rather too heartily, looking upon Morgan with a shrewd eye, as he might examine a prospective son-in-law. "You're in for a rare treat this afternoon. My gels, Melody and Melissa, are twins. And, if I say so myself, two exquisite rosebuds! They would be very upset with their Papa if he failed to introduce them to a handsome young fellow like yourself." He winked. "Dinah and I rarely get up to London, you see, and we have precious few houseguests in this desolate part of the country. As a consequence, all three of my gels are starved for city entertainments."

"Are they, sir?" Morgan murmured politely, wondering if he could be considered a "city entertainment." "And yet your charming home and estate are as elegantly and lavishly appointed as any to be found in London." In fact, the manor house was surprisingly ornate, given the yearly income of a country squire, Morgan thought, mildly curious as to the source of the squire's additional income. Was he both squire, magistrate and free-trader, too? Did that explain the origins of his fine cognac?

"You're too kind, dear boy. But Dinah will be delighted to hear it, flattery or no. Right this way, now. Follow me!" Draker urged.

The squire led the way from the study at a brisk stride, passing down a spacious, oak-paneled hallway hung with portraits of the Draker ancestors.

At a slower pace, Morgan followed.

"I believe we shall find the ladies taking tea in the drawing room. No doubt they'll be surprised to—"

"Draker! You naughty man! You didn't tell me

you were expecting a guest!" a female voice declared as Squire Draker was about to open the double drawing room door. "Won't you introduce us?"

The rich, husky tones snapped Morgan's head around as if jerked by a chain.

A striking young woman stood in the doorway, wearing a wine-colored riding habit that displayed her lush hour-glass figure to advantage. The chessboard tiles of the foyer, the dark wood panels and gilt-framed family portraits made a dramatic foil for her rich, dark beauty.

Glossy blue-black ringlets streamed from under her veiled top hat, beneath which her eyes flashed like a sultry Spanish señorita's. Red lips slightly parted, she ran the very tip of her tongue over the pouty lower one, and slapped her riding crop against her thigh, apparently impatient for Draker to make the introductions.

"Allow me, sir," Morgan offered. Coming to a halt before her, he made a gallant half-bow and drew her hand to his lips. "Your obedient servant, ma'am," he murmured, kissing her gloved knuckles.

The burgundy kid was as soft and smooth as butter.

"Morgan St. James, at your service." He inclined his dark head. "Have I the pleasure of making the acquaintance of Miss Melody Draker or Miss Melissa Draker?" Morgan asked, flashing her a dazzling smile.

"Charmer!" the lady accused with a throaty laugh. "You flatter me shamelessly, sir, pretending to mistake me for my step-daughters!"

Her dark lashes swept down like fans, then lifted, revealing golden eyes. The cruel amber eyes of a lioness boldly met his. "I am Lady Dinah, sir," she confessed. "Squire Draker's wife. And I am likewise at your . . . service . . . Morgan St. James."

The invitation in her eyes, her voice, left no doubt as to what services she would provide, were he so inclined.

Morgan saw a man he recognized from Lizard Cove as he was riding away from Windhaven. He was leaning up against a tree trunk, enjoying a smoke. Coppinger, he thought his name was. He was one of the great blond giants he'd noticed at the inn the other evening—the one who'd shot him such a hostile scowl.

What the devil was the man doing here, so far from home, he wondered.

The man cast him a long, suspicious look from under thick, fair brows and spat in the grass as he approached. Not surprisingly, he gave no nod of recognition as Morgan rode level with him, and on.

His mount's hooves thudded on the rutted earth of the winding country lane. The road was lined with deep birch and oak woods that led away from Windhaven and would, at length, take him back up onto the high moors.

As he rounded a curve in the lane at a brisk canter, he spotted something red beneath some trees. On closer inspection, he realized it was Dinah Draker's riding habit. She was mounted on a handsome bay, and seemed to have been waiting for him, because she lifted a gloved hand in greeting.

But in the same instant, her horse reared up on its hindquarters, its forelegs pawing the air. Its shrill whinny rang out through the trees, along with its rider's startled scream.

When its hooves struck earth once again, it was off, fleeing whatever had startled it. Its rider, perched precariously on the sidesaddle, was almost unseated as the frightened bay plunged into the dense woods.

Straightway, Morgan dug heels into his own mount's flanks and raced in pursuit. The woman appeared to be an excellent rider, but she could still find herself unhorsed, her neck broken by a low branch, if her horse was not halted.

His dangerous ride through the trees ended abruptly only moments later, however, when he spied a flash of burgundy upon the grass ahead.

145

The horse had thrown her, then. Odd, when she'd given every appearance of being a seasoned horsewoman. . . .

Reining in his own mount, he dismounted and hurried to her aid.

Injured or otherwise, Dinah Draker made a fetching picture, sprawled upon the grass.

Her arms were gracefully outflung. The back of one hand rested against the flushed curve of a cheek. Her skirts were artfully tossed up to show a glimpse of gartered stocking and the scalloped lacy edge of a petticoat above the top of her riding boot.

Her veiled top-hat lay forgotten among the dried leaves at the base of a tree. Without it, long, glossy black ringlets spilled over the grass. Her eyes were closed above flushed cheeks, her glistening red lips slightly parted, as if she was sleeping.

There was, he noticed absently, something faintly unpleasant about those too-red, too-moist lips. Something almost carnivorous. *Predatory*.

Dropping to one knee beside her motionless body, he took her delicate wrist between his fingers, feeling for a pulse. Much to his surprise, he discovered it was strong and steady, if perhaps a trifle fast.

He was about to release her hand when to his

shock, her tapering fingers cupped his groin and gently squeezed.

"What kept you, St. James?" she asked huskily, looking up at him with a sly, knowing expression in her golden eyes. "Oh, come, come. Don't look at me that way! We're not children, after all. You want me. Admit it! Did you think I couldn't tell?" She laughed. "On the contrary. I can always tell. Lucky man, I want you, too. . . ."

"Do you, now?" he echoed with an amused half-smile. His gut feelings had stood him in good stead where the Lady Dinah was concerned. He plucked her hand from his treacherous manhood. "Tell me. Do you always get what you want?"

"Yes!" She giggled throatily. "*Always*. Aren't you glad?"

In answer, he grasped her wrists and hauled her to her feet. Powerful fingers digging deep into the flesh of her upper arms, he shoved her up against the trunk of a nearby tree.

"What do *you* think?" he rasped hoarsely.

Chapter Seven

"Well, I'll be," Simon exclaimed some two hours later, standing in the doorway of the now neatly appointed keeper's cottage. "Done miracles, you have, Mistress Tallant. Those rag rugs make the place a proper home, they do."

"Thank you, Mr. Longfield. I'm glad you like them. It does look better, doesn't it?" Miranda agreed, looking around the tidy little cottage with satisfaction.

The few sticks of furniture gleamed with polish. A fire crackled merrily in the polished black grate, casting a ruddy glow over everything. An earthenware jug stood on the table, filled with sea pinks. "I hope Morg . . . I hope Mr. St. James will be just as pleased."

"Oh, he'll be tickled pink, ma'am! Not here right now, he isn't, or he'd thank ye himself. Had urgent business in Bodmin, he did. But he'll be home by supper."

"Would you mind if I went up to the gallery? I've never seen the view from up there." With Morgan gone, it was the perfect time to satisfy her curiosity about the lighthouse. "My father says it's breathtaking."

"And so it is! Go right on up, ma'am, but mind your step, aye? It's hard going, for them what aren't used to it. Over two hundred steps, in all, there are. I'll be up t'point out the sights for ye, in a bit. Why, some days, the air's as clear as crystal. Then ye can see as far as Land's End. But when there's a fog rolling in . . . well, then you're lucky t'see the tip o'your nose!" He chuckled.

As Longfield had promised, the spiral staircase that wound up to the viewing gallery was steep. She had climbed only half of the two hundred iron steps when she came upon a door.

Glad of an excuse to catch her breath, and curious, besides, Miranda opened it and stuck her head inside.

The room had been the keeper's quarters, before the cottage was added to the lighthouse, she saw.

This was where Morgan must have slept last night, for he had not returned to his room at the inn. She knew, because she had lain awake for hours, listening for the sound of his tread outside her door, like some foolish twit of a girl.

She caught herself in mid-thought and scowled, cross at the direction her thoughts were taking. Why on earth should she care where the wretched man slept?

Still, she darted a quick glance over her shoulder to make quite sure Simon had not followed her up, and peered into the room.

Spartan quarters, to say the least!

Two curved "banana" bunks followed the curves of the lighthouse's whitewashed walls. Both bunks were tidily made up with pillows and coarse navy-blue wool blankets.

Set neatly beside each bed was a seaman's chest that served as both table and dresser. Only one held any personal items, however. There was a stack of leather-bound books with gold lettering, a bottle of India ink and a pen.

Those were Simon Longfield's, most likely. Morgan did not strike her as the scholarly type. No, far from it! Both chests held chimney lamps. There was an iron brazier, unlit at the moment, in one corner. Wooden pegs set into the wall held articles of clothing, one a dark frockcoat of excellent cloth that she recognized as Morgan's.

She resisted the sudden urge to run across to it and bury her face in cloth that held his scent.

Instead, convinced—perhaps by a guilty conscience?—that she'd heard someone on the stairs, she ducked out of the room, and hurried up to the viewing gallery.

Above it lay the lantern room, reached by a ladder and a trapdoor. The latter had been left open, she saw.

Through the opening, she could see the Argand, the great lamp that used whale-oil for its fuel. It stood at the focus of a parabola of copper, a lens large enough for a grown man to stand inside.

The keepers, her father had told her once when she complained of having to polish the inn's brass and silver candlesticks so often, spent several hours each week polishing that copper lens. It, in turn, magnified and reflected the light of the Argand, so that its beacon was visible from twenty miles out at sea.

She was breathless by the time she stepped out onto the narrow catwalk that surrounded the lighthouse's viewing room.

Immediately, the blustery wind whipped her hair wildly about her head and stole her breath away. Both skirts and ruffled petticoats were flattened against thighs and hips.

Oh, how those fierce gusts exhilarated her!

Hands braced against the fragile railing, she leaned forward, gazing out at the beautiful panorama of sea and land spread before her. She filled her lungs with great mouthfuls of briny air, and her senses with the gulls' keening cries as they dipped low over the blue-green Atlantic.

Sunlight glinted off their white wings and off the white canvas of a small fleet of fishing boats, now little more than a peppering of dark dots on the horizon, as they turned their prows toward harbor. Sunlight also sparkled off scalloped waves edged with lacy froth.

It had been well worth the climb to see such beauty. Not even the highest tor in Cornwall could command such a breathtaking view!

Reluctantly, she turned to go, but was brought up short by a man's hard body, planted firmly across the catwalk in her path.

She was temporarily flattened against him, her nose buried in the coarse knitted fibers of his jersey, her fingers clutching brass anchor buttons.

A small shriek escaped her as she swayed, coming close to losing her balance and slipping under the rail, to the jagged rocks below.

"Whoa!" the man's deep voice cautioned.

153

Strong tanned fingers curled over her upper arms.

It was not Simon Longfield, as she'd expected, but Morgan St. James.

Her heart lurched.

"Steady as you go there, Mistress Tallant. 'Tis a wicked drop to the rocks, aye?"

"So it is!" She laughed nervously, glad of his firm grip, yet perversely unsettled by it, too. "I rarely jump at shadows, but . . . ! Well, I confess, you startled me, sir!"

Startled her? An understatement, if ever she'd made one. For a second, he'd frightened her so badly, she'd almost slipped under the iron railing and fallen from the narrow catwalk to her death. The rail was a flimsy thing, after all. More a reminder to be cautious than a true safety barrier.

She shuddered, thinking of what might have been. As he had said, it was a wicked drop to the jagged black rocks below.

"You may let go of me now, sir. Really. I'm perfectly all right. You have a most annoying habit of saving me when I am in no need whatsoever of being saved!"

"On the contrary," Morgan countered in a taunting tone, drawing her toward him instead. He swept a stray lock of copper hair from a flushed cheek as he looked down into her upturned face, so freshly enticing, so very far removed from Dinah Draker's undeniable yet strangely repulsive charms. "Since you have already escaped me once, I am minded to keep you close, now that I have you where I want you. Very close. . . ."

"You jest, surely, sir?" Miranda replied huskily, her voice breaking with a mixture of excitement and disbelief.

"Do I?" he murmured, his sensual voice a dark, rumbling purr now. The arms around her tightened their hold. "Do I really, Miranda?"

Their bodies were pressed closely together their entire lengths. Like lovers, Miranda thought in that part of her mind that was still able to think. The idea was oddly thrilling, made all the more so by its forbidden nature.

Her cheeks flamed. Her breasts were crushed against his broad chest. Her thighs brushed his, separated only by the fabric of their clothing. Her fingers were still caught over the knobby brass buttons of his navy reefer jacket, worn with its deep collar turned up against the wind.

He wore coarse canvas seaman's breeches and sea boots with the tops cuffed over, yet had never looked more handsome than he did now, with his black hair tousled by the salty wind and the sunlight dancing in his devilish green eyes. More like a dashing sea-rover, newly returned from the China Seas, than any lighthouse keeper. . . .

Her nostrils were filled with his exotic scent. With the lanolin smell of warm, wet wool. The bouquet of French brandy. The spicy aroma of fine tobacco. The salt tang of the sea—and the dizzying scent of the man, himself. . . .

It was, in every respect, a most improper situation for a widowed woman to find herself in, she thought, hastily taking a step away from him. Aye, and especially so with this man, this handsome stranger who made no secret of his attraction to her, and seemed not to give a tinker's cuss if she was married or nay!

Yet, try as she might, she could not ignore the sudden thunder of her own heart. Nor the rush of pleasure and warmth the heat in those deep-green eyes instilled in her.

Excitement fluttered inside her like a trapped bird, beating its wings against the cage of her ribs, just bursting to be free.

Deny it she might, but she was attracted to Morgan St. James. Attracted deeply, and in all the ways a woman could be attracted to a man!

"Enough of your teasing, sir," she said crisply. "I have an inn to tend to, in case you hadn't noticed. Guests to feed. Servants to order. Meals to cook. Let me pass."

She tried to shoulder her way past him, then

to step around him, but he took her elbow and instead drew her firmly back to face him.

"Not this time. I demand a forfeit! If you would pass by me, you must kiss me first, my lovely sea-witch," he taunted softly, huskily, still trapping her arm. He cocked a dark brow at her, a grin just bursting to break through. Even now, it tugged at the corners of his mouth. "Or else permit me to steal one, before your husband catches us, aye?" he challenged.

His hair was ruffled, like a bolt of black silk rippled by the wind's playful fingers. His green eyes danced, sparkling with wicked merriment.

He knows, she realized, relieved and angry at the same time. About Daniel, that is. Someone must have told him she was a widow! There was a new boldness to him now, the rogue. A cocksure determination that wasn't there before.

"Ah, Miranda," he whispered. "Give up, lass. Come here to me."

Before she could protest, he thrust his hand beneath her hair. Splaying his fingers across the back of her head, he drew her closer. *Closer.*

She tried to resist, but it was no use. They both knew it.

He was going to kiss her, and there was not a bloody thing she could do to stop him, even had she wanted to!

It was the moment they'd been moving toward

157

since they first set eyes on each other at the inn. As inevitable as the sunset. . . .

Her body softened as he angled his dark head to hers, claiming her mouth with a savage finesse that robbed her of breath and shattered coherent thought.

Deeper, his magical kiss went, reaching inside her, finding and igniting the deeply sensual, untamed part of her that Daniel had never known existed. The wild, secret heart she'd buried deep under years of convention and propriety, so only the standing stones could kindle it, till now.

Till him!

She tried to remain aloof, to hold herself cold and detached from Morgan's kisses, Morgan's lips, but she could not. What woman could?

At last, with a sob, her soft, ripe mouth parted under his, yielding all, surrendering with a joyous throaty purr of need.

The astonished, contented little sounds she uttered sent Morgan's senses reeling,

He groaned as he tugged the tortoiseshell combs from her hair. Kisses weren't enough, damn it! He wanted more than just the taste of her. Wanted her here, now, beneath him in his bed—and devil take the consequences! And he didn't give a damn who saw them!

Freed from pins and combs, her copper ringlets lifted and twisted on the salty wind as he crushed her against him. Hands splayed, he cupped her buttocks, lifting her against the hard ridge in his breeches front, before his hands rose to clasp her by her slender waist.

"I must have you, Miranda, or go mad, my sweet," he swore thickly as he bit her earlobe. "Let me take you."

She shivered. His deep-green eyes were heated. Smoldering with desire—no, lust. To desire her, he must love her, and she knew he did not.

"H . . . *have* me?" she protested. "You'll do nothing of the sort, Mr. St. James! How dare you speak to me in this fashion? I'm a decent woman, I'll have you know!"

She sputtered, pretending disgust. Outrage. But no matter how she tossed her head in disdain, her insides jangled, wobbly as coltsfoot jelly, and her loins throbbed from wanting him so.

"You're already mad! You must be! I . . . I'm a respectable married woman. What of my husband! What about him?" she stammered in desperation, when she was able to speak at all.

"You, my dear, are a bloody, beautiful little liar," he growled, grinning broadly between nipping the other petal-pink earlobe with his teeth. The bite was hard enough to make her yelp with pain—gentle enough to make her moan with

159

shivery delight. He worried her lower lip until it reddened and grew swollen. "You, my sweet wild rose, are a widow! The Widow Tallant."

That devil! He was mocking her!

"What difference does it make whether Daniel's gone or nay? All that need concern you is that I choose to be faithful to his—to my husband's memory!" she protested as he pushed the neck of her gathered shift down, baring a shoulder for his lips.

"Aye? And I'm a Dutchman," he retorted in a taunting tone.

She gasped, then moaned as he pressed a marauding mouth to that smooth curve of flesh, feeling both her nipples pucker with the touch of his lips, his tongue on her bare skin.

"For the love of *God!* Don't do that!" she begged.

Yet perversely, she tipped her head back, baring her throat for his greedy lips at his slightest nudge, moaning with pleasure as he encircled her throat with a necklace of kisses.

His arms were a like a band of steel about her. Keeping her safe. Protecting her. When he held her this way, she could no longer think. Could no longer reason or protest. She could only *feel!*

"On the contrary, my lovely little liar. I intend to do 'this' everywhere. There will be no part of you I have not kissed, my sweet. No inch of your body I have not tasted. Your breasts. Your belly. The silky satin of your inner thigh. . . ."

His wicked promises made her shiver and arch against his hand like a kitten, her movements as arousing as they were instinctual.

"Sweet Lord!" he growled.

Twisting his hand through her billowing hair, he dragged her head back and fitted his lips over hers.

Hungrily, savagely, he claimed her mouth again and again, stabbing his tongue deep inside it to find her own, and seal his possession.

Daniel's kisses had been sweeter than wine. Tender, gently arousing kisses.

Nothing like these!

Morgan's kisses were fierce, deep kisses that demanded a woman's response. They ripped and tore at her emotions, peeled them away, layer by layer, until another, different Miranda was exposed. Another Miranda, buried deep within. An earthy, wanton Miranda she did not know, whose unknown depths—if she was honest—frightened her.

His kisses stirred hungers, needs she had not suspected she had. And what she hungered for, needed, was *him!*

Morgan St. James.

She wanted him inside her. Filling her. Wanted to cradle him on her hips and belly. To take him between her thighs. To smell him on her skin, his scent mixed with the lavender of her sheets. To see his dark head resting beside hers on the goosedown pillow—so very close, she could roll over and touch her lips to the corners of that dark-rose mouth, to his lean throat. . . .

She wanted him to bed her as a man beds the mistress he adores; as if every coupling was their first, their last, their everything!

For him to make love to her with all the fiery savagery of the Celtic tribes who once raised their magic rings of stone upon the desolate moors and celebrated pagan fertility rites there. To feel their wild life-force pounding through her veins like drums, as she'd so often felt the henges' wild song inside her, filling her with rivers of fire.

She wanted to feel alive, *truly* alive, as she had never felt in Lizard Cove. To experience something quite different from the gentle lovemaking she'd enjoyed in Daniel's arms.

Daniel.

His name, his memory were like cold water, flung over mating cats.

Remembering the decent, kind man who had loved her, married her, cherished and respected her, filled her with shame. It brought her back to her senses as nothing else could.

What would Daniel think, if he could see her now? Of the way she was trampling upon his memory with her flagrant behavior!

Yet here she was, nonetheless, her hair unbound, her lips reddened, her shift sliding off one shoulder like a slattern's, dallying with a strange man in plain sight of the world. Aye, and liking it, too!

Daniel deserved better. He had been a good and gentle man. A loving and faithful husband. Was he even now turning in his grave, she wondered guiltily, her cheeks flaming.

It took but one person to see them together up here, and every tongue in Cornwall would be wagging!

"Let me go," she panted, struggling to escape his arms. Her mind was made up. "Let go of me, I say. Stop it, do!" she insisted, beating at his chest

"Why, Miranda?" Morgan asked softly, trailing his knuckles down over the sweet, flushed curve of her cheek, to her determined jaw. He tilted her chin up, his hot breath fanning her ear so that she shivered. "Don't pretend you hate my kisses, for I know better. You like them very much. You'll enjoy the other, too, sweet. I swear it. I'll show you pleasures you've only dreamed of," he vowed in a lower, huskier voice. "Let me

163

show you, Miranda! Let me make love to you! Here. Now."

It was not a plea, any longer, but a command.

She swallowed. *The other*. There was no question what he meant by that, the bold rogue. Or where he wanted her to go with him. His keeper's quarters were less than a stone's throw away, after all. In a matter of seconds, they could be together, limbs tangled in that spartan bunk. . . .

His words lanced through her. Hot, dark spears of excitement. *Of anticipation*. . . .

"I'll do nothing of the sort," she forced herself to say hotly, her turquoise eyes flashing. She was nettled by guilt, flustered by excitement. He was so bloody sure of himself, the devil. Aye, and far too sure of her. Why, he knew her better than she knew herself!

"Had you not . . . had you not surprised me up here, I would be gone to my inn, by now. I'll thank you to remember that!"

She tried again to push past him, a risky maneuver on the dangerously narrow catwalk. But he stepped in front of her, cutting off her escape route. Blocking her path.

Again.

"Oh, I'll remember, Miranda," he promised in a teasing tone. "I'll remember everything." With a wicked smile, he crossed his arms over his broad chest. "I'll remember the way your lips parted beneath mine, like a rose opening its petals to the morning dew. And I'll remember how you felt in my arms. The way you pressed against me to return my kisses, measure for measure."

His knowing smile was the last straw. That arrogant . . . *bastard!* He saw through her like glass. Knew what she wanted without need for words, better than she knew herself. Damn him.

It was too much to bear.

Drawing back her hand, she whacked him across the cheek with all the force she could muster, pleased yet startled by the vivid welts her palm painted on his cheek.

"Then remember that, Mr. St. James!" she hissed. "What's more, I'll thank you to send for the rest of your belongings within the hour. You're no longer welcome at my inn."

With that, she picked up her skirts, shoved past him and took the treacherously steep iron steps back down to the ground at reckless speed.

Morgan shook his head. "Not welcome, Miranda?" he muttered, rubbing his smarting cheek. "You tempt me to put that claim to the test."

A lazy grin curved his lips. Oh, she would welcome him, and more, were he to put it to the test. He knew it as surely as he knew his name.

Why else had she run, if not from herself?

He walked around the catwalk to the other side of the gallery, and craned his head over the rail just as Miranda exploded from the door below.

He saw her toss her bright curls in withering response to some innocent comment poor Simon made, then Longfield's startled expression as she marched angrily away, headed for the lane between the trees with her red-gold hair streaming behind her like a battle standard.

In moments, her temper had carried her from his view.

Perhaps this evening was not the most auspicious time to take his supper at the inn, he decided ruefully. He had the feeling there would be a decided frost in the air, insofar as he was concerned. Aye, and a definite possibility that his victuals would be liberally laced with poison!

Tonight, he would have to see to his own supper.

Nevertheless, he was still grinning as he climbed up, through the trapdoor, to inspect and light the Argand.

There were few things he enjoyed better than a challenge, and lovely Miranda Tallant was a challenge, indeed. He would have his work cut out for him if he wanted her to spill her secrets on his pillow.

He rubbed his smarting jaw. Still, for a woman who was not only lovely, but perhaps knew the answers to the questions he wanted answered—he would happily endure far more than a slap and a few sharp words.

Aye. Much, much more. . . .

Chapter Eight

Two nights came and went before Morgan, dressed in his best, presented himself at the Gull, bearing a sizeable bouquet of wildflowers he had picked from the hedgerows along Gull Lane. Along with them were some not-so-wild marigolds he had "borrowed" from the window-boxes fronting Lizard Cove's high street.

It was a peace offering of sorts, and a sizeable one at that. As Simon had so bluntly pointed out, speaking slowly and carefully, as if Morgan were a simpleton, if he wanted to find out about the Killigrews, he must go where the Killigrews went. And where the Killigrews went was the

Black Gull Inn, where Morgan was now persona non grata.

There was nothing else for it, Simon had declared with frost in his tone and in his eyes. Morgan would have to eat humble pie and apologize to Mistress Tallant. . . .

And so, carefully shaven and well-groomed, a handful of stinging bay rum briskly applied to cheeks and jaw, he announced his arrival to Big Jan, who was pulling pints behind the Gull's bar, and inquired after the lady of the house.

When Big Jan returned from the inn's nether regions, however, it was to inform Morgan that Mistress Tallant was unavailable, and his presence at the inn unwanted.

"She wants ye t'leave, Mr. St. James," Jan added, his eyes doleful.

"Blast!" Morgan muttered.

"Got her properly riled up, did you?" Rob Killigrew observed with a grin from his post at the bar. "What did you do? Try to kiss her?"

"Aye," Morgan admitted ruefully.

Rob Killigrew snorted. "And got a slap for your trouble, I shouldn't wonder, judging by the size of that great posy you're carrying!"

"You're a perceptive man," Morgan observed with a wry grin. "If your beautiful sister ever decides to toe the scratch in the boxing ring of some country fair, she'll make a fortune in purses with that right hook of hers!"

"You don't have to tell me, man!" Rob chortled. "Who do ye think she practiced it on, eh? Me and our brother, Gil! Oh, she's a wild one, beneath that starched apron of hers, our 'Randa is. But there's none better to have on your side in a fight."

He raised his tankard in salute to his sister, and quaffed the last of his ale.

"Aaah. That's good!" He set the tankard down before turning back to Morgan. "Don't tell her I told you so, but you'll likely find her 'round back, in the kitchen. She dived into the passage when she saw you come in." He chuckled. "Go around by the stable yard, t'the back door. Likely you'll catch her there, aye?"

"I'm forever in your debt, sir," Morgan said with a broad grin. He fished a coin from his inner pocket and tossed it onto the scarred bar. "Halloo, bartender! Another pint for my friend here!"

"After you've brought in the kindling, fetch me some more candles, would you, Tommy?" Miranda murmured without turning to look at whomever had come in.

Her bottom swayed enticingly beneath her skirts as she vigorously stirred the kettle of lamb-and-barley broth that simmered over the kitchen fire.

The huge blond man lounging against the door frame grinned and wetted his red lips. Crossing beefy arms over a brawny chest, he settled back to savor the fetching picture made by Lizard Cove's wealthiest widow.

Her bright hair was twisted into a knot on top of her head and held in place by a jet comb inlaid with silvery mother-of-pearl flowers. Strands of burnished copper fell untidily, yet alluringly, about her rosy face.

The low square neckline of her hunter-green gown exposed a delightful expanse of lace-trimmed bosom; skin that was rosy and glistening from her labors and the heat of the fire.

"Tommy?" Receiving no answer, Miranda straightened and turned around, sighing in exasperation. "That wretched boy—"

Her turquoise eyes widened when she saw the man standing there, instead of the lad she'd expected. "Carl! What are you doing back here?"

"What do you thinking I'm doing, woman?" Carl Coppinger's leer widened to a broad, lecherous grin. "I've come a-courting ye."

Her eyes took on a frosty glitter. Carl was the worse for liquor—the Safe Harbor's liquor, not the Gull's. When he drank, he was dangerous, and his idea of "courting" and her own were quite different.

"Oh, have you, now? Then you'd best be gone right smartly, because I'm not in the market for another husband. And if I was, I'd not be looking at you, Carl Coppinger. Now, go!"

Carl's grin became a belligerent scowl. "Hark at you, Mistress high-and-mighty Tallant! You treat me like dung to be scraped from the soles o' your fine shoes!" he sneered in a tone that made the fine hairs on her nape prickle. "Who do you think you are, to turn your nose up at me, woman?" he demanded, taking two great strides across the room to loom over her. "I've had better women than you, Miranda Killigrew. Ladies of quality!"

The kitchen shrank around him. Carl's bulk filled it as he crowded her into a corner, forcing her to look up at him.

"I'm the owner of this inn, that's who I am!" she snapped bravely, pretending a courage she did not feel. "And I'm telling you to get out, before I have you thrown out!"

"Oh, no. Not this time, you don't. I've had enough of you flaunting yourself beneath my nose. Dan Tallant's gone. You need a man, Miranda."

"Do I now?" she scoffed. Her tone was withering, her aqua eyes blazed as she glared at him. "For *what?*"

"To plant sons in your belly, woman! Sons t'run this inn when we're old and gray. Something your fine Daniel wasn't man enough t'do, eh?" he jeered.

"Don't you talk about my Daniel! He was ten times the man you are, Carl Coppinger! Don't you dare touch me!" She screamed as he reached for her.

Raising the heavy iron ladle she'd hidden behind her back, she swung it at his head, trying to break free of the ham-like paws he clamped about her waist.

"You don't mean that," Carl said thickly. He squeezed her wrist so painfully, the ladle clattered to the floor from numbed fingers. Slamming her up against the whitewashed brick wall so hard that she saw stars, he pinned her there, then forced his bulky knee between her thighs.

"I'm done playing your games, my girl. When your belly starts to swell, you'll beg me to marry you!" His breathing labored, his massive chest rising and falling like bellows, he thrust his hand beneath her skirts.

Fear gripped her in icy fingers. Dear God. If she screamed, no one would hear her above the loud laughter in the taproom. She was on her own.

"The devil I'll marry you!" she panted. "Get off me, you bloody pig!" Bringing up her knee, she jabbed it at his groin.

"Oh, no, you don't, my lass," he warned thickly, stepping back. "Not that old trick!"

Furious, she beat her fists against his chest and tried to push him away, but he was as big and solid as a door. Her efforts to fight him only whetted his appetite.

"Be still, ye damned bitch!" he snarled. Swinging her around, he flung her roughly across the scrubbed table, onto her back, and pinned her beneath his chest. He gagged her with a heavy forearm pressed across her windpipe.

The mask was off now, the beast fully exposed as he roughly fondled her breast.

"You'll soon be singing a different tune, my girl," he rasped as he fumbled with her skirts. "Just see if you ar—*oooaaagh!*"

His scream began deep, but ended on a high, girlish note.

"Sounds as if you're singing a different tune yourself, eh, Coppinger?" Morgan growled. He had reached between Carl's legs from behind, to lift Miranda's attacker off her by certain vulnerable parts of the lout's anatomy. It was a handy tactic he'd learned in a dockside brawl in Macau he'd never known to fail.

175

Sure enough, Carl Coppinger howled like a whipped hound. *Yodeled*, almost.

"Or maybe you've always sung soprano? Is that it, my bully?" he growled, thrusting his dark, angry face into Coppinger's. "Either way, get it into your thick skull, chum," he rasped. "Mistress Tallant and I are . . . well, let's just say we have an . . . understanding. And I don't take kindly to other men pawing what is mine. Right?" He tightened his grip a little. His green eyes blazed.

"Yes!" Carl whispered hoarsely, his blue eyes bulging. Sweat beads popped out on his skin, rolled down his ruddy face and soaked into the too-small grimy collar that choked his bull-like neck.

"I can't hear you." Again, the fist tightened.

"Yeees!" blubbered Coppinger. "Oooooh, God, yeeess!"

"Better," Morgan murmured with a nasty grin. "Now, run along, my bully!"

He swung Coppinger around, planted a booted foot squarely against his backside, and shoved.

Carl barrelled forward, head first. It was only by some miracle he regained his balance before he reached the door.

Rocking on his heels, he swung around to face Miranda and Morgan like a huge blond dancing bear, stabbing a shaking finger in their direction. His face was contorted with pain and fury.

"No man makes a fool of a Coppinger, least of all a bloody lighthouse keeper!" he swore. "You'll be sorry for this, some day, St. James. You . . . you mark my words!"

Coppinger's warning lingered in the air long after the lout himself was gone, like the pungent residue of some foul odor.

"Well, well. It appears I came in the nick of time, does it not, Mistress Tallant?" Morgan asked softly.

Miranda snorted as she tried to regain her composure, busying her trembling hands in adjusting the clothing that Coppinger had left in disarray.

Vivid spots of color bloomed in her cheeks, the only outward sign of her upset. Her apparent composure filled him with admiration. She was quite a woman.

"Did you indeed? And for what, I wonder?" she demanded hotly. "To continue what Carl started? Or to go on where you left off the last time?"

Her unexpected attack stunned him. He winced. A muscle ticked at his temple. "Ouch. You've a sharp tongue, Miranda Tallant! Aye, and a cruel one."

"Do I? Thank you! I also have an excellent

177

memory to go with them. Go away, St. James! Get out of my inn!"

He bristled. His huge hands curled into fists. "The devil I shall! I came here to apologize to you, woman. So don't you dare go comparing me to that . . . that—"

"Rutting animal?" Miranda suggested, rounding on him before he could think of an appropriate epithet. "That great randy goat?" Her fists were planted on her hips, her eyes giving off turquoise sparks now. "Give me one good reason why not? Carl tried to take advantage of me. So did you! Carl kissed me. So did you. Where's the difference, pray?"

"In the intent, madam, at very least. It was my intention to seduce you," he explained, his green eyes sensual. "To woo you in such a way you could not help but succumb. Whereas, he!" His jaw hardened. He shook his head in disgust. "Coppinger was bent on rape! On force and control. He had you pinned beneath him to the table, for God's sake, while I . . ." He shook his head, obviously furious. "There is something you must know, Miranda. I have never forced a woman to my will. Nor would I, under any circumstances," he added, his voice dropping to a low, sensual growl. "Difficult as it may be for you to believe, I have never lacked *willing* bedmates."

"No? Then what brings you here?" she challenged him.

"I came to apologize, and . . . to bring you a small token. A peace offering, if you will."

"Really? I see nothing." She glared at him, her expression one of disbelief, suspicion.

He stepped back outside, and reappeared carrying an enormous bouquet that almost hid him from view. It looked as if a huge posy of wildflowers had grown human legs and arms.

He peered around the floral offering, trying to look penitent with his dark head bowed, his green eyes downcast. But it was no use. No use whatsoever! His thick black lashes made dark smudges against the rugged wind-browned angles of his cheekbones, and to her, his scowling face had never looked more handsome than it did now. . . .

Her anger vanished like smoke on the wind. She giggled. "Are there any wildflowers left in all of Cornwall?

"Just one or two. Friends?" Morgan suggested hopefully.

She sighed. "I suppose so."

"Prove it, Miranda. As Ferdinand said, 'Here's my hand,'" he said softly, quoting the words from Shakespeare's *The Tempest* as he held his hand out to her in a gesture of peace. He had a feeling she would know the lines of the play by heart, since her own name had been taken from it.

"And mine, with my heart in't," Miranda responded easily, tucking her hand in his.

She was rewarded by a delighted, satisfied grin from Morgan as she took his peace-offering in the other.

"Your heart, too, Mistress Tallant?" he teased. "Then I may presume you're no longer angry about the other afternoon?"

"Well, that depends."

"Upon what?"

"On whether you are truly sorry."

"No," he admitted after a second's pause. "I'm not sorry. Not for kissing you, anyway. If I said I was, it would be a lie. You're a beautiful, desirable woman." His eyes caressed her, green shot through with flecks of gold. "I do, however, apologize for my impatience to do so."

"Prettily said, sir. But on second thought, I have come to the conclusion that you were not entirely to blame," she admitted, unable to look him in the eye. "On reflection, it is quite possible that some of my own . . . actions . . . could have been misinterpreted. My . . . um . . . concern for you as one of my guests, perhaps? Or a simple smile of greeting that you mistook for one of . . . encouragement, say?"

He nodded, knowing she was lying, that they

were both lying, but playing along regardless.

"If you truly accept my apology, you must prove it. Walk with me, Miranda," he urged, folding his fingers around her slender hand. "It's a beautiful evening for a stroll along the beach."

"The beach! Now? But . . . it's dark out!"

"On the contrary. There's a huge, silvery, full moon, just made for lovers! Or for the most cordial of friends," he amended softly. "I picked these by its light, just for you. The lane was as bright as it is by day."

She laughed, burying her nose in the fragrant wildflowers. "The lane, my foot! These marigolds weren't picked in any lane, sir! Nor the busy lizzies. Come morning, old Mrs. Pettit will be blaming the 'piskies' for stealing the flowers from her window boxes! She blames all her troubles on the little folk—"

"Even when the not-so-little folk are really to blame!" He grinned down at her, her face made mysterious now by the flickering kitchen fire, and by the play of light and shadow. God, she really was beautiful! And desirable, too. His treacherous body hardened. Truth was, he wanted her now, more than ever. But he would bide his time and court her first. He must, if he ever wanted to win her. . . .

. . . *or uncover her secrets*.

"Well, Mistress Tallant? What say you? Will

you walk with me in the moonlight?"

"Aye," she accepted softly after considering for only a second or two. "I will. But only because you and I have an . . . how did you put it for Carl's benefit? An *understanding*, I think it was?" She smiled. "Hand me my shawl from that peg, if you please, sir? I'll just put these flowers in water, then we can go. The poor things are sleeping. Look here. Their petals are half-closed. . . ."

He was right, she discovered as they strolled down the lane, arm in arm. Outside, it was almost as bright as day.

The straggly hedgerows were still bulky dark clumps, the trees darker still, but silvery moonlight flooded everything. It picked out the tiny faces of wildflowers hidden amongst the grass so that their pastel petals shone like ghostly stars.

Moonlight glistened on drops of dew, too, and gave leaves, grasses, stones and flowers an ethereal glitter, as if hung with tiny diamonds.

Somewhere off in the distance, a dog barked. As they strolled along, she thought she heard the shriek of a nighthawk, or perhaps it was an owl hooting as it hunted up on the high moors.

By silent agreement, their moonlit stroll drew them off Gull Lane proper, and onto a steep path littered with pebbles that led down from the cliffs to the ghostly beach below.

With the help of Morgan's strong arm to steady her, she clambered safely down to the pale sand and moon-kissed ocean below the cliffs.

The breakers beat against jagged black rocks there, sending showers of spindrift high into the air, like mist.

"Beautiful, isn't it? I've sailed the world over, but I always come home to England," Morgan murmured, gazing out at the silver-rimmed waves.

Crystal ripples danced up the sandy ribbon about his sea-boots, their sparkling edges fluted like blown glass.

"Like a lovely woman, her beauty never leaves a man. Instead, it becomes a part of him."

Their eyes met, and there was a world of meaning in their green and turquoise gazes. But, since Morgan clearly expected no answer, Miranda offered him none as they moved on, scrambling and clambering over the rocks. Headed, by silent if mutual consent, farther down the beach.

The tides had strewn their flotsam and jetsam upon the sand. Old King Neptune's treasure trove, Morgan thought.

Green glass fishing balls lay forgotten amongst sand, shells and shingle. A scrap of rot-

183

ting net with a few crumbling cork floats still clinging to it. A piece of oddly shaped driftwood, stag's antlers draped in garlands of brown weed that reeked of iodine and, more faintly, of fish.

Crouching down, he picked up one of the green-glass floats. Holding the small globe cupped in his hand, he brushed grains of sand from its surface, smoothing his hand over the glass like a Gypsy fortune-teller.

The murky green ball gleamed in the moonlight, full of mystery.

"I see a beautiful, heartless innkeeper—and a dark-haired man who is desperate for her love!" He grinned. "Catch, Miranda! Take my future in your hands. Do with it as you will!" He tossed the glass ball to her.

Laughingly, she caught it. "Heartless? Me?"

"Aye, saucy wench! There are few more heartless—or more lovely. Now. Your turn. Tell me what you see in the depths of the crystal ball," he urged, his laughing green eyes the same color as the glass globe in the moonlight.

"Very well, then." Playing along, she passed her hand over the globe's shining surface a time or two, as he had done, tawny brows crinkling as she peered into its depths.

"I see a dark-haired man. A very handsome man who is a mystery to me," she began hesitantly, but truthfully. "A man who confuses and pleases me at the same time, for he is like none of the men I have met before." She risked an embarrassed glance at Morgan, wondering if she had gone too far.

"Being different isn't always bad. Remember that, before you go on," he urged softly.

"This man claims to be one thing, but everything about him says that he's another. He is a man who. . . ." Here her voice wavered a little. "Who attracts and . . . and . . . frightens me, because of my unanswered questions about him."

"And?"

"And the way he makes me feel."

"So, you wonder about me, do you? A good sign, I'm thinking. What is it you'd like to know?" he said huskily, catching both her hands between his. "Ask away."

"Very well," she agreed, looking up at him. "Who are you, really, Morgan St. James? And why did you come to Lizard Cove? Are you truly a lighthouse keeper, as you claim? Or . . . something else entirely?"

He pursed his lips, wondering how best to answer her. "My name really is Morgan St. James. And for the time being, aye, I'm the lighthouse keeper," he murmured, choosing his words carefully. He would not lie to her, unless he had no option but to do so. "I was sent down to Cornwall by Trinity House, to keep the Lizard Light.

But your instincts are sound. I wasn't born to a lighthouse keeper's life, as you guessed. My family is an old and distinguished one in Devon. Very wealthy, too."

"Then what happened? Did they disown you?"

He had her full attention now. And, he thought, her sympathy, depending on what he told her next. She was staring intently at his mouth, her sweet face very serious. He itched to reach out and brush the ball of his thumb across her full lower lip. To touch his mouth to hers and feel her soft weight melt into his arms.

"In a manner of speaking, aye," he admitted. That much was true. Or had once been. "I ran away. Went to sea when I was just thirteen, you see? It happened right after my mother died. Perhaps it was my way of grieving. Or perhaps I just wanted to get away. Who knows? Whatever my youthful reasons, my father . . . well, Father was beside himself with grief. He had lost a beloved wife, a cherished friend. And within weeks he learned he would lose his son to the sea. He warned me that if I left his house, he would disown me. . . ."

"But you left anyway," she finished for him, and sighed. The conclusion she'd reached seemed to satisfy her, like a child who guesses the happy ending to a fairy tale.

"I left anyway." He said nothing more, but instead let his silence and a shrug of the shoulders signify agreement. Nor did he explain that his father had welcomed him back with open arms and open heart some seven years later to embark on a joint business venture that had become the St. James's lucrative shipping line.

Let her draw what conclusions she would.

"Do you miss them? Your family, I mean," she asked gently.

Her concern pricked him with guilt.

"Aye," he said gruffly, knowing she would mistake his brusqueness and reluctance to talk about it for emotion, and a reluctance to open old wounds. "Shall we walk on now, my dear?"

He took her hand in his as they made their way along the rocky shelf, linking his fingers through hers as they crouched down to investigate inky tidepools, half-hidden among their rocky basins.

In the black water, the magical moon swam like a great silver flounder, or a polished abalone shell.

The glittering black ocean, silver-rimmed and restless, continued its shushing refrain as they made their way toward several rowboats, pulled safely above the high-tide mark.

One, painted a dull red, its leaky hull fresh-caulked, had been propped up against some rocks by its owner while the pitch dried properly. It formed a windbreak against the chill sea-breeze.

In its lee, he halted and, removing his reefer jacket, he spread it over the sand for her to sit upon.

She did so, her skirts billowing about her.

There was a new expression in her eyes as she looked up at him. An awareness—perhaps even an eagerness?—that had not been there before.

Kiss me, her expression said.

And this time, there would be no rebuff, no angry protests. No slap. This time, that look said, she would kiss him back.

Lust flashed through his loins like summer lightning, hardening him. The thought of an eager Miranda, a Miranda who wanted him, as wanted her, was arousing, indeed.

Kneeling before her, his shirt a gleaming blue-white in the moonlight, he cupped her face between his hands.

Dipping his dark head, he sealed his lips to hers, gently bearing her down to the cool sand beneath them, still cradled in his arms.

"Miranda," he murmured, pressing his lips to the soft hollow at the base of her throat. "Lovely Miranda."

In some strange way, it was as if Morgan pressed his tender kisses to her heart, Miranda thought with a languorous sigh.

As he pressed a garland of tiny kisses from her sensitive ear to her mouth, her bones seemed to melt within her. Deeply moved by the tenderness of his caresses and by his romantic words, she set aside her mistrust of him. Smothered her suspicions. Surrendered to his lovemaking . . . *forgot her brother's warnings. . . .*

He had kissed her, as Carl had done. But whereas Carl's rough, wet kisses had made her recoil with revulsion, Morgan's lips made her shiver with delight. Carl's coarse, clumsy hand upon her breast had filled her with pain and fear, whereas Morgan's bold touch made her heart race, and brought a rosy flush to her cheeks.

One by one, he unfastened the tiny hooks that closed the bodice of her green gown, parting the two fronts to her waist, much as Moses parted the Red Sea.

Dropping kisses on the tops of her breasts, he deftly worked her busk down, until he had bared them. When she felt the sudden kiss of the breeze on her skin, her nipples tightened, both from cold and from anticipation.

Leaning back to admire her breasts, Morgan traced a circle around and around the delicate areolas with his fingertip, until the small pink buds stood firm as rubies.

"The women of Tahiti bare their breasts," he

189

murmured. "But none are as beautiful as you, Miranda! Like a mermaid on the sand!" Taking one ruby deep into his mouth, he drew upon it.

She bit back a scream of pleasure. It was as if part of her had been drawn into a miniature furnace. Sucked into a swirling vat of melted honey. His mouth was silky. *Fiery*. Odder still, she could feel what he was doing as a throbbing pulse between her legs.

The silvery tug of arousal.

She wanted him to undress her. To toss her garments to the seawinds and bare every inch of her. She wanted to scamper with him along the sands in the moonlight, both of them naked, as Mother Nature had intended. To plunge with him into the waves, and watch his green eyes darken with desire as he gazed at what Daniel had never seen: her naked body.

She did not want him to simply lift her clothing when—if—he made love to her, in respect for her modesty, as Daniel had done. *God, no*. She wanted him to cover every inch of her with kisses, as he was kissing her breasts. To *look* at her, taste her, touch her everywhere. As she, God help her, longed to kiss, caress and taste *him*. . . .

Little gasping sounds of pleasure and need escaped her. She knotted her fingers in the midnight silk of his hair. Cradled his midnight head close to her pale bosom. Just the sight of it nestled there aroused her.

"Oh, yes. Ohh, Morgan, oh, sweet, sweet love!" she cried when his teeth gently worried her tender flesh.

She gasped in surprise as she realized his hand was now beneath her skirts. When had he done that? He was kissing her breasts and stroking her thighs now, fondling the forbidden territory left undefended by her divided pantalets.

"Oh!" She moaned as he gently slid a finger deep inside her, his entry eased by a flood of liquid silk. "Don't stop. Ohhh. No, no, you should not. Oh, *yes, yes.* . . ."

"Make up your mind, my sweet," Morgan murmured against her ear.

His tone was tender, but amused. His hot breath raised goosebumps down her neck and arms. Oh, God, he was laughing at her! She wanted to say something, do something, to make him stop laughing, but then he began moving his finger in and out of her, first one, then two, gently at first, then with a stronger, more insistent rhythm, pushing deeper each time. And she could not find the will to speak.

The erotic friction made her whimper even louder. He stanched the sounds she was making with his kisses, still plying her with the delicious, intimate caresses that made her squirm

191

with mindless pleasure beneath him.

A widow she might be, and a beautiful one, at that, but Morgan knew she had learned very little about the sensual pleasures that were possible between a man and a woman. He smiled. He would enjoy teaching her. Would enjoy making love to her, too, and feeling her supple, exquisitely feminine body soften in surrender beneath his own, then come alive to his touch. But . . . not here on the damp sand. And not in the lee of some leaky old boat. She deserved better than a quick coupling in the shadows, like a sailor's doxy. Besides, a brief postponement would sweeten their ultimate lovemaking.

"Please, mmm, please, Morgan . . ." she was murmuring against his shoulder.

"Aye, I know, sweet. Let me finish you, aye?" he soothed. He deepened his thrusts, moving his hand more swiftly, parodying the act of lovemaking with his motions.

After a few moments of nothing but breathy sighs and moans, she began to utter little gasps of delight and astonished pleasure.

Her cries built until suddenly she arched her hips against his hand and grew rigid. He felt her lovely body contract around his fingers as she found her release.

His erection was painful against the coarse canvas of his sailor's breeches. So painful, he clenched his jaws. The temptation to sweep her beneath him, to bury himself deep inside her sweet hot flesh was enormous. But, for some reason, he could not. When he made love to her—and he would, someday soon, he promised himself—it would be because she wanted him. Not because she could not help herself, or because he'd given her no choice.

Jaw set, he withdrew his hand, trying to think of anything but her as he smoothed down her skirts and fought to regain his self-control.

When he had restored her modesty, he cupped her chin in his hand and gently kissed her, startled to taste salty tears on his lips and on her damp, hot cheeks.

"What . . . what must you think . . . of me?" she mumbled, some words lost, for her face was buried in his shirt. "Like a common . . . no decency. . . . I never intended . . . my Daniel's memory."

"Stop it, Miranda," he chided, giving her a little shake. "I think none the less of you for enjoying what I did. Nor should you think less of yourself. Next time, it will be my turn. And rest assured, when that time comes, I'll not ask forgiveness for taking my pleasure of you."

Clasping her hand, he raised her to her feet, then retrieved his reefer jacket and brushed the sand from it. "The wind is chilly. Will you wear my coat?"

"Yes, thank you," she murmured, looking away, still too ashamed to look him in the eye.

He draped the coat over her shoulders, then cupped her chin. Tilting her head up, he gazed deep into exotic, slightly slanted turquoise eyes, awash with tears in the moonlight, then ducked his head.

Pressing his lips to hers, he gave her a long and lingering kiss that surprised even him with its tenderness.

Then, slipping his arm about her, he walked her back along the sand to the cliff-path, and thence to the Black Gull Inn.

At the foot of the cliffs, in the shadow of a rocky overhang, Carl Coppinger watched them, still nursing his aching middle.

He saw the expressions on their faces as they passed within feet of where he stood, but they were too busy eyeing each other to even notice him.

So. That's how the wind blew, was it? St. James hadn't lied when he claimed he and the Tallant woman had some kind of understanding. The way that bitch Miranda's face glowed as she smiled up at the keeper was enough to tell Carl exactly what that "understanding" might be. She was giving the keeper what she'd denied him and every other man in the Cove since Dan Tallant had been planted six feet under!

Had a taste for men of property, Miranda did. Or gentrified coves, like Morgan St. James. What would the little bitch say if she knew the true depths of his own pockets, he wondered smugly? She'd spread her legs for him right smartly then, and no mistake!

Meanwhile, St. James had best watch his back, before he found six inches of Spanish steel slipped snugly between his ribs some fine dark night. . . .

That night, Miranda lay sleepless in her brass bed at the inn, thoughts of Morgan St. James chasing themselves around in her head like kittens playing tag.

If she closed her eyes, she could still feel the heat and pressure of his lips on hers, and where he had gently nipped or licked her skin, as if his flesh had the power to imprint—nay, brand!—itself on hers.

Her body still hummed with the afterglow of what he'd made her feel—and with the hunger to know what other pleasures he could show her.

Dreamily watching the tossing shadow of a great tree cast upon her whitewashed chamber wall, she wondered if Morgan lay sleepless in his circular room at the lighthouse, his long, lean body curled in the banana-shaped bunk, and thought of her . . . *wanted her!*

"Moon madness." That's what Mam would have called it, had she still had her wits about her. The lovesick yearnings of a girl who had been wed once, and was now a young woman, quite old enough to know better.

Still, the urge to get out of bed, throw a cloak over her nightgown, and run down the lane to the lighthouse and Morgan's bed was a powerful one. It was only the possible consequences of such an act that kept her huddled there beneath the quilted counterpane.

She finally fell asleep with the last stroke of the clock in St. Breoch's stone tower.

'Twas the hour of midnight—the witching hour! But where Miranda was concerned, all was far from well. . . .

Chapter Nine

It began that night, she decided later. Loving Morgan. Wanting him. A fever took hold of her in the lee of that leaky old rowboat, and refused to let go.

Several times a week, she found an excuse to wander down Gull Lane to the lighthouse, bearing gifts of bread loaves or sausage or garden vegetables that she insisted, always, were for Simon Longfield, but which all three of them knew were really for Morgan.

Morgan, in his turn, took to attending St. Breoch's church each Sunday morning, and to shooting her long, sinful looks from the pews that were the talk of the Cove, and of a certainty had no place in any house of worship.

He also visited her inn almost every night and would sit, watching her, from one of the settles in the taproom as she tended her patrons. And if her step was lighter, her laughter more ready and musical, her cheeks rosier when the keeper was there than before his arrival, well, where was the harm in that?

Sometimes, the kittens, Kit and Kat—half-grown now—would follow him down the lane. They sat at Morgan's feet in the sawdust that was sprinkled over the taproom flagstones while he lingered over his pint. When he was done, they padded back to the lighthouse in his wake, their furry tails carried erect like gray and ginger rudders.

While at the inn, Morgan chatted with patrons, be they farmer or fisherman, tinker or squire. They talked about the weather and the crops, about their livestock and their fields. And, little by little, his easy ways, his casual banter and innocuous comments stilled their mistrust and made them forget they'd ever been suspicious of the handsome green-eyed stranger in their midst.

Besides, his looks—his smoldering smiles—were all for Miranda. The occasional kiss and cuddle they managed to steal in the passage behind the bar or in some shadowed corner of the inn were all the sweeter for their rarity. The danger of discovery sharpened desire, too, and gave each clandestine moment an added excitement.

Still, to the would-be lovers, each parting, each moment of separation was agony.

"You need a man in your bed, Mistress Tallant," Morgan declared one night in September when he surprised her in the drafty kitchen passage. His green eyes danced wickedly in the shadows as he drew her closer. Such comments angered her, he knew, for they smacked of what Carl Coppinger had said. *"Tonight."*

As he'd expected, she stiffened in his arms. "I do not! Men always talk about the 'needs of widows,' but precious little heed is paid to whether those needs are real!" She glowered up at him, stabbing her index finger into his chest. "Contrary to what you and others may believe, Keeper St. James, I am quite content in my widowed state. Both in bed and out of it!"

She'd convinced herself that a proper wife would honor her dead husband's memory, and so tried half-heartedly to push Morgan away, to lift his hands from her bosom and scold him for his boldness. Then she would run, and keep on running!

But she would not—*could* not—bring herself to lift his hands from her body. She was too busy holding her breath, and praying there would be more. . . .

She was still a young woman, after all. A woman of flesh and blood who had needs and desires. One who was vibrantly alive!

He was right, damn him, she realized! She *did* need a man—but not just any man.

She needed *him*.

"Are you really content, Miranda?" he asked huskily, strumming callused thumbs over her sensitive nipples. The velvety buds tightened, pebbling beneath the stuff of her bodice. "In every way?"

"Yes! So . . . so you stop that, you wicked devil," she lied, flustered yet almost drunk with longing for him. But there was no snap to her protest. No sense of anger or urgency. Moreover, the invitation in her eyes, in the softening of her body, denied her claims. "Please. I must go! My patrons!"

But it was too late to avoid the moment they'd been hurtling toward ever since they met. Too late to go back. There was certainly nothing *she* could do to stop it, Miranda thought, dizzy with desire, even had she wanted to. Nor, it seemed, could he.

"I'll come to you tonight," he promised her. "Hush, don't bother pretending anymore, woman. We both know what we want, aye?

Leave the kitchen lock unbolted for me, sweet," he urged.

His voice was husky with lust sparked by the heated kisses they'd stolen in the drafty passage behind the bar. He pressed her up against the brick wall, then reached beneath her skirts to stroke her warm, secret flesh as if she were a twopenny whore.

The threat of imminent discovery, coupled with the cold and discomfort, heightened their hunger for each other. Gave it a deliciously dangerous, doubly exciting edge.

His heart was thundering, Morgan noticed as he dipped his head to kiss the pale ridge of her collarbone, just above the ruffled neck of her gown. And, judging by the throaty catch to her breathing, so was hers.

"I want you, Miranda. More than you know. Tonight, sweetheart. I'll come to you tonight. Upstairs." His voice was low and urgent. Excited. . . .

"No. You must not. Not here, anyway," she amended in a shaky whisper.

Her eyes were closed, her spine pressed to the cold brick of the wall. It was chilly in the stone-flagged passage, but her face burned nonetheless. Could he tell? Did he suspect? Had Morgan any idea just how badly she wanted to fling herself into his arms? To let him do as he would

201

with her, and devil take the consequences?

Surely he must be able to feel how her heart pounded as he slipped his fingers deep into her bodice? Cupping the fullness of her breast in one large hand, he teased the nipple until her breathing became little more than gasps.

"It's too risky here. Big Jan or Maisie could see us. Go home. I . . . I'll come to you," she promised shakily as he tweaked the sensitive buds between his fingers. "At the lighthouse. But . . . oh! What about Simon?"

"He sleeps in the keeper's cottage. Don't worry about him. When will you come?" he pressed.

"After closing. Give me a few minutes to lock up."

He nodded. "Ten. Not a minute longer." He gave her a quick, hard kiss, a fierce embrace. The lambent heat in his green eyes made her shiver. "I'll be waiting, Miranda. And Miranda, my sweet? My darling?"

"A . . . aye?" she murmured shakily. Dear Lord, even his whispered endearments caused a fluttering in her womb!

His eyes smoldered. "Don't dally. I'm not a patient man. Not patient at all. . . ."

Darkness came late to this corner of England. The golden evenings of late summer seemed to last forever, before melting into black-velvet nights.

That September's eve was no exception. The hands on the mantle clock seemed to move with agonizing slowness. Miranda wished they would fly!

It was eight before the sky turned to flame with the setting sun. Nine before charcoal shadows pooled over moors and countryside like spreading ink, and the last of the drinkers were gone.

In her room at the inn, Miranda stepped from the basin she'd filled with steaming water. She patted her glowing body dry, then lightly dusted herself all over with rose-scented powder, using a powder-puff of fluffy down feathers.

Trying not to look at the gleaming brass bed she'd once shared with Daniel, she dabbed French perfume on the pulse spots at her wrists, behind her ears and in the valley between her breasts. The fragrance of lilies-of-the-valley hung sweetly in the air. The small flacon of perfume had been a gift from her father and brothers. One of many similar luxuries they'd smuggled ashore, untaxed, as part of the smugglers' trade.

She was breathless with excitement as she sped down the moonlit lane, her red-gold hair flowing loose over her shoulders, her fringed

Spanish shawl thrown on over her night-chemise.

Silvery light glistened on dewy leaves and on blades of grass as she hurried along. Her heart was pounding as she began climbing the lighthouse's iron steps. The wild song of the standing stones swirled through her veins like hot wine as she swung open the door to Morgan's round room.

Hesitantly, she stepped inside, eyes widening as she looked around her.

Since bidding her farewell at the inn, Morgan had filled the room with lighted candles—dozens of them! And the trouble he'd gone to, for no other reason than to bring her joy, made love overflow her heart.

Scented beeswax candles stood in dishes upon every barren surface. Pools of quiet golden light softened the round, whitewashed room, and made it a lovely place; the romantic tower of some fairytale castle, of which she was the princess.

There were wildflowers, too. Hundreds of them! Flowers stolen from window-boxes and tiny cottage gardens, as well as wildflowers picked from hedgerows or woods. They graced enamel bowls, blossomed in earthenware jugs, trailed from china ewers and spilled from chipped pitchers.

Their delicate herbal perfumes mingled with the scent of burning wax, the briny, seaweed tang of the sea, and the exciting, masculine scent of the man himself.

She wanted to bury her nose in the good clean scent of him. To taste his salty flesh on her tongue and learn his body's subtle differences from her own with her lips and fingertips.

She wanted to lie with him on fresh-laundered linens that smelled of sunshine, sea-winds and flowers. To bask in the glow of the candles, and in the heated glow of his eyes.

"At last," he murmured, coming to meet her.

"You were so sure I'd come," she said huskily, looking up at him, suddenly shy. To cover her uncertainty, she hugged herself with her arms and walked over to the window.

"Not at first, no," he denied. Following her, he placed his hands on her shoulders, drew aside her hair and kissed her neck. "But on my way back from the inn, I saw a falling star—the first of the evening—and wished upon it."

His voice was husky as he gently rested his chin upon her head. Slipping his arms around her waist, he drew her back against his chest. "I wished for you, Miranda. In my bed. In my arms. In my heart. And, here you are. Wish granted."

Before and below them, the sea swept away to

the bloody horizon that cupped the sun like a fiery ball. Its last bright rays gilded the water with bronze and gold, and painted a glittering trough from the far distance, to the foot of the granite point on which the lighthouse stood. The tops of the clouds were still flushed with the last pink blush of day, their underbellies charcoal with the coming night, which already blanketed the land in darkness.

She turned in his arms and, looking up at him, saw that his green eyes were dark in the glorious light that poured through the window.

"Love me, Morgan. Love me," she whispered urgently.

"You're sure?" he asked on an uneven breath, his eyes searching her face. Cupping the fullness of her breast as if he cradled her heart, he asked again, "Really sure?"

His mouth hovered just above her ear. Its warm current stirred the fine hairs at her temple and tickled her ears. *Oh, God*. His pliant, sensual lips were slightly parted now. Ready, she knew, to kiss her. . . .

As it had before, Daniel's image rose up before her eyes, but his features were fainter now. The edges were softer, less sharply defined.

"Go on, woman," she heard his low voice in her mind. *"You were a grand wife to me, and I loved you with all my heart. But I'm gone now.*

*Don't cling to my memory. Don't grieve for me.
Live your life to the fullest, with my blessing. . . ."*

She felt his spirit move through her, like a whisper of wind, and then he was gone—*truly gone*—for the first time since he'd left his mortal shell.

And in her heart of hearts, Miranda knew he'd never return.

There was only Morgan now.

Morgan, whose midnight head dipped to hers.

Morgan, whose hot breath she felt on her cheek and whose hungry mouth covered and captured her own.

Morgan, whose touch made her come alive. Whose searing kisses and caresses left her hungry for more.

"Yes," she murmured, turning to face him. "I'm sure. Oh, Morgan, hold me!"

A delicious shiver ran through her as she raised her arms and curled them about his neck, plunging her fingers into the thick, dark waves at his nape.

Her eyes closed on a sigh. Dark lashes fluttered against her cheeks as his sweet, hard lips came down and stole her breath away. And then he was cradling her, holding her in arms of steel, and it felt so wonderful, so right, she wished she need never leave!

His hands slid down from her breasts to cup

207

her bottom. To lift her against the hard ridge she could feel through his breeches. His tongue stabbed deeply inside her mouth, sliding against her own.

The intimate contact made her shudder. Her heart pounded. Her fingers clenched over the rough silk of his hair. She gasped as heat lanced through her breasts, her belly, her womb.

Whispering her name, he lifted her into his arms and carried her to the narrow, curved bunk. There, he set her down as if she were made of finest crystal.

The Spanish shawl fell away to pool beneath her as he dragged her ruffled nightgown down, off her shoulders.

She wore nothing beneath it.

"Sweet Lord, look at you!"

Breathing raggedly, he whispered endearments, calling her his sweetheart, his love. He caressed and kissed her everywhere with such reverence, his kisses became prayers, his caresses a reverent celebration of their passion.

She began to tremble as he worshipped her with lips and tongue, teeth and hands, instead of words alone, until he'd filled her with a honeyed languor. A dreamy heaviness filled her limbs and belly and she wished it would last forever.

The sun's last rays had become shafts of

moonlight, joining the candles' flickering glow to drench the whitewashed walls in shadows, light and magic, when he knelt between her thighs.

By the candles' glow, he saw her eyes darken to a deep, dreamy aqua as he lifted himself over her. Her lips parted on a sigh. Her hair spilled a shining swathe of red-gold through his fingers, cascading like molten copper across the snowy bolster and playing hide-and-go-seek with the nipples that stood up, like rosebuds carved of angelskin coral, against breasts as flawless as pearls.

Dipping his head, he drew her pouty lower lip between his teeth, and nipped it. At the same time, he slipped his finger between those other, softer lips below, crowned with auburn curls.

He groaned. She wanted him as badly as he wanted her. The proof—had he needed any—was right there in the silky moisture that sheathed his finger. And the heat—ah, such heat!

She sighed at his intimate touch, arching herself against his hands and lips like a kitten, pressing belly and hips to his aching loins.

He groaned at the sight of her, beautiful, naked before him. So ready and eager to be loved.

"Hurry!" she urged him, tugging the shirt from his belt. She slid her hands under the fabric to rub his belly and chest. "Take me now! Oh, God, Morgan, *hurry!*"

His dark head disappeared briefly as he lifted his shirt up and off, ripping the fine linen in his haste. Flinging the garment aside, he bared a broad-shouldered, lean torso, a tanned chest bisected by a narrow T of black hair, and a belly as flat and firm as a washboard. His sea-boots followed, thudding to the polished wood floor; then he slowly unfastened his canvas trousers, knowing her eyes traced the line of dark hair below the fly opening as he stepped from them.

"I am," he growled in answer to her urging. In a deeper, huskier voice, he added belatedly, and quite unnecessarily, "ready, that is."

The sight of him, standing there, gloriously male, in all his ready nakedness, made the spit dry up in her mouth.

It did not, however, cause her to cover her eyes.

Nooo. Far from it.

St. Breoch and all the little piskies! She had never seen a man completely naked before, despite having been married for three years!

Daniel had been modest by nature, and had taken pains not to embarrass or offend her modesty, even on their wedding night. Consequently, they'd always made love in the dark. Never naked, as they had come into the world, with a hundred candles blazing . . . *and everything showing!*

Morgan looked, she decided, her cheeks reddening, like a disgustingly healthy male animal. Tanned, virile—and decidedly dangerous. Nor was his claim that he was ready a lie. Hardly!

His manhood was huge, erect and carried well to the fore. It jutted like a great ruby-and-marble battle spear from a fistful of coarse, ink-black curls. His backside, by contrast, she saw as he obligingly turned, was round and hard with muscle. . . .

Her blush deepened as she realized he knew very well that she was staring at him. Knew—and liked it!

"Soo? Do you still want me to hurry, sweetheart?" he drawled, his lilting voice a silky, rumbling purr now. His fists were on his hips, and an arrogant, devilish grin tugged at his lips.

"Yes! Even more so," she whispered. "Oh, God, yes, hurry! I . . . I want you i . . . inside me!"

He nodded, his eyes, hooded now, never leaving her own. "Then you must open your legs for me, Miranda," he commanded softly, gobbling her up with those wonderful dark-green eyes. His hand swept down her body in a single, possessive caress. It was like the kiss of wildfire, and

211

made her tremble uncontrollably. "Take me inside you."

Her eyes still locked to his, she did as he asked.

Dropping to his knees between her parted thighs, Morgan lifted her hips, and drove into her.

His first powerful thrust went deep. It wrenched a groan of pleasure from him, and an answering sob of delight from her. Again and again, he thrust into her, flexing his muscular flanks to send her passion soaring, until she found herself poised on the brink of something wonderful and new. A dizzying precipice of pleasure she'd never reached before.

"Oh, Morgan!" she sobbed. The night shattered into a thousand golden splinters that left her sobbing his name, over and over. Her slender body arched beneath his, rigid as a drawn bow. Her fists clenched in the rumpled sheets.

Morgan grunted an oath as he felt her climax drawing him deeper, deeper, into her lovely body, hastening his own release.

When it came, he gave a great shudder. Sweat sprang out on his brow as he roared her name aloud, gripping her hips. Holding her fast.

His chest heaved as he bucked against her, and his shout echoed like thunder through the lighthouse tower.

"Miraaaanda!" he roared. *"Ah! Miranda!"*

*   *   *

They made love twice more that night—slower, gentler matings than the first explosive joining. Just as Miranda was about to drift off to sleep, Morgan squeezed her shoulder to wake her.

"Come on, sleepyhead! Let's take a moonlight swim," he urged. "You can wind the sheet around you. No one will see."

"A swim?" she said incredulously. "*Tonight?* Have you gone mad? The water's freezing out there!"

"No, it's not. The ocean retains the heat of the day. It will be warmer in the water than on the shore."

"I'll take your word for it. You go, then come back and tell me all about it," she urged, snuggling back under the covers. "I'm exhausted."

"I wonder. Are you really exhausted—or is it just that you can't swim? At the lake, you said you knew how, as I recall. But now? I'm not so sure."

"I swim like a fish, I'll have you know. A fish that will not be tricked into taking your bait, sir!"

"Then prove to me you can hear the stones sing, as I do!"

"How could I do that?"

"Take a chance! Take a risk, innkeeper! Give in to impulse and do something dangerous! Something reckless and out of character! Something wonderful! Get up! Come swim in the ocean with me!"

With that challenge, he headed for the door.

"It's not working. I'm not going with you."

No answer. The door closed softly behind him. With or without her, he had gone.

She cursed in a very unladylike fashion and muttered, "Madman!" under her breath. Nonetheless, she wound the bed linen around her body like a toga and scampered after him, finding him waiting for her halfway down the lighthouse's wrought-iron steps.

"What kept you, my sweet?" he asked, grinning.

"You! How did you know I'd follow you?"

"I didn't, but I hoped. Did I ever tell you just how lovely you are?" he murmured moments later, when they stood facing each other on the smooth, cold sand. "The Birth of Venus, come to life."

Despite his tan, their nude bodies were pale in the moonlight. Bare skin gleamed like satin as the nightwind lifted her hair, and made the long, soft ringlets swirl about her face and body.

"I think you did, once or twice."

He took her hand in his and drew it to his lips, kissing the tips of her fingers, then he padded down the sand, and waded into the shallows, leading her after him by the hand.

She gasped as chilly black water, agleam with moonlit waves that were rimmed with silver and white and spangled with diamonds, rose up to her armpits, then she kicked free, and let the tide lift and take her, swimming after her lover like a mermaid with only a flick of her lithe tail.

As she swam after him, doubts chased themselves around in her head, like dogs chasing each other's tails.

What if someone saw them together, both naked, she wondered? What if they drowned, and their dead—and naked—bodies were washed up upon the beach, for all the people of Lizard Cove to see and speculate about?

But then, she amended, if she was dead, she supposed what people thought of her would no longer matter. . . .

Morgan swam up alongside her, his black head jutting from the inky, gleaming water like a seal's, streaming silvery cascades as it broke the surface. He was laughing at her, she realized.

"Enough, Miranda! Enough worrying about what people might think. Enjoy the moment, instead. For just this once, surrender to the other Miranda who lives inside you. The Miranda who yearns to be wild and free, and not Widow Tallant, the proper innkeeper, at all."

"How did you know? About the stones singing,

215

I mean?" she whispered, treading water.

He grinned. "You told me, at the lake that day. Remember? You said you'd heard them humming. But when I asked you to repeat yourself, you refused. I couldn't believe my ears, because *I feel it, too*, Miranda. That faint humming, like a song. The stones' vibrations call to something in my blood. They kindle some ancient memory!"

"Yes! That's exactly how it feels," she agreed eagerly.

"How do you like the water?" he asked, taking her in his arms. "Warmer now?"

"Warmer than I expected, aye," she admitted. In fact, the water felt wonderful, like cool silk, flowing all around her, in sharp contrast to her head and shoulders, which quickly grew chilled by the wind.

"Have you had enough yet?" he challenged.

"I think so, yes."

"All right. Come on out, then."

Except for her shivering, she stood quite still on the cold damp sand while he briskly rubbed her all over with a corner of the sheet, then wrapped the rest about her tingling body.

They raced back to the lighthouse, hand in hand, giggling like children as they sprinted past the keeper's cottage where Simon slept on, blissfully unaware, past the horse shed, where Morgan's horse neighed in greeting, then on up the iron staircase, to Morgan's round room.

Moments later, curled warm and snug under several coarse blankets, spoon fashion, their bodies glowing from the combination of cold water and brisk toweling, they drifted into exhausted sleep, wrapped in each other's arms.

When they next awoke, the candles had burned down to half their lengths, and the sky glimpsed through the room's small rectangular windows was black, spangled with tiny glittering stars.

"Are you awake?" he asked. The question was redundant, he realized immediately, for he was looking down into open turquoise eyes that reflected the candles' dying flames, and had the dreamy, heavy-lidded look of a woman who has been well-loved.

"Hmmm, I'm not sure," Miranda murmured lazily, smug as a cream-fed kitten. "I could be dreaming."

She reached out to run her finger down his cheek. It felt scratchy now with new beard. From his square chin, she traced the narrow T of sparse dark hair down over a rock-hard abdomen to the small well of his navel.

Ticklish, he sucked in a breath, grabbed her hand and laughed huskily.

God, he was handsome, his torso tanned

217

golden brown from working, stripped to the waist, under tropical suns.

"Perhaps everything that happened last night was a lovely dream?" she suggested softly.

He lifted her hand and kissed her fingertips. "It was no dream, my sweet. And I thank God it was not."

"You do? But, why?" She frowned, wrinkling her nose delectably.

He grinned, dropping a kiss on that nose. "Because dreams are rarely repeated, Mistress Tallant. And I have every intention of repeating what we did last night," he threatened. "Time and time again. . . ."

She giggled. "Hmmm. I'd like that," she murmured, snuggling against him like a small, sleepy animal.

He ducked his head, and kissed her lips this time. A long, deep kiss that in some strange way confirmed what had passed between them.

"Get some sleep, love. It will be dawn soon enough. And you, my love, have an inn to run, remember?"

She made a face. "How could I forget?"

The night sky was the color of ashes, the moon faded to a fingernail crescent of pale light when she slipped from the lighthouse door.

She sped past the keeper's cottage where

Simon Longfield slept, his shutters still closed against the coming day.

Where the rocky point gave way to Gull Lane, lined on either side with hedgerows, ditches and trees, she halted and turned back to look at Morgan, leaning over the rail of the catwalk. He was barechested, and wore only his canvas breeches.

Smiling, she pressed her fingers to her lips and blew him a farewell kiss. A slender woman whose nightgown was molded to her figure by the wind, and whose glorious hair and fringed Spanish shawl whirled like dervishes on its blustery breath.

He lifted his own hand in salute, stabbed by guilt as she gave a last wave, then turned and headed home.

He and Miranda had been good together, he mused. And their lovemaking had seemed especially pleasurable for her, as if the depths of her own sensuality had stunned her.

It didn't surprise him. From what little he knew of the man, Daniel Tallant had been a decent husband, a moral, God-fearing man, but also one who—like most men of his class and generation—had not expected his wife to seek pleasure in their marriage bed.

In fact, he doubted Tallant had known decent, moral women *could* find pleasure in it. Most men thought only lower-class women enjoyed bedsport. Prostitutes. Seamstresses. Nurses. Actresses. Camp followers. Domestic servants. Mistresses.

Married women merely suffered their husband's attentions to get children, or to satisfy their spouses' animal lusts, for men were known to be of a far baser nature than women.

Morgan knew better. Women were as capable of sexual pleasure and fulfillment as their male counterparts. Perhaps even more so. All it took was a partner who had both the patience and the desire to show them the way.

As he watched Miranda's bright head vanish into the morning, he was filled with remorse and no little guilt. Miranda was a desirable, beautiful, intelligent woman. A woman any man would be privileged to call his own. And God knew, he'd wanted to bed her. That much had been no lie.

What had been wrong was for him to let her give herself so trustingly to him, believing her surrender would lead to a betrothal, then marriage. Oh, yes, she'd marry him, if he asked her! She was more than half in love with him already. He had seen it in her eyes when she kissed him goodbye. It was in her touch, her voice and kisses, too. Besides, a woman like Miranda did not casually take a lover, as did widows of the gentry, unless she loved him and believed his intentions were honorable.

Aye. He'd encouraged Miranda to think he wanted more, when in fact, all he'd wanted was the answers to his questions. . . .

She would despise and loathe him when she learned he'd used her.

Although he was only doing what he must, to expose Geoff's killers, the knowledge saddened him.

Chapter Ten

Morgan was nowhere to be found a few mornings later when Miranda walked down to the lighthouse to deliver a letter that had come for him. The round room where they had made love so gloriously was empty except for the kittens who were playing with a length of twine.

"A good day to you, Mr. Longfield!" she sang out cheerfully, taking the last few stairs back down to the ground. Kit and Kat sprang down the stairs after her and ran, meowing, to wind about Simon's legs.

"And to you, ma'am," Simon murmured, tipping his sailor's peaked cap to her. Bending, he petted the cats.

"Is Keeper St. James not here this morning? A letter came by this morning's post coach, but he isn't tending the lantern," she said.

She held up the letter as proof. The stiff cream envelope, addressed with exquisite script was, she'd already decided, penned by a female hand. A blob of red sealing wax closed the flap.

"Gone to empty his lobster pots, he has, ma'am," Longfield replied, indicating the beach with his pipe-stem. "If ye hurry, happen you'll catch him before he rows out to 'em."

"Thank you." Tucking the letter into the pocket of her coat, she hoisted her skirts and scrambled down the rocky path to the beach.

Summer was waning, and autumn on her way to Lizard Cove. In just a few days, the sea pinks, the thrift and all the other bright flowers of summer had vanished. In the woods, the first of the leaves were turning scarlet, russet and gold. Others were ready to fall. The damp wind that blew in off the sea this morning had sharper teeth than it had a week ago, when they had swum in the moonlight.

Miranda was glad of her short jacket as she hurried down the path.

There he was! She could see his tall, dark figure, dressed in a navy-blue fisherman's jersey, canvas trousers and sea boots, farther down the beach. He was dragging a red rowboat down the shingle into the shallows.

"Morgan!" she called, waving. "Wait for me!"

"Come on, then! But I don't have all day! Shake a leg!" He waved in return, shading his eyes to watch as she pelted down the beach toward him. Shingle sprayed, crunching under her feet. Great clods of wet sand flew up behind her.

"Simon says you're going to collect your pots," she began, breathless as a girl, the letter forgotten when she reached him.

"Aye. I caulked this old tub last week, then Simon and I took her out and set a few pots around the cove. It's a fine spot for lobster. They'll be big bullies, too, I'm hoping! The waters around here are deep and cold, and the currents are strong. Perfect for lobstering, aye?"

"Yes. Whose boat have you borrowed?"

"This one belonged to Billy Ashe. I'd say it's mine now, as the light's new keeper, wouldn't you?" He grinned.

"Oh, of course."

"Well, then? Are you coming out with me, woman?"

"Just try to stop me!" She snorted with laughter, her turquoise eyes sparkling as she quickly bent to unlace her boots, and peel off her stockings. "I'm the daughter of a Cornish fisherman-

225

turned-farmer, remember?" she boasted as she hopped on first one bare pink foot, then the other. "Wild horses couldn't keep me away. There. Ready!"

"Good. But if you're planning to eat *my* lobster, you'll have to do more than just stand there and look beautiful." He laughed. She really did look beautiful, with her face all pink and glowing and her eyes shining like jewels. "Heft that end of the boat for me, woman! On three. One . . . two . . . threeaaggh!"

Together, Morgan pulling, Miranda pushing, they shoved the sturdy little craft down the shingle and out, into deeper water.

Hitching up her skirts, Miranda struggled to scramble aboard the bobbing craft, squealing as she splashed about. "Owww! Hold her still! This water's f . . . freezing. Look! My poor feet are blue from paddling in it!"

"Blue! It's not cold enough for that, you bloody weakling!" Shaking his head in mock disgust, Morgan shoved her into the rowboat with a hefty boost that required planting both of his hands firmly on the cheeks of her bottom—and keeping them there far long than was necessary.

"You wretch!" she accused, turning an indignant red as he sprang into the boat after her, and took up the oars. "I didn't need *that* much help."

"Aye, I know," he admitted, grinning. "But I

226

did. What an inspiration you are, Miranda!"

"You!" she accused, dipping her hand over the side and splashing water at him.

He flicked his head aside. "Missed! Do you like lobster, then?"

"I love it!" she confessed.

Sunshine glinted off her coppery head, so that her hair shone red-gold, like the beech leaves in the woods he noted. Her eyes were the color of the sea this morning, green, gray and blue and all the myriad colors between. A man could lose himself in their depths, he thought absently.

"Why do you ask?"

"Oh, I was thinking that maybe—just maybe, mind—I'd give you some of mine."

"You'd better, St. James," she teased, adding, "if you know what's good for you! Lobster's tasty, all on its own. But lobster meat dipped in drawn Black Gull butter, and some baby potatoes boiled with mint and sea-salt, and perhaps a crusty loaf and some chilled hard cider to wash it all down, hmm, that is heavenly!"

"You drive a hard bargain, innkeeper," he murmured, offering her his hand. "Done!"

Laughing, she shook it heartily to seal their bargain, then drew his long, callused fingers to her lips to be kissed, before settling back to watch through half-closed eyes as he rowed.

From her seat, she enjoyed an uninterrupted

227

view of Morgan at the oars, which he plied in the same fashion he did everything else: intelligently, expertly, and with a minimum of wasted effort or fuss.

"You're a very handsome man, St. James. But of course, you already know that," she drawled.

"Aye," he agreed devilishly. "I do!"

She laughed, liking the way the wind tousled his black hair, and the way he narrowed his green eyes against the glare of light reflected by water, so that his dark brows crashed down like thunderheads. She liked the way his broad shoulders filled out his knitted jersey, too, and the smooth, sleek way he bent to the oars.

"Don't look at me that way, woman," he cautioned. "There are things that are better not tried in a rowboat. And what that gleam in your eyes is suggesting is one of them!"

"Really? And what's the other?" she asked cheekily as he rowed them over to a bobbing cork float that marked where he'd dropped his first lobster pot.

"Standing," he replied drily in answer to her question.

They were several hundred yards out now and, as always, the off-shore angle gave her a completely different perspective of Lizard's Cove and the surrounding area.

Over Morgan's shoulders, Miranda could see

all the ins and outs of the pretty Cornish coastline, the many bays and inlets, the harbors and river estuaries.

From the sea, the coastline and cliffs appeared to have been whittled willy-nilly from a piece of old black walnut. A lunatic's dining table, spread with the emerald tablecloth of the moors.

To the west lay the slate-and-cob cottages and shops of Lizard's Cove, straggling down the steep, winding high street to the little stone quay like limpets, gamely clinging to the granite cliffs.

From the harbor rose the masts of those few vessels that had not sailed at dawn with the fishing fleet, seeking the shoals of pilchard and mackerel that were the village's livelihood.

To the east, she could see the chimneys of her inn, and beyond it, the tower of St. Breoch's church, while the Lizard Lighthouse seemed even larger and loftier from this viewpoint, soaring majestically from the point itself.

On the stretch of golden sand farther down the coast, she spotted two familiar dark figures. Forbes and Archer, the artists, both guests at her inn. But there was no sign of either their canvases or their easels anywhere, unless they were the lumpy-looking arrangement abandoned by the sea-walk.

"How strange!" she exclaimed.

"What?"

"Mr. Forbes and Mr. Archer. Look, over there by the caves. D'you see them? They're not painting."

"Aye? What of it? Are the poor devils not allowed a day of rest, then? *Whoa!* Will you look at these bully-boys!" Morgan declared, hefting a dripping lobster pot over the side.

There were two sizeable lobsters in it, huge blue claws waving madly about. Having taken the bait, the poor creatures had been unable to find their way out of the wicker lobsterpot to freedom.

"Not feeling sorry for them, are you?" he asked, eyeing her askance. "You know what they say? They'll be tough as old boots, if you are."

"No, not in the least! To be honest, I was wondering if my kettle was large enough to hold both at once. Hmm. My mouth is watering already!"

"Bloodthirsty wench."

She smiled sweetly. "Aren't I?"

His other three lobster-pots held only one lobster apiece, none as big as the first two, but sizeable, for all that.

"One for Simon, one for tomorrow's lobster stew, one for each of us, and the other . . ."

"For Maisie and her mother, Mrs. Pettit, perhaps, if you're offering? They're of limited means, poor things."

"Would Mrs. Pettit be the old woman who huddles over her ha'penny worth of stout, and glares at me as if I were Satan incarnate?"

"That's her, bless her."

He sighed. "Ah, well. Maisie and her mother it is, then. Let's head home. My belly's growling."

They'd almost reached the shallows when she remembered the letter she'd tucked into her bodice.

"Oh, I almost forgot. This came for you, on the morning posting coach."

He shipped the oars and took it from her, giving the handwriting only a cursory glance.

"Is it from Trinity House? From your employers?" she inquired.

"Possibly," he murmured noncomittally, tucking the letter inside his jersey, unopened, and springing over the side.

Taking the tow rope, he waded ashore, tugging the bobbing little craft behind him until its bottom touched sand.

"Well, now! Here's a pretty handful I've caught in my net, aye, sweet?" he murmured. "A mermaid, as I live and breath!" Giving Miranda a quick kiss, full on the mouth, he scooped her up into his arms and swept her over the side.

He carried her through the shallows to the sand, where she'd left her neatly arranged boots and hose. Dropping a kiss on her nose, he set

231

her down, then went back for the rowboat and the lobster pots while she pulled on her stockings and shoes.

"Go home and set your biggest kettle to boil. I'll bring these bully-boys up to you," he told her, nodding at the lobster pots.

"Is something wrong, Morgan?" she asked. He seemed preoccupied suddenly. Did he want to get rid of her so that he could read his letter in private, she wondered? Was that it?

"No, nothing. Go on home, now, sweetheart. There's a nip in the air. I don't want ye catching cold with those wet feet. Tell Simon I'm bringing him his supper, if you see him."

"All right," she agreed, bending down to button her second boot.

Morgan's reassurances that nothing was wrong rang decidedly false, she decided as she walked back down the sandy lane to the inn. Who, she wondered, eaten up with curiosity, had the letter really come from? Certainly not from Trinity House, despite what he'd let her think! The blob of red sealing wax that closed the envelope flap had been stamped with a curlicue monogram. The letter C, rather than an official seal, as might be expected of Trinity House. What on earth, she wondered, did the letter say? And who was this 'C'?

She scowled. Unless Morgan decided to tell her, she would probably never know.

And for some unknown reason, it seemed terribly important that she should.

Chapter Eleven

"There's nothing else for it, love. Your mother must see another physician. Old Doc Hardee can't help her, and we can't care for her alone anymore. We don't know how. So, I've decided to take her to Bodmin tomorrow morning. I'd like you and Juliet t'come with me."

"But what if the physician there . . . what was his name?"

"Trethgallen, Dr. John Trethgallen."

"What if he wants to commit her? What then?" Miranda whispered, her throat choked with tears.

The possibility of their mother being committed to one of London's dreadful asylums was a possibility that had terrified them all ever since Catherine Killigrew began acting strangely, although they had been too terrified to voice their fears.

"We can't let her go into one of those horrid places. We just can't!" Miranda was pale and unsmiling as she set the lobster before her father.

A crock of drawn butter and a dish of boiled baby potatoes were set before him on the checkered blue-and-white cloth. A loaf of warm bread lay, half-sliced, on the breadboard.

Thad Killigrew slathered butter onto a thick "doorstep" of crumbly fresh bread, then scooped a morsel of lobster meat out of the giant shell, which had turned bright red with boiling. He munched a bite of buttered bread and lobster meat with every evidence of satisfaction.

Not unlike Morgan had done earlier, Miranda thought—although watching her lover devour the lobster with such relish had been a peculiarly sensual experience, and nothing like watching her own father do the very same thing.

"You've a grand touch at bread-making, love."

"Hmm?" She flushed guiltily. Her thoughts had been miles away. A quarter mile, anyway. . . .

"I said, this bread's very tasty," he murmured between great bites. "Just like your mama's, before she took sick."

"Don't you dare switch subjects on me, Papa. Did you even hear what I said?" she demanded, exasperated, her hands planted on her hips now. "About mama, I mean? What are we going to do?"

"Weell, this doctor's younger than most. Squire Draker told me about him. He thought he was worth talking to. I wrote to Trethgallen a while back, told him what was going on with your mother. He said he'd heard of something similar in Italy or some such place. Another farmer's wife, it was, too. He'd like to see her. He thinks he may be able t'cure her, Miranda!" His blue eyes shone, filled with new hope. "We have to give Cate that chance!"

"What did she do now, Da'? What happened, to make your mind up?" she demanded sharply. She held her breath, not at all sure she wanted to know the answer. "You didn't mention this new doctor or going all the way to Bodmin the other evening."

"She pushed Kitty down, love," Thad admitted wearily, his shoulders slumping, his eyes filling with tears.

"What!"

"Aye." He ran his hands through his silver-streaked hair. "Last night, it were, after supper. And Gil's poor lass so heavy with child, she couldn't get out of her way! Poor little Kitty started having pains soon after, so Juliet put her to bed with a hot brick. She was better this morning, and the pains have stopped, but I can't risk it happening again. I won't risk it!"

This was it, then. The turning point. The end of the road. They had to do something, had to get help, before Mama hurt someone, or hurt herself. She sighed. "All right, then. What time do we leave?"

"I'll bring the cart 'round for ye tomorrow morning. We'll stay the night at the Duke of Cornwall. They have a Harvest Fair and market there this week, so we'll have ourselves a look 'round, then drive back the next day. Rob'll keep an eye on the Gull for ye, lass. And ye've Big Jan and Maisie to see t'things here. Ye've no need to fret."

She nodded, resigned. She still had time to boil a ham for her guests' luncheon tomorrow. A larger one than usual, so that a few wafer-thin pink slices wouldn't be missed for sandwiches for the four of them to take. "All right. I'll come. I'll pack us a nice picnic basket to take with us, shall I?" she agreed, resting her head on his shoulder and hugging him. They had to do something, and this was as good a plan as any. "Why don't you bring mama here tonight?"

"I don't know about that." He looked deeply troubled.

"Room nine is vacant," she assured him. "Bring her and Juliet in through the kitchen entrance. No one will be any the wiser that she's here. That way, we can make an early start in the morning."

"All right," he murmured, trying to keep his voice normal and even. But it was too late. His daughter's support and gentle comforting had undone him. "You're a good girl, 'Randa," he said thickly, his throat choked with tears. He put his arms around her and held her close, something he'd not done since she was a little girl, except on her wedding day. "I don't tell you near often enough, and that's a fact, but you're a fine, good lass."

She smiled through a mist of her own tears. "Aye, but then, I had a good teacher."

Thad nodded. "The very best! And, God willing, this Dr. Trethgallen will help t'bring her back to us."

"Where's your mistress, Jan?" Morgan asked that same evening, coming around back to the inn yard, where Jan was forking hay and drawing water for the horses. There was no sign of Miranda.

"Blowed if I know, sir. Ain't she in back?" Jan responded. He paused in his forking to cock a gleaming eye at Morgan. It was obvious from his knowing grin that he'd guessed which way the wind blew between the lighthouse keeper and his mistress, and was amused by it.

"Not that I can see."

"Ah. Then 'tis likely she's upstairs, sir. Mr. Forbes, the artist gentleman, was complaining of a draft when he came in from his paintin.' Reckoned he couldn't sleep a wink last night for a stiff neck, besides. Happen she's gone upstairs t'take a look at the window sash."

Morgan grunted. "Very well."

He took the steeper, back staircase, running Miranda to ground just as she was leaving the room at the end of the hallway. Number nine— the one opposite her own.

When she saw him, a decidedly shifty, guilty look crossed her face. Why? he wondered. What was she up to?

"Found you," he murmured, slipping his arms about her waist and drawing her to him in an amorous way.

"Stop that! Morgan, don't," she insisted, trying to squirm free. "What are you doing up here, anyway?"

"What else would I be doing? Looking for you, my sweet. Hmmm." He sniffed her hair. "Baking day, was it? You smell of cinnamon from Ceylon. Vanilla from Madagascar! Good enough to eat."

She squealed as he nipped her earlobe with his teeth. "Grrr."

"Morgan, stop that. Come downstairs with me. *Now*," she insisted sternly.

"Scared?" he taunted. She certainly seemed very nervous. In fact, she was breathless. *Why?*

He cupped her breast, and could feel her heart racing through the stuff of her gown as the small nipple quickened and hardened under his hand.

"You were far from scared the other night, remember, my sweet? What happened since then to change your mind, hmm?" he wondered, crowding her back against the door to room nine—the one she'd been leaving with such a guilty look on her face.

He ducked his head to kiss her, fumbling for the doorknob behind her as he did so. "All we need, my love—he began thickly—is a bed. Preferably one with clean sheets. Or failing that, any reasonably flat surface will serve our purpose. . . ."

His words made her shiver, he noted with satisfaction. But despite his best efforts, the door at her back resisted his best efforts to open it.

"Blast. The bloody door's stuck—or locked. Have you a ring of keys dangling from your pretty waist, I wonder, my little chatelaine?" he whispered.

He pretended to look for one, but instead of

241

giggling, as she would usually have done, Miranda seemed genuinely frightened. "Stop that! Let me pass. I must go back down. My guests!"

"Wait! Just let me say a proper goodbye. That's all I wanted. Then I'll go."

That got her attention. She suddenly went very still.

"Go? Why? Where are you going? You didn't mention leaving when you were wolfing down the lobster I cooked for you this morning," she accused.

He could see panic fill her eyes. "I hadn't made my mind up then. Don't look at me that way! It's only for a day or two. I'm coming back. Remember the letter that came for me? I just wanted you to know how very much I'm going to miss you."

His cajoling tone and dancing green eyes had the desired effect. They softened her, so that he could see the indecision, the yearning now in her lovely turquoise eyes.

"Come now. Surely you have time for a wee cuddle before I leave, hmmm, Miranda? . . ."

His lips on her cheek, he reached past her, trying the doorknob at her back again as he did so.

Nothing. To his surprise, the door really was locked.

"Well, now. A locked door to an empty room! What secrets are you hiding behind this locked door, I wonder, Mistress Tallant?" he teased, dipping his dark head to plant a quick kiss on her lips. "Casks of fine French cognac, perhaps? Baccy from the Americas? Tea from Ceylon? Or . . . a bolt or two of Brussels' lace?"

Such luxury goods were brought ashore by Cornish smugglers, to avoid the excise tax. Was that what she was hiding, he wondered? Smuggled goods? Or . . . something more sinister? The ill-gotten gains of a shipwreck?

Just as his lips brushed hers, the locked door behind the pair flew open.

Morgan leaped away from Miranda as if she were red-hot, for Thad Killigrew's wiry frame and angry face suddenly filled the open doorway.

The man stepped out into the passageway, firmly closing and locking the door in his wake before Morgan could sneak a look inside.

"Well, now. A good evening to ye, Mr. St. James. Lost your way t'the public saloon, have you?" Killigrew demanded, fixing a cold eye on Morgan, then one of concern on his daughter. "All right, are ye, 'Randa?"

"Quite all right, thank you, Papa," Miranda said demurely, although there was a hectic flush to her cheeks.

"Glad to hear it," Killigrew declared. "I'd not

like t'think Mr. St. James here was trying t'take advantage of ye."

"Papa!" Miranda hissed, her face very red now.

"On the contrary, Mr. Killigrew, sir. Mistress Tallant and I have become friends over the past few weeks," Morgan explained smoothly. "I came to tell her that I'm going away for a day or two. She would not have thought well of me, had I left without a goodbye."

Thad's brows lifted. "Leaving the Cove, are you? Well, then. We won't keep you, St. James." He bared his teeth, but it could hardly be called a smile. "A good evening to you."

Morgan hid a smile. He had to admire Killigrew's paternal instincts! They were very sound when it came to his beautiful daughter! There was little doubt in his mind that the older man knew exactly what sort of "friends" the keeper and his daughter had become. . . .

He was about to hastily offer his apologies and say his goodnights when a muffled cry and a series of loud thuds behind the door to room nine sent both Killigrews whirling around.

"What the devil was that?" Morgan demanded, frowning at the other two.

"The wind?" Miranda suggested hastily.

"Mice," her father declared firmly in the same moment.

"Hmmm. Restless little brutes, aren't they?" Morgan murmured, his eyes meeting Thad Killigrew's directly. "Big bully-boys, too, from the sound of those thuds."

"Aye," Thad murmured, meeting Morgan's questioning stare without flinching. "But harmless, for all that, rest assured. My word on it."

Again, their eyes met, green boring into brilliant blue.

"I'm sure they are, sir," Morgan agreed with a nod.

Killigrew's shoulders slumped a little. "A very good night to you, St. James." He sounded slightly less hostile now. "And a safe journey."

"A good night to you, too, sir. And to you, ma'am . . . Mistress Tallant . . . *Miranda*. Good night." He made them both a dashing half-bow. "I shall call upon you as soon as I return."

"I . . . I shall look forward to it, sir," Miranda said firmly. She shot her father a defiant look and amended, "*Morgan*."

With a farewell nod, Morgan turned on his heel and strode away down the landing.

"Nosy bastard! What was he doing up here, sniffing around? He's not a guest here anymore! He has no place above stairs."

"He told you, Papa. He was looking for me."

"Asks a lot of questions, does he? Wants to know the where and why of everything?"

Penelope Neri

She hesitated. "Sometimes, aye. Yes, I suppose he does," she added defiantly.

"And? Do you answer them?"

"Of course I don't! What do you take me for? A fool? He knows only what I want him to know—which is nothing at all."

"Good girl. Mind ye keep it that way."

Despite what she'd told her father, Miranda couldn't help wondering if Morgan had seen inside the room, and if he had, what he had made of it.

Perhaps it was better he knew the truth about her mother than suspect her father was a freetrader, storing smuggled contraband in one of her empty guest rooms. After all, the keeper would never find where the goods were really hidden.

And smuggling was, after all, a hanging offense. . . .

246

Chapter Twelve

The following day dawned with an overcast sky, and clouds the color of pewter that held the promise of a soaking before the day was out. There was, too, a distinct nip in the air, ample proof that even here, in sunny Cornwall, summer was giving way to autumn.

Miranda and her family set out by pony-trap soon after sunrise, the three women well-cloaked and bonneted against the morning chill, Thaddeus swathed in a great-coat and cap. They followed the rutted cart track that skirted the moors and the winding coast and would, eventually, lead to the market town of Bodmin, set between gently rounded hills.

It was a long ride, and noon had come and gone before Miranda and her family, having got down only twice to stretch their legs and make water, reached the Cornish county town of Bodmin, which lay on the edge of the moors to the northeast of Lizard Cove. By then, the sun had come out, and the day was unseasonably warm, persuading them to remove their cloaks and coat.

As they entered the charming little town, they encountered considerable traffic going in both directions.

Coaches, pedestrians, carts and wagons were going into and away from the ancient Buttermarket in the very center of town, which was overlooked by a turret clock. Some were laden with farmers and their wives, bound for outlying farms, others with travellers headed to distant London, others with produce and livestock, going back to their own little moorland villages nearby.

Thaddeus drove the cart past austere Bodmin Gaol, past the county Assizes, and St. Petroc's church, which housed a four-hundred-year-old casket reputed to contain the remains of one of Cornwall's patron saints, St. Petroc himself. From there, he proceeded to the Duke of Cornwall Public House and Inn on Barracks Street, where he took two rooms, one for his two daughters, the other for him and his wife.

The Duke of Cornwall's Light Infantry was housed in the town's barracks nearby. Scarlet-uniformed soldiers were strutting about, their gold buttons winking, white breeches dazzling, black knee-boots highly polished. Like soldiers everywhere, they had an eye for a pretty female face or a fetching figure, and to a man, their eyes snapped in the direction of the two lovely young women helping their mother down from the cart.

"Perhaps I could be of some assistance, miss?" offered a moustached young soldier, extending his strong arm to take Juliet Killigrew's place.

"How very kind of you, sir," Juliet murmured, turning a furious red. "Our poor mam has not been well and we have traveled some distance. We are going up to our rooms, so that she can lie down and rest," she explained.

"I'd be happy to help you."

Miranda hid a smile as the gallant young officer took her mother's right elbow, while a glowering Thaddeus supported her left. Together, the two men easily escorted Catherine Killigrew up the stairs to the two clean, airy rooms the innkeeper's wife showed them into. She and Juliet followed the little group, with Miranda looking eagerly about her at the inn and its appointments as she went.

249

Penelope Neri

It was a beautifully maintained establishment, and the landlord and his wife, Mistress Mevagissey, were justifiably proud of it.

"You have a most charming hostelry here, ma'am," she told the innkeeper's wife. "I must compliment you on your sparkling brass and shining floors, and upon the excellent manners of your servants. I have my own inn over in Lizard's Cove. The Black Gull, by name. Perhaps you have heard of it?"

"Indeed I have, ma'am. And only the finest of reports," the woman said with new respect. "As for my servants' manners—well! Thank you kindly for your compliments, ma'am, but they had best be polite, else I'll know the reason why!" the red-cheeked, plump woman declared stoutly. "I pay my servants a goodly wage, aye, and feed and outfit them well, besides. There are many eager to fill their places, if they've a mind to be lazy or insolent."

A pert little maid swung open the door of the room assigned to her mother and father. Bobbing a curtsey, she bade them enter with a smile and a promise to bring jugs of hot water for washing. "Here we are, Mam," Juliet murmured, ushering her mother inside. "And thank you kindly for your help, Captain—?"

"It's Dickerson, miss. Harry Dickerson."

"Captain Dickerson. Thank you," Juliet mur-

250

mured, bobbing him a sketchy curtsey. "We don't know what we would have done without you," she added, ignoring her father's sudden scowl.

Harry beamed and brushed a cowlick of fair hair off his brow. "It was my pleasure, miss." He turned to Thaddeus. "A very good day to you, sir. Ladies." He made them all a smart salute, then snapped his heels together.

Thad Killigrew shot him a sour look. "Aye, aye, lad. Run along with ye now." Then, noting the way his younger daughter's face dropped in abject disappointment, he added gruffly, "Perhaps we'll run into you later, aye? At the harvest market."

The soldier brightened. He flashed a smile at Juliet. "I'd say that's a distinct possibility, sir!" he sang out.

Cramming on his cap, he made a smart exit, bootheels thudding down the landing as he left.

"Arrogant young puppy!" Thad growled. "Helpful, my arse."

"Oh, thank you, Da'!" Juliet exclaimed, throwing her arms around her father's neck. "He was so very handsome, and extremely charming— didn't you think so, 'Randa?"

"Very," Miranda agreed. She unfastened the ribbons that tied her mother's dark-green bonnet beneath the chin, took it off, and set it carefully on the hat-stand in the corner.

Smoothing down the faded red hair, which she'd dressed in a simple coil, she poured eau-de-cologne onto her palms, rubbed her hands together, then massaged her mother's brow and temples, to soothe her. "He seemed very kind, too. Mam, lie down. You've time for a bit of a rest, before you see Dr. Trethgallen."

Catherine Killigrew seemed unusually composed. Miranda wondered if she was still groggy from the laudanum they had given her that morning before they set out.

Catherine looked uncertainly up at her oldest daughter, standing beside the brass bed. She frowned, her blue eyes troubled. "A doctor, did you say, Miranda?" she murmured.

Miranda gasped, stunned that her mother had recognized her after so many weeks without having done so, and that she had understood what was being said.

"Yes, Mam," she said gently, endeavoring to remain calm. "How do you feel today?"

"I'm not sure. Everything is so . . . so confusing," Catherine muttered. "I . . . I've been forgetting things, haven't I?" She raised her hand to her brow and kneaded her temple. "I do not know what is wrong with me. It is . . . difficult to hold on to my thoughts. Is that why I must see a physician?"

Goosebumps rose on Miranda's neck and arms as she exchanged glances with a wide-eyed Juliet and her open-mouthed father. These words were the first coherent ones her mother had uttered in several weeks! What had brought about this small but very significant miracle between Eastmoor Farm and the Duke of Cornwall's Inn and Public house?

"Yes, mam, it is. But you're going to get better, I just know you are," Miranda assured her with tears in her eyes. "We've found a very good doctor to examine you. Dr. John Trethgallen. I'm sure he'll be able to help you. Please. You must not fret."

To everyone's amazement, Catherine's own eyes filled with tears as she squeezed Miranda's hand. "All right, my dears," she promised simply. "I'll try not to."

"I believe a simple change of scenery is exactly the reason Mistress Killigrew seems somewhat recovered," Dr. Trethgallen declared, making a steeple with his fingers on his desk top while the Killigrew listened in astonishment and disbelief. "The other patients that I wrote to you about, Mr. Killigrew? Those women in Italy? They all enjoyed a similar improvement when removed from their places of residence. Indeed, the longer they were away, the greater the improvement in their conditions! Which led their physicians to draw a somewhat obvious conclusion."

"That something—or someone—in their homes was the cause of their condition," Miranda suggested.

Dr. Trethgallen appeared annoyed that she had guessed, and so stolen his thunder. With an irritable grimace, he removed the gold pince-nez spectacles from his nose and polished them upon a huge, white-silk kerchief. "Why, yes, young lady. How very clever of you! That's it, exactly. I strongly suspect something your mother has been ingesting on a regular basis has caused her erratic behavior and her mental confusion. A poison, in fact. An educated guess on my part, going by the symptoms you've been describing, would be arsenic. Now that she's been removed from the source for—what is it? A day?"

"Almost two now."

"Two days, yes. It appears the ill effects you described are beginning to wear off. To reverse themselves."

"Arsenic! But, we don't have arsenic at Eastmoor!" Thad Killigrew growled.

"Oh, but we do, Da'," Miranda whispered, her

lower lip quivering. "There's arsenic in the rat poison. Remember?"

"But that can't be it, surely? Dr. Trethgallen says your mam's been taking whatever it is on a regular basis!" her father exclaimed. "Who would feed your mother poison, tell me that?"

She shrugged. "I don't know how it happened any more than you do. But we'll find out when we get home and we'll get rid of whatever it is, if it's the last thing we do!"

"Oh, sir, is she really going to get well?" Juliet eagerly asked the physician.

Trethgallen smiled. He was not so old that her golden-haired, blue-eyed beauty did not have some effect on him—as did the flattering way she deferred to him for answers, unlike her older sister.

"I am encouraged Mistress Killigrew will improve greatly, my dear child. However, whether she will ever be completely her old self again remains to be seen. I would recommend that you seek out the source of the poison, remove it completely, and pray for her recovery. We physicians are not God. We can only do so much."

"Thank you, Dr. Trethgallen," Thaddeus said, sliding a small purse of gold coins across the desk, along with a pouch of tobacco and a bottle of brandy. "Thank you, sir. For everything!"

"Why, Killigrew, this is most generous of you,

man. Most generous!" Trethgallen declared, beaming with pleasure.

Her father, overwhelmed by such promising news after so many weeks of anxious days and sleepless nights, elected to take their mother back to their rooms at the inn to rest. He arranged to meet his daughters in the inn's taproom at dusk, so that they could all take supper together and celebrate. Catherine leaned forward and patted Juliet's cheek.

"How lovely you're becoming, my dear," she murmured wonderingly. "You know, you are the very image of my sister, Jenny, as a girl."

Miranda and Juliet set off alone in high spirits to visit the stalls in the Buttermarket, delighted by such a promising visit to the physician. Juliet, Miranda suspected, was more interested in running into handsome Captain Harry Dickerson than she was in any wares to be had there, or in the delicious aromas that wafted from the food stalls. Hot Cornish pasties were filled with minced lamb, onions, carrots, diced potatoes and peas, their crumbly crusts running with gravy. Roasted capons turned slowly on a spit over beds of glowing coals, so that their juices bubbled and glistened as they oozed from golden-browned skins.

Tarts filled with strawberry and raspberry

jams, or Miranda's favorite, tangy lemon-curd, glistened like jewels.

Other stalls were heaped high with the bounty of the harvest. Cabbages and potatoes, carrots and beets, cauliflowers and marrows. Wicker baskets held apples, pears, blackberries and nuts.

Miranda and Juliet meandered amongst the stalls, stopping every now and then when something caught their eye. Miranda bought some pretty mother-of-pearl buttons for a gown she was sewing, while Juliet kept a weather eye out for Harry Dickerson.

Her delighted expression when she spotted the dashing captain making his way toward them through the bustling crowds had Miranda shaking her head in disgust, very much the older sister now.

"Juliet Portia Killigrew! Are you completely lacking in pride?" Miranda hissed, tugging her younger sister behind a handy tinker's stall. "You don't even know the man, and yet you smile as if the sun's come out the very instant you set eyes upon him! At least pretend you haven't seen him, for modesty's sake, if no other reason!"

"Oh, all right. I'll try," Juliet promised with a sigh, yet looked very little less delighted. In fact, her lovely, heart-shaped face, framed by long blonde ringlets and her best bonnet, a deep-rose creation boasting a brim that was decorated with silk roses, beamed with delight. "Now, please come back to where we were, do, Miranda, in case Harry can't find us," she pleaded, tugging Miranda back around the stall by her elbow.

But Harry, as Miranda had fully expected, experienced very little trouble in locating the pair of them. Or at least, in locating Juliet.

Like a homing pigeon winging back to its loft, he had almost worked his way to their sides when Juliet gaily exclaimed, "Now, there's a man for you, sister dear! Such a handsome fellow would surely make even you throw off your widow's weeds! What a pity he has a wife!"

"Where is this paragon who's caught your eye?" Miranda demanded, laughing as she turned to look in the direction Juliet was pointing.

The smile froze on her lips.

The tall, elegantly dressed, black-haired man was handing a lovely blonde-haired woman wearing a delicate oyster-colored woolen cape into a private carriage. A curlicue initial "C," topped by a coronet, was painted in gilt upon the hunter-green door.

The man was Morgan!

Stilled by shock and disbelief, Miranda held

258

her breath as his delightful companion leaned from the carriage doorway to kiss his cheek and accept the small bundle, swaddled in lacy shawl and bonnet, that he was holding, and which he now carefully lifted into the woman's arms. Then he sprang after her into the carriage.

Morgan St. James—and a blonde-haired woman with an infant! What were they to him?

The obvious explanation for that kiss, for the tender way he'd handed the woman up into the carriage, then placed the infant in her arms was one Miranda could not bear to contemplate. *His wife and child.*

"Don't you think he's handsome?" she heard Juliet say as if from very far away, as the blood turned to ice in her veins.

"Very," she heard herself respond woodenly.

"It must be wonderful to be married to someone like that," Juliet said wistfully. "Why, hello, Captain Dickerson! What a lovely surprise to see you again." She dimpled and giggled.

"I was hoping you would allow me to escort you and Miss Killigrew through the market, Miss Juliet," Captain Dickerson sang out in a hearty voice. "There are always pickpockets and ne'er-do-wells about at such goings on. I would not want you or your charming sister to run afoul of such ruffians."

"How kind of you to offer, Captain. We would

259

appreciate Captain Dickerson's protection, wouldn't we, Miranda?"

"Very much," Miranda whispered, her thoughts a lifetime away. "Yes."

Dickerson offered his right arm to Juliet, his left to Miranda. She slipped her arm through his like a sleepwalker.

Morgan!

The silent scream seemed to begin very deep inside her, and force its way up into the light, the air. It was a marvel to her that no one else seemed to hear it. . . .

"I want to visit the needlework stalls first," Juliet suggested. "It's so hard to come by the silks I need for my embroidery at home. The tinkers never carry a very wide selection of colors. And the embroidery hoop I have is cracked and will not hold the cloth quite tightly enough. . . ."

Morgan, oh, Morgan!

"I saw such a stall down here," the captain was saying gallantly. "Ladies, shall we?"

One on each arm, as proud as a peacock with two fine hens, Harry Dickerson led them both away.

Try as she might, Miranda could not remember later what had transpired for the remainder of that afternoon. Not which stalls she had visited, nor what she had purchased nor why, nor any detail of what had been said, nor who else they might have encountered.

She only knew that her heart ached in her chest. That her head hurt. That the enormous feeling of violation, of betrayal, blotted out all else and was like a sort of sickness. Perhaps even a small and violent death: the death of trust.

She swallowed over the painful knot of tears that clogged her throat like leaves in a drainpipe. Blinked back smarting tears. She had fallen in love with, had taken to her bed, a man who was married to another. Someone who had already fathered at least one child. . . .

"You're so quiet this evening, lovie," her father observed as they sat at a celebratory supper that evening in the tap room of the Duke's of Cornwall, enjoying the innkeeper's tasty supper of roasted beef and Yorkshire pudding.

Harry Dickerson had been invited to join them, and had needed no second urging to do so. He'd also cleverly won their father over by standing them all a bottle of fine claret, purchased from the landlord's personal cellar.

"And ye haven't eaten a bite of Mrs. Mevagissey's fine beef roast. Not coming down with a grippe, are you, my girl?"

"Noo. No, I'm quite well, thank you, Da'."

"You're not jealous of me and Harry, are you, 'Randa?" Juliet asked anxiously that night as

261

they undressed by the light of a pair of candles. "Um, Captain Dickerson, I mean. I never intended to ignore you so this afternoon, truly I didn't. But Harry was . . . well! He was so very . . . charming, and so attentive, too! I just couldn't help myself."

"On the contrary, I'm delighted Harry has asked Da's permission to visit you at Eastmoor, truly I am. It is just that my spirits are at a . . . a very low ebb this evening. I know I am very poor company. But don't let my wretched mood cloud your own."

"Is it Daniel? Do you miss him terribly?" Juliet inquired, her lower lip trembling. She brushed a lock of hair away from her sister's face. "Did Harry remind you? Oh, darling, Miranda, I'm so sorry. All I've been thinking about all day is my happiness. I never once stopped to consider how you might feel, seeing me laughing and chattering with Harry! And when I thoughtlessly said you should throw off your widow's weeds? Truly, I never meant to be so cruel! It must be dreadful for you."

"I'm quite all right, Juliet. Really. Don't fuss. It's not Daniel, nor anything to do with you or your new admirer. Please, Julie, darling, just try to sleep, there's a good girl. We must be up early in the morning, remember?"

Miranda leaned over, blew out the candle, and slipped between the sheets.

"I'll try, but I doubt I'll sleep a wink." Juliet's voice came from the shadows beside her. "Oh, Miranda! I just can't seem to stop thinking about how blue his eyes are. Nor how fine and determined his jaw. Harry really does have a very fine jaw . . . did you notice, 'Randa? 'Randa?"

Juliet was still chattering like a magpie when Miranda, exhausted both physically and mentally, plummeted into a deep and troubled sleep.

She awoke in the wee hours to find hot, salty tears streaming down her cheeks; the pillow beneath her head was soaked. But they were tears that neither Juliet nor anyone else would never see. . . .

Chapter Thirteen

"So. How are you really, Nan?" Morgan inquired, frowning as he accepted the cup and saucer his cousin handed him.

The almost translucent porcelain seemed far too fragile, too flimsy in his large hands, he thought absently. Almost as fragile as Nanon, who looked as if a strong breeze might whirl her away.

"Milk?" she offered, indicating the dainty matching jug and ignoring his question.

"No, damn it!" he snapped. "Stop avoiding the bloody question, and answer me, Nan! How are you?"

Forgetting its fragility in his impatience, he

slammed his cup and saucer down with such a loud clink, he thought he'd broken it. In a gentler tone, he added, "I've been worried about you, damn it all, Nan. I hate to think of you all alone."

"Alone! Hardly. Uncle Robert made quite sure that I was never left alone to dwell on things while I was still at home, bless him! He was truly wonderful when my darling little Bobby was born, the very picture of the doting grandfather."

"I'm not surprised. Father has been eager for grandchildren for quite some time now, as well you know. God knows, he has completely abandoned all hopes of my producing an heir for him anytime soon. You were his best shot, Nan," Morgan said with a sad smile. "I understood from your letter that little Robert—Bobby—arrived early? Was there some question of his surviving his birth?"

A shadowed crossed Nan Christopher's lovely, grave face, and darkened her gray eyes with pain. "Indeed there was. I'm sure it was the shock of Geoff's . . . of his Papa's drowning that brought on the birth." She bit her lower lip. Swallowed. "You can imagine how devastated I was. . . ."

She swallowed, but the slender fingers clenching the lacy handkerchief in her lap soon stiffened, as did her spine. Her fair head, blonde hair elegantly upswept, tilted bravely as she forced herself to continue. "As I explained in my letter to you, your godson arrived some six weeks earlier than was expected. And both my physician and the midwife were doubtful that he would survive. But, praise God, my darling little boy is just like his father. Stubborn and tenacious! He clung to life with his every breath, growing bigger each day until he is as you see him now. A plump little cherub! But were it not for him, Morgan, I would be inconsolable, I fear." Her lip quivered. "Bobby is my reason for living, now that my darling Geoff is gone from me."

The baby, cooing in his nurse's arms, suddenly crowed with delight, as if agreeing with his mother.

"He's a fine boy. You have every reason to be proud of him, Nan," Morgan murmured huskily, reaching out to squeeze her hand. "Nothing could make me prouder than becoming his godfather."

"Silly man! You and Uncle Robert are the only two I would trust to be Bobby's godfathers. And my dear friend, Amanda, will be the perfect godmother. I'm so very glad you were able to come for the christening tomorrow. But . . . what of you, Morgan? How are you faring, my dear cousin?" Nan asked, leaning across the low table and taking his hand. "I have been so worried

267

about you. Truly. You and Geoff were closer than most brothers. . . ."

"We were, aye," Morgan admitted with the ghost of a smile. "I valued Geoff's friendship more than I can say. You know that."

"Yes, I know. Morgan . . . Uncle Robert told me you are not convinced that Geoff was drowned, or that his death was even accidental?"

Relief washed over him. She knew! "No, my dear. I'm not. Did he . . . did he tell you everything? Did he mention the lighthouse keeper, Ashe, and what he saw?"

"He did. Once he had convinced himself that knowing would not send me into further decline." For the second time, her lower lip quivered. "I cannot comprehend how anyone could commit such a barbaric act! To cold-bloodedly club the survivors of a shipwreck as they struggled ashore! Why, it defies the imagination! Have you been able to learn anything, as lighthouse keeper of this wretched place?"

"Not as much as I'd hoped, no. But I'm far from abandoning the investigation! Unfortunately, with wrecking being an . . . opportunistic endeavor by its very nature, unless a similar situation arises, those responsible may not show their hand again."

"You mean, another vessel carrying a similarly tempting cargo must first be wrecked upon the same shores, in order for those rogues to try it again?"

"That's it, exactly."

"Well, then, you must engineer such a circumstance, since one is unlikely to occur naturally!"

Morgan's dark eyebrows rose. A slow grin erased the sad, grim expression from his face. "Never a dullard, were you, Nan? By God, I do believe you're on to something! I hadn't thought of that."

Nan shook her head. Her gray eyes gleamed with amusement now. "You have changed very little, Morgan dear. And, for all that you're a man of the world, you're still the worst of liar! Don't try to flatter me into good humor, sir! I am quite certain that you have entertained the idea of arranging such a scenario yourself. The question is, what has persuaded you to put it off?"

"No one, Nan," he denied quickly. Earnestly. *Too* earnestly. "Hhhrrmph. That is to say, nothing. Nothing at all."

Nanon stared at her cousin. "You said no one. Who is she?"

"There is no 'she', I tell you. It's just very difficult to identify who was responsible!" he insisted with a scowl.

"Oh, pish! I don't believe you for a minute. You have met someone," she guessed. "Ah. I was

269

right! You have!" she crowed, delighted by the guilty expression he now wore.

His shoulders slumped. He threw up his hands. "All right! I give up. Yes, you minx! I have met someone. A woman. But it's not what you think."

"No? What is it then? Explain yourself, do!" Nan insisted, leaning back in the wing chair with a smile of genuine delight as she sipped her tea. "Nurse, you may take Master Bobby up to the nursery now, if you will, then have your own tea."

"Very well, ma'am. Come along with Nanny, my fine young master. Off to your cradle we go! Upsadaisy! We'll see your mama later, won't we, my love? Oh, yes, we will. . . ."

Still crooning, the nurse bobbed her mistress a curtsey, then carried the baby away, leaving Morgan and Nan alone in the sunny conservatory, where wicker peacock chairs with green-and-pink flowered pillows, flowering rhododendrons, camellias and numerous potted palms created the illusion of the tropics.

"I was surprised to hear that you'd come to live here with Geoff's parents. Are they kind to you, Nanon?"

"Oh, yes, very! In fact, Mother Christopher and Sir Alec dote upon both me and their grandson. I believe raising Geoff's child here, where they may watch him grow up, is the very least I could do for them. Geoff was their only child, after all. And with him gone, Bobby is Sir Alec's only heir."

"I'm glad they're good to you."

"The beauty of this arrangement is that here, we are not so very far away from you and Uncle Robert in Devon. Now, never mind changing the subject, you wretched man! Answer my question."

"What question?" Despite the innocence with which he asked, Morgan could not help the wicked grin that twitched at the corners of his mouth.

"You know very well which question, sir," Nanon Christopher said sternly. "Tell me about this woman you have met!"

"Very well. If you insist," he agreed with a great sigh. "Her name is Miranda. Miranda Tallant. She is a lovely, intelligent young woman."

"And? What is wrong with her? Is she married?"

"Lord, no. She's a widow." He glanced quickly at Nanon's face to see if his comment had upset her. It did not appear to have done so.

"Her husband was the innkeeper of the Black Gull Inn in Lizard Cove. Since his passing, she has become the hostelry's proprietor—and a very competent one, too, I might add. The place is flourishing. Such places being the hub of gossip in such small communities, it was my intention to—"

"Get to know this Miranda, then find out what you could about the wreck and the community?"

"Exactly."

"By . . . whatever means?" Her fair brows arched in inquiry. She had obviously seen something more in his expression than he had intended her to. But then, Nan had always been a very perceptive woman—not unlike his mother, Anne.

He squirmed. "In a manner of speaking, aye."

"Then what is the problem? Is it that you consider her of a lower class than yourself?"

"Good Lord, no!" he exploded, full of indignation. "I may be many things, but a snob is not one of them. How could I be? My own mother was the daughter of a gentleman farmer, with no claims to nobility whatsoever."

"And yet no nobler, more gracious lady ever lived!" Nan finished for him.

"Exactly."

"Then what, pray, is the reason for that scowl?"

Morgan, still scowling, sighed heavily and crossed his arms over his chest. "The lady's maiden name was Killigrew."

"And?"

272

"Killigrew was the only name Ashe heard the wreckers utter! The sole clue to their identity."

"Aaaah. And since you have fallen for her, you find your conscience torn in both directions?"

"Fallen?" He snorted. "As in 'fallen in love?' The devil I have!" Morgan exploded, his green eyes flashing with indignation. He sprang from his chair and began pacing the length of the conservatory. Back and forth, back and forth he strode, muttering under his breath, and setting the palms to rustling with the violence of his pacing.

Satisfied that she was right, Nanon Christopher poured a second dish of tea and allowed herself a smug little smile as she sipped.

Unless she missed her mark—and she knew Morgan far too well to have missed it by far—for the first time in his life, her freedom-loving cousin was in love!

She could hardly wait to meet the widow who had won his heart. Of one thing she was certain: This Miranda would be no humdrum innkeeper. Nanon fully expected her to be like darling Aunt Anne, Morgan's wonderful mama.

As Morgan had said, Anne St. James had been the daughter of a gentleman farmer when she caught Sir Robert's eye, yet she had been a lady in the truest, finest sense of the word. The couple had raised her with their only son, Morgan, after

Nan was orphaned by the death of Sir Robert's widowed sister, Lady Margaret Dubois, in France.

Morgan's Miranda would be a high-spirited, strong-willed, adventurous woman, she had little doubt. Aye, and one of great beauty, wit and intelligence, too. She could hardly wait to meet her.

"Morgan St. James, you, sir, are a liar!" Nanon declared in a most unladylike fashion. " 'Else I'm a Dutchman."

And with that, she raised her dainty cup to the ceiling, then drained it to the dregs.

Chapter Fourteen

Miranda went to great lengths to ensure that she saw nothing of Morgan for several days after her return to Lizard Cove, and for that, she was grateful. Her wounds were too raw, too new—too painful—to confront him as yet.

When a few days became two weeks, and the pain seemed not a whit less, she threw herself headlong into the running of her inn. In an effort to drive him from her thoughts, she embarked on what she described as a "pre-Christmas cleaning spree" of immense proportions, and participated in helping her family search the farm for the substance that had sickened her mother.

"Whatever it is," Rob wisely pointed out after several days of fruitless searching, "it must be something that only Mam ate. No one else is ill or acting strangely."

"I presume you're not speaking for yourself, brother?" Gil suggested, grinning and poking Rob in the ribs. He seemed more lighthearted than Miranda had seen him in weeks. Slipping his arm about Kitty's hugely expanded waist, he kissed his wife's cheek. "He acts very strangely, does my brother! Isn't that so, Kitty, my love?"

Much to everyone's relief, the answer to the question of what had poisoned Catherine Killigrew was found far sooner and far more easily than they had expected.

In one of the barns, Juliet discovered a burlap sack containing what was left of the rat poison. It had been crammed into a forgotten corner on a high, rickety wooden shelf. And, unnoticed by anyone, holes in the bottom of the sack had been allowing small but steady amounts of powdery rat-poison to sift down into an apparently empty storage bin below.

But upon lifting the bin's lid, Juliet discovered a white paper twist that contained several lemon-shaped bonbons, each dusted with powdered sugar. Or was it *just* powdered sugar? Could some of it have been arsenic powder that had drifted down from the sack on the shelf above?

It had to have done, and Miranda said as much. "I think you've found it, Julie, I really do!" she exclaimed, hugging her sister.

"Dear Lord. Mother's sherbet lemons! Who would have thought it? You know how she loves them, Miranda, how she always rations herself, one or two bon-bons at a time, like a little girl? Da'! Rob! Gil! Come look at this!" she shouted. "Oh, Miranda, just think! Poor Mam must have hidden these bonbons away in here so that we wouldn't tease her for her self-indulgence!" Juliet exclaimed. "Poor, poor Mam! Her little secret was almost her undoing."

Catherine Killigrew was a generous woman with but two weaknesses. Her love for her husband and children—and what she had always considered an embarrassing fondness for a certain French bonbon known as sherbet lemons!

The hollow centers of the lemon-shaped, boiled sweets were filled with tangy sherbet powder, and they could be bought only in France.

Thad Killigrew, knowing how much his wife adored the sherbet lemon bon-bons had asked the captains of the smuggling ships to bring paper twists of the sweets for his wife from time to time. And, like a greedy little squirrel, she had hidden them here in the barn, reluctant to share her favorite treats with anyone, including her beloved children.

Such a touchingly human weakness had almost cost her her life.

And, like all mysteries, now that the puzzle was solved, it seemed incredible that they had not thought of it before.

With a curse, Thad snatched up the paper cone and the forgotten sack, and flung them onto the great pile of fallen leaves and broken branches heaped in the stableyard ready to be burned.

"Toss me a match, Gil!" he commanded. "The sooner this lot has gone up in smoke, the better I'll feel! I'll be sure there are more in the next shipment, my love," he added, drawing his wife to him in a hug.

With the source of her poisoning discovered and removed, Catherine Killigrew gradually improved.

After two weeks, there was no longer any need for Miranda to haunt the farm. It was time, she decided with a sigh, to concentrate on the running of her inn. She would have to hope that she could avoid coming into any contact with Morgan St James.

Morgan.

Devil take the rogue! She had told herself to forget him, to cast him out of her life and out of her mind. Any man who could betray his wife with another woman was not worthy of such anguish or pain.

But it was far easier said than done.

At night, after an exhausting day spent sweeping, polishing, dusting, washing and scrubbing in her efforts to stay busy and preoccupied, she lay awake in her wide brass bed beneath the inn's eaves, listening to the wind and the creaks and groans of the old building settling around her, unable to sleep for imagining his hands stroking her breasts, or the feel of his lips on hers.

Her longing to be with him in that way was unbearable. Her treacherous body ached for his with a pain that was physical. Her nipples grew hard as sea shells at the very thought of his caresses. And between her thighs, she grew wet with longing, yet no ease would come from touching herself. It was Morgan she wanted. Him and nothing less would serve, damn him. . . .

And so, rather than make the situation even more difficult than it already was, she decided to forgo the walks she'd once enjoyed along the seashore, and instead took to tramping the moors and woods on those rare afternoons

279

when she found herself with time to spare. There would be less chance of running into him there, so far from the lighthouse, she told herself.

One afternoon, she left Maisie to mind the beef stew she'd set to simmer over the fire, threw a shawl over her shoulders and escaped to the woods.

The air was filled with the smell of autumn woodsmoke, and the weather was more crisp and invigorating than truly cold as she walked between the boles of trees that in springtime were bright with the nodding blue and yellow heads of bluebells and wild daffodils, or the smaller blooms of snowdrops and grape hyacinths.

But at this time of year, the flowers and most of the leaves were gone. Acorns and nuts were scattered amongst the tree roots, winter fodder for the red and gray squirrels she saw gathering their stores. Those leaves that still remained were glorious in their autumn colors. Reds, russets, golds and coppery browns, they either clung gamely to the branches or rustled in great drifts beneath her feet as she strolled along.

Glad to be out, she wandered along the mossy banks of a burbling brook. The water rushed over large pebbles worn smooth and round by its rushing current, and time. Using the small, sharp paring knife she'd brought with her, she cut tall, leafy twigs here and there to use in the brass flower vases or woven baskets at the inn. Several tall, elegant twigs with brightly colored autumn leaves still attached made as pretty a decoration as summer flowers in their season, as did a selection of colorful harvest fruits and nuts spilling from baskets.

She had gathered an armful of such leafy branches when she heard voices from the small spinney ahead of her.

From the low pitch of the voices—a man's and a woman's—it was immediately obvious that she had stumbled across a courting couple who had made the woods their romantic rendezvous.

Fearing the couple might think her a peeping Tom if they saw her, she hastily turned away—though not before catching a glimpse of Carl Coppinger on his knees in the leaves!

His broad back was to her, his breeches were pulled down about his ankles, baring a broad pair of hairy white buttocks!

Any question she might have had about what Carl was up to was answered by the shapely pair of female feet that were angled over his broad shoulders. Whose, she could not have said.

Clamping her hand over her mouth to stifle her cry of surprise—and her laughter—she turned and plunged back into the bushes,

281

breathing heavily in her haste to get away.

But she'd gone only a few yards in panicked flight when a hard hand closed over her elbow.

"Don't run! They'll hear you!"

The imperious edge to Morgan's low voice stopped her in her tracks like a pistol ball. She froze, flinging off his hand without looking around.

"You! Let go of me!" she hissed. "Let me pass!"

"The devil I will," he hissed back. "You've been avoiding me for days, damn it. I followed you to find out why." It was a lie: He'd been following Coppinger, but she didn't need to know that.

"Did you, indeed? Well, I don't have time to satisfy your idle curiosity, Keeper St. James!" she flung back in a low, jeering tone. "So, let go of my wrist. I have guests to be shown to their rooms. Supper to see to. Servants to instruct," she snapped as he walked around her, blocking her escape. "Step aside. Let me pass, I say!" she insisted thickly, unable to look him in the eye.

"No." He placed himself squarely in her path, refusing to budge by so much as an inch. "Not until you tell me what's wrong. What have I done?"

His green eyes searched her pale, set face. There were lilac shadows beneath her lovely eyes. Lines of strain about both eyes and mouth.

Clues that she was suffering and sleepless, but for what reason?

"Why have you been avoiding me since I came back? The good Lord knows, I've missed you, Miranda. Our closeness. The nights we shared. Every night, I think of how you looked in my bed, or swimming in the ocean, wearing only the moonlight . . . and sleep escapes me."

His voice dropped to a husky purr that was caressing, almost hypnotizing. She could feel herself growing mesmerized by it—by *him*. Her eyelids drooped. Her body grew peculiarly fluid and loose, before she caught herself.

"I'll just warrant it does, St. James!" she retorted, flaring up like a Roman candle, all sparks as she turned to face him. "By virtue of your conscience, not me! Did you tell your wife about us, when you met with her in Bodmin? Did you tell her you'd missed our *closeness*? And what about your baby? Did you tell your little son or daughter about me, too? *Get out of my way*, do you hear me? *Step aside and let me pass!*"

His handsome face was like thunder as he took a step toward her, closing the gap between them. He looked dark, stern, ready to explode. And, although she took a hasty step back, he thrust his face into hers.

This close, she could smell the faint, pleasing aroma of the sandalwood soap he had shaved

283

with that morning. Could feel the crackling anger that sizzled inside him.

Anger, not guilt, a still-thinking part of her noted. If he were married, surely he would feel guilty, rather than angry.

"If you want me to step aside, Miranda, then by God, you'll have to make me! I'm not going anywhere until you hear what I have to say, damn it!"

"That can be arranged, St. James," she declared hotly, adding with a nasty little smile, "Making you step aside, I mean!"

An unholy grin creased his dark, handsome face. "Go ahead, my dear. *Try it*," he taunted in a low, challenging voice. "Nothing would give me greater pleasure than to lay my hands on you—even if only to defend myself."

His nasty grin deepened as, reckless and defiant, she raised the twigs she'd gathered above her head, whipping them back and forth like a headmaster's birch rod.

"Whenever you're ready, darling."

She was magnificent! Her turquoise eyes blazed. Her hair was the fiery hue of the leaves that crunched beneath their feet. Her bosom heaved. With her bright copper tresses flying behind her, she reminded him of the Saxon warrior queen, Boadicca of Suffolk, likewise red-haired, preparing to ride into battle with sharpened blades fastened to her chariot wheels.

"Come on, then!" she tossed at him.

"Ready, are you?" he murmured. His green eyes were sensual as he remembered a different encounter entirely, and quite another sort of readiness. "Good. So am I, my sweet."

His wicked expression, the roguish gleam in his eyes, left her in no doubt as to what he meant. The color that filled her cheeks left him in no doubt that she remembered that night. But, although her knees almost buckled, she was far too angry, too hurt, too betrayed to back down so easily.

Lifting her bundle of twigs a little higher, she slashed them down, half-heartedly trying to lash him across the face and shoulders.

But, with a low laugh, his hand shot out. He grasped her makeshift whip, wound his hand through the twigs and used them to jerk her toward him.

In one lighting move, she was brought up short against his chest with a startled squeak of shock and protest.

"I win," he said huskily.

Her turquoise eyes flew open. Her lovely, furious face was only scant inches from his as he flung the twigs aside and snaked his arms about her waist, cupping her bottom and pulling her snugly against him.

"The lady you chanced to see me with was my cousin, Nanon. . . . *Wait, damn it, woman! Stay still!* You'll hear me out, or I'll know the bloody reason why!" he added, panting as she bucked violently, trying to break his hold upon her. His arms tightened, steel bands that surrounded her and would not let her go. "The infant was her little son. She asked me to be Robert's godfather. The letter you delivered to me the day we emptied the lobster pots? The one with the monogrammed seal? It was from her. An invitation to little Robert's christening."

"Liar! If that were so, why wouldn't you tell me?" she demanded hotly. "You had no reason to lie about a . . . a simple christening!"

"Who lied, Miranda? Not I! As I recall, I told you only that I had to go away for a day or two, and that I wanted to say goodbye. That's all."

She grew still, torn between wanting desperately to believe him—*needing* to believe him—and knowing, deep in her heart of hearts, that there was more to it than that, regardless of what he claimed, and despite what he had told her. Perhaps it was just female intuition, but she knew it, nonetheless. Sensed it.

He was keeping something back.

"Why did you not tell me where you were going, then?" she demanded. "If you truly had nothing to hide?"

He shrugged. "It's a long story. Nan and I were raised by my parents, after her mother passed away in France, you see. When my own mother died, I ran off to sea. Since then, I've been considered the black sheep of our family. And so, Nan and I prefer to. . . ." Again, he shrugged.

"Meet secretly?" she suggested almost eagerly, to his relief. "You have kept up your ties with her, unknown to your father?"

"Hmm, something like that, aye," he murmured, relieved that she'd supplied her own answer—perhaps one she wanted to hear?—without any need for him to lie.

"How so? Has your father disowned you?"

A smile curved his lips. "Aye, love. Many times. In fact, more times than I care to count!" But each time, his love for me has forced him to recant just moments later! he added silently. "Well? Am I forgiven?" he asked.

Without waiting for her answer, he drew her down beside him onto a a heap of fallen leaves in a dense thicket of bushes. "Am I?" he murmured again as he nuzzled her throat, her ears, until goosebumps rose on her arms.

He could feel her blood racing under his fingertips. Could see the quick flutter of the pulse beneath the warm, silky skin of her throat. There was a deliciously husky catch to her breathing when he delved into her bodice to fondle her lovely breasts.

"Noo," she protested as he unknotted her shawl. "Don't! Morgan, stop it! Not here. . . ."

But perversely, her fingers plunged deep into his thick dark hair, and her lips hungrily sought his own as she drew his handsome head down to hers in a greedy kiss.

The knowledge that another couple was making love in the deep woods, just a stone's throw from the woody thicket where they lay upon a heap of fallen leaves, worked as a catalyst of sorts. The risk of discovery lent a sense of urgency and danger to their own secret liaison, heightening sexual appetites that had been denied for too many nights.

His lips muffled her cry as he thrust up her skirts and petticoats. Reaching beneath them, he eased his fingers inside her. She was already wet, swollen and silky and oh, so ready for him. . . .

"Miranda . . ."

"Morgan, oh, God, I've missed you so. Hurry, my love!"

He needed no second urging. Shoving up her petticoats, he positioned himself between her thighs, ducking his head to press his lips to the hollow at the base of her throat as he freed his aching shaft from the confines of his breeches.

The hard, hot flesh sprang forth, and was soon sheathed deep within her silken body, sliding home as smoothly as a knife through butter.

She moaned, eyes fluttering shut with delight as he began to ride her. Deepening his strokes, he lifted her hips a little higher, groaning with pleasure. Perhaps unconsciously imitating what she had glimpsed in the thicket between Coppinger and his female companion, she brought her legs up and over his shoulders and lifted her hips to the rhythm of his.

Her head was tipped back, coppery hair pooling on the bright leaves beneath them. Her eyes were closed, the dark, tawny lashes like tiny fans upon her rosy cheeks, while her full lips were parted and moist. Her breasts rose from the gathered neck of her shift so that the coraline nipples peeked over the lacy edging like deep-pink shells, delicately whorled.

He was forced to muffle her cries of pleasure—and his own—as he moved inside her, riding her strongly, more deeply with each thrust.

Not long now. Sweet lord! Not long!

He told himself he must withdraw, spill his seed on the leaves, and by so doing, lessen the chance of getting her with child. But she clung so fiercely to him, he could not do it.

Too late, ah, God, too late!

He clenched his jaw to staunch the roar of tri-

289

umph, of unbridled male pleasure, that would have burst from his throat as his climax shuddered through him.

He grew very still, braced on his palms above her, his body taut with the pleasure that roiled through it as his manhood bucked, filled her with his seed.

Her own shattering release accompanied his as her body arched beneath his. Muted, fluting cries broke from her parted lips and lost themselves in the chill, misty air, like the cries of some exotic bird. Her nails dug deep into his shoulders. Seconds later, he felt the rippling contractions of her womanhood, and knew she, too, had found her release.

"Ah, love, sweet love," he murmured, still breathing heavily as he fell to her side. Gathering her into his arms, he cradled her against his chest, kissing her tenderly.

Lost in their kiss, and in the velvet aftermath of their passion, they heard the horse that whickered in the woodland hush only dimly.

"Someone's coming!" she whispered urgently, tearing her lips from his. "I heard a horse!"

"It's been here all along. Be still, my love. No one will see us here," he assured her.

There was no moon that night as a small fishing ship hovered off Lizard Cove, and flashed a lantern signal from the port bow to those huddled, waiting, on shore.

Two rowboats had been dragged down the shingle to the sand, and thence into the shallows. The rowers handled their oars with hardly a splash, sending the two small craft skimming over the water to the lofty side of the far larger vessel.

After a few whispered words, several bulky parcels, kegs, pouches and bolts were lowered over the side to be stowed in the bows of the two row boats.

The rendezvous was completed in a matter of moments, with hardly a word exchanged. Conversation was dangerous. Sounds—especially voices—carried great distances over calm water at night, and there was always the chance the Preventives might be laying low, watching for them.

To a man, the smugglers heaved a sigh of relief as their rowboats skimmed safely into the dark waters closest to shore. The oarsmen had broken a sweat to evade the great shaft of light that shone out from the Head every few seconds, sending a path of dazzling brightness across the ink-black water.

When the rowboats scraped bottom, the men inside the small craft shipped their oars, and with the help of those waiting, began unloading the vessels with an economy of effort.

Forming a human chain, they tossed the contraband from one to the other, not stopping until their smuggled cargo of lace, brandy, tobacco and tea had been stacked deep in the bowels of a sea-cave.

Miranda, their lookout, was waiting at the mouth of the cave.

"All clear, lass?"

"All clear, Da'," she assured her father as he swung a hefty tea-chest down from his shoulder and added it to the rest. "Let Rob or Gil take those. They're too heavy for you," she scolded.

"I'll be the judge of that, my girl," Thad said with a scowl. He fiercely resented any suggestion that he was aging or that his strength might be waning.

Morgan—hidden farther down the beach— watched the men vanish into the bowels of the cave. It was only after the last of them had disappeared that he saw the glint of the wan moon off something metal upon the cliffs above. Heard the sound of harsh voices, quickly muffled, carried to him on the wind.

Glancing from the cliffs to the sea-cave, he cursed softly and thoroughly, and sprinted toward the cave.

Chapter Fifteen

Miranda was the last to leave the tunnel, following Jeb Bent, the Cove's blacksmith, the Tremayne brothers, Tom and Quentin, Big Jan, her father and Rob over the still-warm hearth, into the inn's kitchen.

While the men milled about, Miranda carefully closed the secret entrance behind them, then knelt and set a new fire on the hearthstone.

The smuggled goods would remain safe in the secret cache behind the chimney until yet another moon-dark night, when a string of ponies would spirit them away from the inn, on the final leg of their journey.

But as Miranda touched a match flame to the

heap of dry woodshavings she used for tinder, she heard a loud thudding sound. A gust of cold air rushed past her, the draft making the tiny flame gutter and go out.

The outside door to the taproom had blown open, and slammed against the wall. But how—?

"Find the bastards!" a voice roared. *"They're in here, somewhere!"*

The tramping of booted feet followed.

Not the wind at all. Dear God, no! Someone—several someones!—had forced their way into her inn!

White with shock, she whirled to face her father, her frightened question dying on her lips when she saw the ashen faces of him and the others.

As one, they surged toward the kitchen door, only to hear other voices in the yard beyond. Deep, rough male voices, questioning Tom, the stableboy, whose own sleepy voice sounded high and scared. Voices that demanded to know where they could find his mistress and her family.

Preventives!

And they were surrounded—trapped like fish in a barrel!

The men tensed and exchanged uneasy, apprehensive glances.

"Back into the tunnel with ye, lass," Thad commanded quietly yet urgently. "Lads, get ready to follow her!"

"Aye, Thad. You and me can hold 'em off, until these young 'uns get away," Jeb offered.

"It's too late, Da'," they all heard Rob say softly.

Someone was coming down the passageway, toward them!

"We must bluff our way out of this one. Well, well! A good evening to ye, sirs!" he declared, louder and with false cheer, going forward to meet their visitors and crowding them back out, into the saloon proper, before they could see exactly who was with him in the kitchen.

"Mr. Archer from room seven, isn't it?" he added in a louder, overly hearty voice. "And Mr. Forbes from room three. I'll be! I didn't recognize you in those uniforms, gentlemen! Now. What can I get for you? An after-hours pint to take the chill off? Or a bowl of my sister's soup?"

"Enough of your play-acting, Killigrew!"

"Play-acting, sir?" An innocent frown.

"Aye! It's not Mr. Archer at all, as you know damned well. Not in this uniform! *The game's up, man!* It's Sergeant Percy Archer, of His Majesty's ninth dragoons, and I'll thank you to remember it!" Archer corrected him with a sneer.

Shoulders back, pointed chin up, he reminded Miranda—who'd followed them into the taproom, bearing the kettle of soup and a ladle—of a bantam cock, strutting about.

"And this here is Corporal Forbes. Corporal Albert Forbes. For some weeks now, we've had this inn and the doings of its proprietor—you, Mistress Tallant and your family—under close surveillance. Tonight—gentlemen, madam—it gives me great pleasure to tell the lot of you that you're all *under arrest!*"

"Arrest?" Rob snorted with laughter, then spat into the brass spittoon to show his disgust. "The devil we are! For what crime are you arresting us, sarge? For enjoying a late supper?" He grinned as Thad Killigrew joined them, carrying earthenware bowls and a long bread loaf. Gil carried in the spoons and a crock of butter, the Tremaynes the bread board and a jug of cider.

A supercilious little smile lifted Archer's thin moustache. "Smuggling, Killigrew," he said with every evidence of satisfaction. "Free trading. Which, as well you know, sir, is a hanging offense!"

An uneasy murmur rippled through the other men behind Rob and Thad. The false smiles they'd plastered on became scowls. They exchanged nervous glances, with Tom and Quentin Tremayne muttering that, with the numbers unevenly matched—six dragoons against the eight of them—it would be easy to set upon the

Preventives and quickly overpower them.

"After all, dead men tell no tales, do they, now?" Big Jan muttered under his breath, eyeing the cocksure pair.

"Jan's right," murmured Jeb Bent, the village blacksmith, flexing his burly forearms. "They don't. I could snap the skinny one's neck, easy as winkin'. Aye, and the big lout's, too! Be damned if I couldn't!"

"You'll do nothing of the sort, Jeb Bent," Thad growled softly. "Leastways, not while I have aught to do with it! Smuggling's one thing. No one gets hurt, and the Crown's pockets are deep enough that they won't miss our little bit of revenue. But I'll not be a party to murder, lads," he added quietly, unaware that Morgan had followed them out of the tunnel and was waiting and listening intently to the goings-on from the darkened passageway behind the bar; he had heard every word Thad said.

"Not even to save your own neck, Thad?"

"Not even then." In a louder voice, Thad began, "*Smuggling*, you said, Sergeant? Surely you're funning us, lad? We're law-abiding, hard working farmers or fishermen, that's what we are. What reason have you to accuse us of such doings, tell me that?"

Archer smiled his superior smile. "When the reinforcements I've sent for arrive—as arrive

297

they shall, within the hour—we'll have all the proof we need. By God, sir, we'll tear this wretched inn apart! Lift every floorboard, search every cupboard, peer into every crevice, nook and cranny, until we find where you've hidden the contraband!"

"Contraband!" Rob snorted. "There is no bloody contraband here, I tell ye, ye blasted fool!"

"I'll thank you to keep a civil tongue in your head, Robert Killigrew! If you won't talk, perhaps our lovely innkeeper will tell us what we need to know, hmm?" Archer murmured.

His hand snaked out, fingers closing around Miranda's wrist. Before she could break away, he jerked her towards him. "Perhaps you can explain what these persons are doing in your public house, so long after closing time, ma'am?"

"Let go of my sister, you miserable little worm, or I'll break your bloody fingers, one by one!" Rob growled threateningly.

"See here? It was just as you said, my sweet!" declared a loud hearty voice. "I found this little bottle of the '90, but there wasn't a trace of the '88 you said I—Why, messieurs Forbes and Archer, a good evening to you, sirs! Glad you could join us. Well, Miranda, my love? Don't just stand there, gawking! See to our guests! Find more chairs for the gentlemen and their friends!"

298

Morgan urged, appearing nonchalantly from the dark passageway behind the bar.

With his reefer jacket unbuttoned, a smudge of something on one cheek, and one hand tucked casually in his pocket, he looked as if he had just stepped down to the wine cellar in search of a special bottle.

"Here you go, Rob!" he urged, tossing Rob a cobwebby bottle of champagne. "Champagne's the only wine for a proper celebration! Uncork this one for us, there's a good man! We'll have a toast, shall we? To the good health and good fortune of my future bride, Mistress Miranda Tallant and myself, God bless us. Soon to be the happiest of couples!"

Without further ado, Morgan passed empty glasses out to the dragoons and the villagers, then caught Miranda about the waist and hugged her. As he drew her into his arms, out of the sergeant's spiteful hold, he accidentally stepped upon Archer's booted toes. He was in no great haste to lift his weighty foot away.

"My . . . my toes!" Archer grunted, his face turning crimson to match his jacket.

"Hmmm? Your pardon, sir? What did you say?"

"Your f . . . foot! Take . . . take it off."

"My what? My foot? Oh. My *foot*! My apologies, sir," Morgan murmured with no sincerity whatsoever.

Across the room, Big Jan snickered.

Rob drew the champagne cork with a loud pop. Everyone cheered or clapped as sparkling wine frothed over the sides of the green glass bottle. Wrapping the bottle in a cloth, Rob went from one man to the next, filling empty glasses.

Soon, Archer's men were laughing and guzzling wine along with the rest of them, muskets propped casually against the wall, tricorn hats pushed back.

"What the devil are you doing, St. James?" Archer bellowed. "And you! Have you men lost your wits?" he asked his soldiers, looking around the room. "Can't you see I'm arresting these people?"

"Arresting? Ho, that's a good one! Did ye hear that, Thomas?" Morgan asked, nudging Thomas Tremayne, the cooper, in the ribs with his elbow. "Our artist friend says he's arresting my guests—and on the night of my betrothal, too! Now, now, Archer, leave off, do, man! Your games are better suited to the highjinks of the wedding-night!" Morgan declared, winking at a scowling Archer and Forbes. "Surely this one can wait till then?"

Taking Morgan's lead, the other men snorted with laughter, slapped their thighs and hooted, apparently highly amused at Archer's "blunder."

Miranda laughed, too. Curling her arms about Morgan's neck, she went up on tiptoe to soundly buss his cheek in a loving display of affection, and whispered, "Thank you!" in his ear.

" 'Twas my pleasure," he murmured, drawing her closer to give her a smacking kiss, full on the lips.

Their eyes met and a current of understanding passed between them as she dabbed the streak of soot from the hearth—or was it only cobwebs from the winecellars?—off his cheek with a corner of her apron. "I'll take some butter for my burned fingers later," he murmured.

"Butter be damned. If we escape this mess, I'll kiss them better for you," she promised softly, patting his cheek. "Now, now, my love. Don't you go giving these rogues any ideas," she said in a much louder voice. "You'll stay snugly at home on our wedding night, or I'll know the reason why!" she scolded, teasing him as a doting sweetheart might do.

Percy Archer had looked confused when Morgan arrived. So had Albert Forbes. Now both men appeared utterly dumbfounded.

"Open up, in the name of the King!" rang out a deep voice from behind the closed door.

"Well, I'll be damned!" Morgan exclaimed mildly. "Who else have you invited to our betrothal, Archer? More of your 'artist' friends?"

"Shut up!" Archer barked, furious. The rest of his foul epithets went unheard as the stout wooden door flew inward.

Once again, several uniformed dragoons spilled into the flagstoned taproom, their bayonets fixed, their muskets leveled at the small group before the bar, who were casually swigging champagne. In with them came a burst of frigid air.

The dragoons were followed at a slower pace by a solitary officer, a tall, strapping, fair-headed man.

"What the devil's going on here, Sergeant?" the officer demanded, smoothing down his fair moustaches.

"*Harry?*" Miranda exclaimed, her turquoise eyes widening in disbelief. "Why, it really is you! Oh, Captain Dickerson! How wonderful to see you again! My sister will be ever so pleased!"

"Mistress Tallant! What a pleasure it is to see you again, ma'am. And you, too, Mr. Killigrew, sir!" He nodded courteously at her father.

"Sir?" Archer said uncertainly, looking from Miranda to Dickerson, then back again. "Captain Dickerson?"

"What's going on here, Sergeant?" Dickerson demanded crisply. Removing his black bearskin hat, he tucked his gauntlets inside it, then handed both to his adjutant with a smart military flourish.

"Earlier this evening, sir, Corporal Forbes and myself observed these people unloading goods from an unlighted sailing vessel that hovered offshore," Archer reported, standing stiffly at attention. "Before we could apprehend them in the act for smuggling, they and the contraband . . . well, they . . . er . . . it had . . . um, disappeared, sir."

"Disappeared, sergeant?" Dickerson murmured in a world-weary, disbelieving tone.

"Well, yes, sir. You see, for several weeks now, we . . . er . . . we have been staying here, at the Black Gull, trying to find the opening to a . . . um . . . a secret tunnel leading from the sea-caves on the shore, sir, up to the inn. It . . . it was all Lieutentant Foxworthy's idea, you understand, sir?"

"And?"

Archer's dark brows rose. "And, sir?"

"Have you found any such entrances?" Dickerson demanded impatiently. "Or have you been taking the King's shilling while enjoying a little holiday at the seaside for yourselves?"

"Why, never, sir! We, er, we would never. . . ."

"Speak up, man! Have you found any blasted tunnels?" Dickerson thundered.

"Er, no, sir," Archer admitted lamely. "I regret to inform you that we have not."

"And have you, Corporal Forbes?"

"No, sir. Nothing yet."

"And the contraband? Have any untaxed cargoes been uncovered in this vicinity?"

"No, sir," both men whispered. "Not that we know of."

"I see. Then, since you have found neither the entrance to any secret tunnel, nor any contraband hidden here, what the devil is your business here? Why did you send to Bodmin for reinforcements? And by whose authority were you fools intending to arrest these innocent folk?"

"I sent for 'em because . . . because we knew we'd need more men to search the inn properly, sir!" Archer began eagerly. "It's the dark of the moon, after all, is it not, sir? That's when they do their dirty work! And there must be another opening t'the tunnel here somewhere, Captain, I just know there must.

"See, one minute, they were on the beach, below us, and the next . . . why, they'd vanished! We found them here, not ten minutes later. Yet no one passed us in the lane! Explain that, sir, if you can," he added triumphantly.

"Can you be sure, against all measures of doubt, that these men are the ones you saw?

Could the men you saw on the beach, and these before you not be two quite different, separate groups of men?"

Archer deflated like a pricked balloon. "Weell, I suppose they could be, yes, but . . . no, no, I think not!"

"Think, Sergeant. Can you? Can you swear on the Good Book that they are one and the same? Before a magistrate, in a court of law? 'Tis the dark of the moon, after all, as you so rightly said. A man cannot see his own hand before him, on a night like this!"

"Not swear, perhaps, but I can—"

"Not swear, man? But swear you must, for there are men's necks at stake here!" Morgan interjected angrily. "Good men's lives."

"And who might you be, sir?" Dickerson demanded, his eyes narrowing as he turned to Morgan.

"Morgan St. James, Captain. Soon to be the husband of this lovely creature here"—he smiled down at Miranda—"which is why we have all come together here tonight for a late supper. To celebrate the fact that this evening, Miranda agreed to become my wife! That is what I was endeavoring to tell the sergeant before you arrived, Captain." He chucked Miranda beneath the chin. "But unfortunately, Sergeant Archer proved most reluctant to hear me out."

"St. James. The name is familar to me," Dickerson observed, frowning.

"My father is Sir Robert St. James, Captain. Former magistrate for Plymouth, now retired. Perhaps you have heard of him?"

"Indeed I have, sir! And of the St. James Shipping Line. Your family is well regarded in the town of Plymouth, sir.'Tis an honor to meet you, Mr. St. James.

"Now. I say again," Dickerson continued with a brisk nod, turning back to the artists-cum-soldiers before him. *"Can you swear?"*

"Uh, no, sir. I can't," Archer whispered, crushed, looking anywhere but into his captain's steely blue-gray eyes. "There was only six men on the beach, ye see? But now there's seven, not counting the woman."

"I cannot swear, either, sir," Forbes agreed unhappily.

Dickerson snorted. "I'm relieved to hear it!" His blue eyes—twinkling now—boldly met those of Thaddeus Killigrew. The firm chin Juliet Killigrew had so admired came up determinedly. "For it would hardly endear me to the father of the young lady I intend to marry, were I to place her papa under arrest for smuggling! Would it, now?"

"Marry, you say, Harry, my boy? Well, well! Who'd have thought I'd be marrying off two daughters in a single night! By God, that's double reason to celebrate! Hand me that bottle, *son!*" Thad growled, sticking his hand out to Morgan. "Your health, lads!" he declared, tipping the almost-empty bottle to his lips and downing a generous swig.

"Our pleasure, *Da'*," Morgan murmured, grinning at Harry.

Everyone—with the exception of Messrs. Forbes, Archer and the other soldiers—laughed heartily, as much with relief over their narrow escape from the hangman's noose as for any other reason.

"What's going on here? What has happened?" exclaimed a quavering female voice from the doorway.

"Cate!" Thad said, hurrying to take the shivering woman by the arm and lead her to a settle by the hearth, where it was warm. "What the devil are you doing here, lovie? And how did you come?" He used the gentle tone he'd used when she was sick of the poisoning.

"I rode Petal. Oh, don't look at me that way, Thaddeus Killigrew! I had to. For Gil, bless him." She pulled free of her husband's arms and stumbled over to her oldest boy, taking off the shawl she'd drawn over her faded red hair as she went. "It's your Kitty, son. The baby's coming!

307

We need Dr. Hardee and the midwife at East-moor, post haste!"

Gil's face blanched. "I'll fetch them home, Mam. That is—I will, if I'm free to go?" he looked inquiringly at Harry Dickerson, who nodded, before he left the taproom at a run.

Thad ran his hands through his silver hair. "Well, I'll be blowed! Two offers of marriage and a grandchild coming, all in one night! Fair makes a man dizzy, it does! Pull me a pint, Miranda, there's a good lass. Aye, and pour a glass of brandy for your mam. She's chilled to the bone. And while you're at it, give all our friends here a drink on the house, too! I don't know about the rest of you lads, but I feel the need for something a bit stronger than this Frenchie wine, aye? 'Tis all dazzle and no guts. . . ."

Chapter Sixteen

Bianca Katherine Killigrew, perfect from her crown of dark auburn curls down to the tiniest pink toe, was born the following frosty morning.

Loud squalls from a pair of robust lungs announced her safe arrival into the world. Her birth ushered in the dawn of a new day, and likewise heralded a fresh beginning for her parents and adoring family.

Baby Bianca was christened at St. Breoch's on the second Sunday morning in December, wearing the long lace-trimmed christening gown that had been in the Killigrew family for over a century.

Freshly laundered, the delicate gown had

been starched, smocked and trimmed with new
eyelet for the occasion. Several snowy shawls,
delicate as cobwebs, a bonnet, booties and mit-
tens, all knitted by her adoring mama, aunts and
grandmama, muffled the little beauty against
the cold as she slept contentedly in her father's
arms. She awoke only when the Rev. Boreham
took her from Gil to dip cold water from the font
and make the sign of the Cross upon her petal-
pink forehead with his wet fingers. And even
then, the little darling only whimpered for a moment, her rosebud mouth turning upside down
in a pitiful sob that touched even the hardest
heart in the congregation, despite the absence of
even a single tiny tear.

"I baptise thee Bianca Katherine Killigrew, in
the name of the Father," Boreham intoned as he
made the sign of the Cross, "and of the Son, and
of the Holy Ghost. Amen. . . ."

Afterwards, they all trooped from the church,
into the churchyard to find the first white flakes
of the season drifting down. Stamping and chaf-
ing cold hands and numbed feet, the laughing,
noisy throng made its way down the lane to the
Black Gull, where Miranda had prepared a de-
lightfully lavish hot luncheon in the new arrival's honor, by way of a christening party.

She also presented her darling little niece with
a silver christening cup, inscribed with her

name and her birthdate, and a small silver platter, mug and spoon she'd had engraved in Bodmin.

"Tim, fetch more logs for the fires! I want them both roaring!" Miranda declared, tying an apron over the fine black, white and hunter-green plaid gown she'd worn to the baptism. "Maisie, heat the poker and mull some more cider for our guests. Hurry now, there's a pet! Brrr, it's freezing in here this afternoon!" she declared, rubbing her hands together. "Everyone's chilled and half-starved! Jan, I'll let you slice the ham for us. Da', the turkey's yours to carve! I'll serve the sausage stuffing. Hmm, just smell that sage and onion! Heavenly!"

For pudding, there was warm gingerbread with fresh cream; wedges of fragrant spice cake, plump with currants, sultanas and raisins; both blackberry and apple pies drizzled with a creamy vanilla custard, as well as the sliced ham and turkey, gravy, dressing and potatoes—oh, more food than they could possibly have eaten at one sitting!

Drinks were poured and toasts offered with raised glasses and tankards to "wet the baby's head." So many toasts, in fact, that the poor little mite, fast asleep in her carrying basket, could have swum in their good wishes, had they been taken literally!

311

Half the people from the village and the surrounding cottages thronged the trestle tables set
up in the taproom, along with Harry Dickerson,
of course, who'd ridden all the way from his barracks in Bodmin for the special occasion, and
Harry's friend, Captain Samuel T. Trent, as well
as Morgan and Simon from the lighthouse, and
Mrs. Pettit—Maisie's sour-faced mama—from
the village.

The Coppingers had come, too, although no
one had invited them, along with a couple of
their rowdy cronies from the Safe Harbor. But
rather than cause unpleasantness, Miranda decided to feed them and say nothing. It was
Bianca's christening party, after all, and there
was more than enough food for everyone, invited or otherwise.

To her mind, harsh words and hard feelings
had no place at such a joyful occasion.

Following the night Archer and Forbes bungled their attempt to arrest them for smuggling,
Harry had ridden out to the farm to court Juliet.
And to no one's surprise, later that day, he had
formally asked their Da's permission to marry
his youngest daughter.

"I've already told Miss Juliet that I loved her
from the first moment I laid eyes upon her,"
Harry had declared softly and with obvious sincerity as he smiled down into Juliet's glowing

face that evening. "And she's made me the happiest man alive by saying she feels the same. The only thing that could make the pair of us even happier, Mr. Killigrew, ma'am, would be your blessing on our marriage."

Her father had looked into Harry's earnest eyes, and into Juliet's; then he'd reached out and put Juliet's hand in Harry's. "You have it, lad. All the blessings in the world. Besides," he added, "what choice have I, when it comes right down to it?" he demanded with a roguish twinkle in his eyes.

The lighthouse keeper and the dashing captain had risked their own lives, their futures, to save him and his sons and friends from certain hanging.

Although it would never again be spoken of directly, Thad, Morgan, Harry and the others all knew *exactly* what had really happened that night, and on many other, similar moon-dark nights. But by mutual, if tacit consent, it was a secret they would carry with them to their graves.

Exactly one week from that night, Morgan came to Miranda in her darkened chamber at the inn, his arrival unannounced and unexpected.

With a gasp of shock, she awoke from a light doze to find him looming over her bed, as he had in her dreams, his fine head, broad shoulders and lean hips silhouetted against the winter storm she could see raging through the casement window behind him.

"You came out in this!" she murmured, holding out her arms to him. "You silly man! You must be soaked through."

His hair was damp with rain, his cheeks cool to her lips as he tore off his jacket and came into her arms.

"Soaked," he agreed, smiling and kissing her. "But it was worth every bloody raindrop, for the sight of you."

"Flatterer!" Laughing softly, she tossed aside the covers. "Let me get something to warm you. A bowl of hot soup and bread, perhaps? No? A cloth to dry your hair, then? Not even a mug of chocolate?"

"Ssshh. All I need is you, Miranda. Your arms. Hmmm, this lovely body. Your lips. . . ."

Still cradling her in his arms, he eased her down to the feather bolster, until he was stretched out beside her.

She parted her lips on a contented sigh, murmuring endearments, making contented little sounds low in her throat as he began to shower her with kisses.

As he kissed her, he untied the drawstring that gathered the neck of her bedgown and pushed it off her shoulders, kissing the fragrant flesh he bared. Flesh that was as smooth and opalescent as moonflowers in the flickering firelight.

Cupping both bared breasts, he kissed and suckled the velvety, raspberry nipples until they grew hard as pebbles.

His lovemaking stole her breath away. Robbed her of reason. She sighed with dreamy pleasure as he smoothly turned her over. She purred and stretched like a kitten as he ran his hands lightly over her shoulders and back, then down to her bottom, following the feathery touch of his lips with scattered little kisses.

Leaning over her, Morgan swept aside her hair and nipped her neck with his teeth, hard enough to make her gasp with pleasure and clench her fingers in the lavender-scented linens. As he nibbled her shoulders, he lazily stroked her bottom, aroused by the peachy firmness of each round cheek beneath his hand. Quickly yielding to his lust, he slid his fingers deep into her quim from behind.

Wet, hot silk sheathed his fingers, as if he'd dipped them in warmed honey. Her obvious arousal made his shaft throb. His own body hard and taut with desire, he deepened his caresses. Quickened his strokes.

With a soft, incoherent cry, she arched backward against him, moaning as she grasped fistfuls of the rumpled linens and pushed her face blindly into the pallet with her need.

"Morgan, aaah, Morgan. . . ."

"We've never made love this way, have we, my sweet?" he murmured in her ear as he stripped off boots, shirt and breeches.

Raising her hips, so that she knelt before him, he grasped her shoulders and eased himself inside her from behind. Thrusting deeply, he withdrew, repeating the slow deep thrusts again and again, until he was sheathed to the very hilt in her sweet, hot flesh.

As he reached beneath her to fondle her breasts, or to strum the delicate, tiny bud of her passion, she arched back and rubbed herself against him until he groaned with pleasure.

"Does this please you, Miranda?" he whispered. His voice was thick with lust.

Reaching beneath her, he rolled both hardened nipples between his thumbs and fingers and rocked against her until she was moaning with desire, tossing her head from side to side and shamelessly crying out her pleasure with each thrust.

"Say it," he commanded. "Tell me. Does it please you?"

"Yes . . . oh, yes! Oh, God, don't stop! Don't! It . . . it pleases me more than . . . more than I can saaay!"

Moments later, they found their release together as waves of delight lifted them, bore them away.

They slept then, Miranda curled on her side, Morgan curved protectively around her. Their hands were clasped, their legs entwined, their hearts beating as one.

Miranda's last thought before sleep claimed her was that nothing was as perfect as their love-making.

I love him, she admitted with a blissful sigh, pressing a hand to her swelling belly. I am hopelessly, deeply in love with him. And it is just as well, since there is no turning back.

Not now.

Chapter Seventeen

The storm was still raging, she noticed drowsily some time later, when Morgan shook her by the shoulder to wake her.

She could see eerie lavender flashes of lightning through her casement window, which faced the wild Atlantic. Still more than half asleep, she nevertheless counted silently:

One-one-thousand, two-one-thousand. . . .

Again, the thunder clattered, rattling the windowpanes in their frames.

The storm was still two miles out to sea, but it was fast coming inland and would soon be directly overhead.

"Miranda? Wake up! We need to talk," she

heard Morgan say urgently. "There's something I have to tell you, and there's not much time left now! Come on, love. Wake up."

"What is it? What's wrong?" There was an edge to Morgan's voice that frightened her.

"There's something you should know," he said heavily, his voice so low she had to strain to hear him. "Something you *need* to know, so that whatever happens tonight, you'll understand my role in it. . . ."

The chill that had begun creeping through her with his announcement began to spread through her veins like a cold, malevolent fog. Each word that followed would be a nail, hammered into her heart. She just *knew* it!

"Morgan, don't! Stop it! You're frightening me!" she implored, covering her ears with her hands. "Whatever it is, I don't want to hear it!"

"I know you don't, sweetheart. But you must. Miranda, I didn't come to Lizard Cove to keep the lighthouse. My father and I are the owners of the St. James Shipping Line of Plymouth. I came here to investigate the wrecking of one of our ships off the Point, and to find out why both her captain and crew perished. You see, the captain was a very dear friend of my family's. I intend to bring his murderers to justice!"

"Who . . . ? Who was he . . . ?" she wondered aloud. Her inn had sheltered the survivors of many shipwrecks until they were able to return to their home ports or their families.

"The captain of the *Lady Anne*. Remember the schooner that ran aground back in August? Captain Geoffrey Christopher."

Her belly squeezed, like a snake tightening its coils. "God, no!" she whispered.

"My cousin, Nanon Dubois and I—the woman you saw me with in Bodmin—were raised together like brother and sister," he explained. "Nan met Geoff when I brought him home from boarding school one holiday."

Remembering, he grinned.

"A romantic fool, that's what Geoff was," he added without rancor. "He fell for pretty Nan at first sight. After a stint in the merchant marines, and a suitably long engagement, my father gave Geoff his first captaincy, along with Nan's hand in marriage. Needless to say, Geoff was . . . well, he was over the moon! He loved Nanon more than anything in this world, you see?"

A muscle ticked at his temple, betraying the conflicting emotions that roiled beneath his controlled exterior.

"She was just a month from delivering their first child when Geoff was . . . when she heard he'd been drowned."

"I remember the wreck as if it was yesterday," she whispered. The pitiful bodies, sewn into simple canvas shrouds, that her family and others had seen carted up from the seashore to a communal grave in St. Breoch's churchyard. All those who lay now under a simple white stone that Lady Dinah Draker, in a rare gesture of generosity, had herself donated, as lady of the manor. The inscription she had the stonemason carve upon it read, "*For Those In Peril On the Sea*."

"The shock of it all brought on the baby's birth," he said.

"Oh, God. No!"

He nodded soberly. "Aye."

"But . . . their deaths were a tragic accident!" she protested. "The storm . . . the ship running aground . . . those were acts of God. If you must hold someone to account, then blame Him. Or . . . or blame Keeper Ashe, the lighthouse keeper. It was he who let the Lizard light go out, after all. If the wretched beacon had been lit that night, the *Anne* would have been nowhere near those rocks!"

"That's what the wreckers wanted everyone to believe. But Keeper Ashe came to me after the *Anne* was lost. He was recovering from a severe beating and telling a very different tale. One, I might add, that both my father and I believe."

"Why?" Her eyes searched his grimly handsome face for an answer. She had never seen his

322

green eyes so filled with pain, nor so dark and troubled with memory. "What did Ashe tell you?"

"That not all of the *Anne's* crew drowned that night. That a handful survived the rough seas and being dashed against the rocks to struggle ashore—only to fall victim to the wreckers awaiting them. No, not wreckers," he amended, eyes blazing now, fists knotted at his sides. "Those coldblooded, murdering bastards went beyond simple salvaging! They bludgeoned to death the poor devils who crawled ashore. Murdered them in cold blood for the sake of the *Anne's* cargo and her fittings!"

"You believe Ashe's story?" she asked incredulously.

"Aye. In here," he added, touching his chest, then his gut.

"Then you're more gullible than I would ever have thought!" Clearly dumbfounded, she shook her coppery head. "If Billy Ashe had been a soldier, he would have been shot for his desertion that night! He was sworn to keep the Lizard beacon lit, as well you know. But instead, he fell into a drunken stupor and deserted his post. Why, his drinking was . . . was common knowledge in the village. . . ."

Her voice trailed lamely away. Had Billy's drinking *really* been common knowledge, she wondered suddenly? Had she ever heard the man called a drunkard before that dreadful night? Or was the first time in the days *following* the wreck of the *Anne*? . . .

A chill trickled down her spine like melted ice.

Keeper Ashe had always seemed a shy, courteous fellow on those rare occasions when their paths had crossed. In the months before his disappearance, there certainly had been nothing about his neat if threadbare demeanor to suggest he drank heavily. If he had ever been a heavy drinker, he had certainly not acquired his liquor in her public house.

"I had occasion to meet with Mr. Ashe several times following his first visit," Morgan continued while she tried desperately to remember. "In fact, he was a welcome guest at my home until he left to recuperate with his sister in Suffolk. Not once, in the entire month he was with us, did I ever see him imbibe, except on the one occasion when I pressed him to do so, for medicinal purposes. Nor did Simon or I find any evidence of his drinking at the cottage. Not a single bottle, cask, or what-have-you. We also found the Argand well-filled and ready to light, except for the thick layer of dust clouding the lens.

"I'm convinced the claims that Ashe was a heavy drinker, and that he was beaten for neglecting his duties, are nothing but lies, Miranda. Ones the wreckers circulated to account for Billy's injuries, should he be found, and also to explain the mysterious 'failure' of the Lizard light that night.

"When he vanished without a trace, his attackers were desperate to discredit his version of what had happened that night, in case he'd survived. In reality, it was they who came to the lighthouse. They who overpowered Keeper Ashe and extinguished the beacon he had filled. And afterward, they beat him within an inch of his life, to ensure that the Argand remained unlit.

"Unfortunately for them, Ashe was hardier than they realized. He came to before they could finish their dirty work—and saw the survivors of the *Lady Anne's* crew murdered on the shoreline below the point!"

"Then surely he can name the men who killed them?"

Morgan shook his head. "Alas, no. In the dark and confusion, forced to flee for his very life, Ashe could not identify the guilty parties. However, before he fled for his life, he did hear one of them yell a name."

"What name?" she whispered bitterly, hating what he would—must!—say. It was the only name that explained why someone like Morgan—

a gentleman—had ever looked twice at someone like her. . . .

"Killigrew."

Although she'd expected it, she gasped as if he'd struck her a physical blow to the belly.

The color drained from her face, and she felt— aye, she felt as if she'd died a little inside, if such a thing was possible.

"Ashe told you that *my* family murdered those poor men?" she echoed in a whisper.

The shock was too much. Her body seemed numb on the heels of his revelation, even as the blood roared in her ears.

"That explains your—your interest in me," she whispered hoarsely. "Why you courted me so single-mindedly. Took me to your bed. You hoped, in the course of our . . . our pillow-talk, that I would betray my family's secrets, did you not?"

The pain in her eyes, the catch in her voice, were razors that cut him to the quick. A nerve ticked at his temple. His Adam's apple bobbed in his throat. In that moment, he ached to reach out and hold her. Would have cut out his own heart, to have spared her the truth. *To have lied.* But, he could not. He loved her. He knew that now. And because he loved her, he owed her the truth. There could be no love where there was no honesty.

"Answer me!" she demanded, her voice rising, shriller than before.

"At first, yes," he admitted heavily. Before his eyes, she seemed to crumple like a lovely flower. "I never considered you as someone who might be hurt by what I intended. In my ambition to unmask Geoff's killer, you were just a . . . a pretty means to an end. *My* end. Furthering my investigation, and uncovering the truth. In that, I did you a terrible injustice, Miranda."

"Yes," she said woodenly. "You did."

"But before long, all that had changed. I realized that I—"

"Devil take your excuses, sir!" she hissed at him through clenched jaws, springing from the bed. Her turquoise eyes blazed like St. Elmo's fire. Her body was rigid with outrage, hurt and fury, each nerve strung taut as wire.

Fists balled at her sides, she itched to strike out at his handsome face. Instead, she flung her glorious hair over her shoulders, and glared at him with all the fire and fury of a Celtic queen.

"You claim you were searching for the truth, but admit it, sir. You did not need to bed me to achieve your end. No. You *used* me, Morgan! You held me. Kissed me. Swore you loved me. But it was all *lies! All of it!*"

"No!" he denied, his voice like the crack of a whip. In two strides, he had crossed the room.

A third, and he'd taken her by the upper arms and turned her to face him. "Those plans were made before I met you. Long before I came to know the true and lovely woman you are—and lost my heart.

"Miranda, despite how we met, despite my first intentions, *I love you!*" he swore, his green eyes searching her face. "If you'll give me the chance, I'll spend the rest of my life proving it. But for now, my sweet, my only love, our future must wait. You see, the trap has been set. To-night, it will be sprung and, God willing, Geoff's murderers will be caught and punished. There's nothing I can do to stop it. Not now."

"What trap? You speak in riddles! *Explain.* Tell me where you're going," she demanded, frantic for her family as he began dressing. "You can't mean to go out? Not in this?"

An unfastened shutter somewhere was bang-ing violently in the storm, and she could hear the high-pitched shrieking of the inn's sign as it was batted to and fro.

The wind was howling and groaning in the hollows and crannies of the old inn, whistling like a banshee as it swept in from the sea, then fought its way up, onto the high moors.

The sounds it made were unearthly. Fright-ening. Like the sounds a monstrous beast would make as it hunted its terrified prey.

She shuddered. Tonight, the image of hunter and hunted was an all-too-vivid one.

Morgan was a hunter. A dark and dangerous, powerful predator. . . .

"I must go!" His darkly handsome face was stern, his sea-green eyes hooded, his expression set and determined in the sudden brilliant flash of lightning that lit the room.

Tonight, by the storm's cruel white light, the furrows that winged away from his eyes were more deeply carved, his black brows darker, giving his face a dangerous, saturnine cast.

Why had she never thought of him as dangerous before? As a very real threat to her family? Had he convinced Forbes and Archer that her family were not smugglers so that they would trust him? Did he hope to prove them guilty of murder, instead?

"Don't go," she whispered, trailing her hands down over his broad, tanned chest, tugging at the shirt he was trying to pull on.

His nipples hardened with the light caress of her fingertips. The nubs jutted from the pelt of coarse dark hair that surrounded them. She buried her face in his chest. Kissed the warm, supple flesh.

"Stay here. With me. If you love me, as you say, prove it. Don't go!"

Her tone was no longer hurt or outraged, but soft and cajoling. Seductive. . . .

"Let me love you all night long, Morgan," she murmured. Adding silently, for I will gladly play the whore, to keep my family safe!

"I wish to God I could! But it's too late. It's gone too far. This morning, when I saw the storm clouds gathering on the horizon, I knew the time had come, that there might not be another chance. It's been hours since I sent Simon to Windhaven for Squire Draker's help."

"Windhaven?"

"Aye, love. By dawn tomorrow, it will all be over—with our upstanding Squire Draker's assistance," he added with a grim, mirthless smile. He could not forget the casual way Draker had offered to send reinforcements to help him apprehend the wreckers, if ever need be. Soon he would know, one way or the other, if that offer had been sincere. "Tonight, God willing, we'll unmask the men responsible for the murders of Geoff and his brave crew. So you see, Miranda? I cannot go back nor undo it. Not now. 'Tis far too late! The trap is primed and set. Within the hour, it will be sprung!

Cupping her chin in his fingertips, he tipped her head up. She was stiff and unresponsive, yet he dropped a kiss on her chill lips nonetheless. A kiss she made no effort to return.

Her jaw was set, her lovely turquoise eyes glacial.

"I know you're upset. But I want you to promise me you'll stay here, where it's safe, until I come for you. Swear you won't try to follow me, Miranda? When this is over, we shall talk, you and I. I shall make you understand."

"I won't promise anything! I'm not like you," she accused bitterly. "I don't make promises I can't keep."

"That's a pity. You see, I have to be very sure that you keep this one," he said with an air of resignation.

Yanking open the drawer of her armoire, he withdrew a handful of silk kerchiefs.

"Wh . . . what are you doing? Why do you need those?" she demanded, shrinking back against the wall as he selected two kerchiefs and strode purposefully toward her. "Get away from me!"

"It pains me to do this, my sweet," he said regretfully. "But . . . I'm going to tie you up. Unfortunately, you leave me no choice. Give me your hands, Miranda—"

"The devil I will. *Don't!* Let *go* of me, damn you!" Too late, she tried to flee him.

But his hand snaked out. His steely fingers caught her wrists in a vise-like grip as he dragged her up against his chest. Crowding her toward the brass bed, he bound her wrists together with a length of silk and tied the ends with a sailor's knot.

Then, ignoring the blazing fury in her eyes, he gently pushed her back, onto the bed, trapped both legs and lashed her ankles together.

Drawing the quilted counterpane up, over her half-clad body, he stared down at her for several moments before he bent and kissed her brow.

"I wish to God there was another way, but you left me none. I'll be back," he promised softly.

Her eyes were murderous as he headed for the door. He could feel them boring holes in his back.

"What will you do?" she called after him, straining her wrists to no avail. The bonds that held her, although of silk, refused to break. "Who is it you're hoping to catch? Won't you tell me their names, at least?"

Her voice rose at the end, unsteady, hoarse. But he would not answer her. Could not! Something might yet go awry, and too many lives depended on his silence. Hers. His. Her family's. Others'. . . .

His face was dark and closed as he buttoned the reefer jacket and pulled up the collar. Jamming the captain's cap down over his dark hair, so that the peak cast his stern face in deep shadow, he bent low and roughly caught her chin between his fingers. He pressed his lips over hers in a quick, hard kiss.

"I can't. Not yet," he said when he broke away. "Damn it, I love you, Miranda! Whatever happens tonight, remember that. Remember—and *trust me.*"

With that, he stepped through the door and out, onto the upstairs landing. After a moment's pause, she heard the quick stride of his boots on the stairs as he went down them.

Then the thunder clattered, drowning out all other sounds, and she was alone.

Alone, bound and helpless.

"Morgan! Morgan, come back!"

Her voice sounded weak and frightened, compared to the storm's monstrous, loud fury.

But it was no use. He had gone.

Chapter Eighteen

It seemed an eternity before a means of escape occurred to her. And then, like all simple solutions, she could not believe she had not thought of it sooner!

In one corner of her bedchamber stood a sturdy sewing chest with a padded needlepoint lid. Inside it, stowed in one of the wooden drawers that lifted out, was a pair of sewing shears. With any luck, she might be able to use them to cut through her bonds and free herself. But first, she had to get them out.

By wiggling her fingers, she managed to lift the brass latch, thanking the good Lord she had not locked the chest.

Using fingers, mouth and chin in turn, she managed to lift the heavy lid, exposing two sets of small drawers on either side that lifted out on hinges.

The sharp shears she cut fabric with were at the bottom of the chest, alongside her inchtape, some papers of pins, and a lumpy pin cushion that Juliet had pieced together from red-flannel scraps when she was still a little girl. It was shaped like a strawberry.

Managing to hook the handles of the shears over her fingertips, she gingerly lifted them out, almost sobbing when they slithered free and clattered to the floorboards.

She crouched down and, bracing the scissors against the wood with the fingers of one hand, she managed to pry open the stiff blades with the other, promising herself she would oil the shears and the Gull's swinging sign herself, if only she got away.

With another muttered prayer of thanks, she managed to angle her hands so that one of the heavy, sharp blades slid between her wrists and the length of silk.

Hurrah!

The need to concentrate and go slowly and carefully made drops of sweat spring out on her brow. Impatiently, she flicked them away, telling herself she must stay calm.

So far, so good. Now, all she had to do was close the blades with enough force that they cut through the silk kerchief, and her hands would be free! From there, it would be a simple matter to untie her ankles. . . .

The kerchief was wound about her wrists— but not so tightly she could not maneouver her fingers.

After several botched attempts, she managed to brace the lower blade and the lower handle of the shears against the floorboards, then curled two fingers through the upper handle. The kerchief now lay between the opened blades.

"Please God, help me!" she prayed silently, and pushed down.

With a rasping sound, the silk parted cleanly in two and fell free!

She let the shears fall, untied her ankles, then dressed as quickly as her trembling hands would allow, her mind furiously churning.

What had Morgan meant about setting a trap? What was it? More importantly, *where* was it, and *how* would it be sprung? Whom did he hope to snare, that he would not tell her their names?

The obvious answer was her brothers and father. The Killigrews, and all the other free-traders of Lizard Cove! It was the only answer that made sense. Why else would he not tell her?

She had thought that he and her Da' and brothers had reached some sort of understanding. After all, he had stuck his own neck into a noose in order to help them outwit Archer and Forbes that night.

Perhaps he'd helped her and her family only to lull them into trusting him, believing all along that they were wreckers, as well as smugglers?

She was shaking as she hooked her skirt, her fingers clumsy. He was wrong about them, terribly wrong! The free-traders had not killed his friend, nor the survivors of the *Anne's* crew. She had to stop him, before it was too late, and innocent men were hanged!

As she drew on her stockings, she found herself remembering the scene in the taproom below, just a few evenings ago, following little Bianca's christening. . . .

A heavy haze of pipe smoke had hung about the blackened rafter beams that evening. The smells of burning tobacco, horseflesh and damp wool had been sharp to the nostrils. The faces of her patrons, some ruddy, others weathered and seamed in the lanternlight, had been rapt with fascination—and perhaps with greed, too—as Morgan described the rich cargo carried by the schooner, *Jade Moon*, a vessel of the St. James shipping company line that belonged to his father. . . .

"She set sail from the Indies weeks ago," he had said, slurring his words and grinning broadly as he spoke. His green eyes had danced with merriment as they met her father's. "And is winging her way home to Plymouth Harbor, even as we speak, her holds laden to the gills with prime goods. Rum, tobacco, sugar, tea! My father and his blasted agents expect her any day now," he'd confided with a sly wink.

His face had been devilishly handsome than night, his expression more than a little cocksure as he looked around the circle of faces.

"Will none of you brave lads help me to thumb my nose at the lot of them?" he'd demanded, sounding a little loud, a little drunk. Very much the angry black sheep of the family, bitter at having been disowned.

She had been puzzled that night. On other occasions, Morgan had drunk as much as Big Jan had poured for him at the christening party, yet he'd been none the worse for wear. . . .

Had he been *pretending* he was tipsy? Was that it? Was that when Morgan had baited his "trap?" And was the "bait" the promise of the rich cargo carried in the holds of his hated father's ship?

"Are there none among you," he had added in a softer, silkier, taunting tone, "who will help me

. . . relieve . . . a rich old fool of his cargo?"

"What you're planning is piracy, lad," her Da' had pointed out, drawing the pipe from his mouth and waving it about to give emphasis to his words.

His and Morgan's eyes had met, dancing green to faded turquoise. A look she could not fathom had flickered between them. Had it been conspiratorial? Or, much more likely, a challenge? Had a gauntlet been tossed down that night? " 'Tis nothing short of robbery on the high seas!"

"Not if there's a storm, Killigrew," Carl Coppinger had been quick to point out, his wet lips red and fleshy as he grinned. He'd snickered, blowing the frothy head off his pint. "Ain't that so, my lads?"

The others had nodded.

"If a gale should cast this *Jade Moon* onto the teeth o' the Point, then what the keeper's suggestin' is lawful salvage, pure and simple. And salvage is a Cornishman's right, guaranteed 'im by King James's royal charter. Aye, Killigrew?"

"That it is, Coppinger. But the lion's share of the salvage still belongs to those who survive the wreck," her brother, Rob, had softly pointed out.

"Phaggh. You Killigrews! Always so bloody quick to split hairs! That's why you'll never amount to anything more than the dirt-grubbin' farmers you are now! A man has to turn what

340

happens in this life to his own good. What if there are no survivors? What then, eh?" Dane Coppinger, Carl's father, had demanded hoarsely, wetting his lips.

"The good Lord helps those who help themselves," the Rev. Boreham had observed with what had seemed to Miranda at the time a most ungodly smirk.

Dane's left eye had seemed even cloudier than usual that night. Milky and half-blind, it gave him a vicious, pitiless cast.

"What if the crew perishes t'the last jack-tar aboard her? Who gets the goods then, eh?" Dane had asked again. He'd nudged his son in the ribs, and the pair had chortled, as if the idea of an entire crew perishing appealed to them. "Young Carl here 'ud be a rich man, then, he would, aye, son? Rich enough t'wed any lass he wants, eh, Killigrew? Even a rich Cove widow what thinks herself a cut above the likes o' my boy, aye?" he'd added, with a pointed sneer.

Looking over his shoulder, Dane had cast her a triumphant leer. The old man's evil glance had made her flesh crawl.

"Believe me, Mr. Coppinger, no man—and especially not your Carl!—could ever be *that* rich," she had tossed back, tight-lipped and furious. "There isn't that much gold in the world!"

Her withering response had made the other

men snort with laughter. They'd punched a scowling Carl in the chest and told him, "By God, Carl, lad, you've picked yourself a feisty lass, t'be sure."

But the look Carl shot her when he thought she wasn't looking had been far from amused. On the contrary. It had been filled with cruelty and the burning desire to get even, at any cost. Now that she had belittled him before the others, not just Morgan, she knew she must take care never to find herself alone with him.

Could Carl and his father be the ones? Was that horrid old man, Dane Coppinger, the wreckers' ringleader? The man Morgan wanted so badly to snare?

She frowned, trying to remember who else had been there that night besides the Coppingers. Racking her memory for names to go with the faces, she counted them off on her fingers.

Squire Draker and his lady, Dinah Draker, had arrived later that afternoon, breaking the lengthy carriage ride between Bodmin and Windhaven House to present the newborn with a christening cup and a gift of five gold sovereigns.

Alan Draker, she recalled, had exchanged a few polite words of greeting with the locals before he and his wife withdrew to a wooden settle in the corner, set apart from those who were not wealthy landowners like themselves.

There the Drakers had sipped their drinks and traded glances—one adoring, the other bored and easily distracted—out of the crush of perspiring bodies ranged along both sides of the trestles.

Miranda remembered Alan Draker nodding a civil good evening to Morgan. Then the pretty, tinkling music of "Greensleeves" had issued from the gold pocket watch he withdrew from his coat pocket, distracting the man.

The squire had not offered any welcome to Simon Longfield, seated next to Morgan, she recalled. Had the slight been an oversight, or intentional?

Big Jan had been serving behind the bar, dispensing pints along with tidbits of dry, west-country humor as he polished tankards and mugs. She'd seen Squire Draker chuckle and nod at some comment the bartender made.

Maisie had been moving around the taproom with her metal serving tray, her cheeks flushed, her eyes sparkling as she sidestepped the amorous arms of saucy young shepherds or fishermen.

Gil, her parents and Kitty had occupied another worn wooden settle, foaming tankards set before the men in wet rings of beer. What had the looks they and Morgan exchanged really meant, Miranda wondered now?

Had Morgan—believing them guilty of murdering his friend—been challenging them in some subtle fashion? Or was she misreading those looks? Had they meant something else entirely? . . .

Thomas Tremayne and his brother, Quentin Tremayne, the cooper and chandler from the village, had been propping up the bar, their beefy fists jammed into the pockets of their moleskin breeches.

Jeb Bent, the huge, red-faced blacksmith who kept the smithy on the far side of the woods, had been there, too, wearing his Sunday best of brown jacket, breeches, and yellow satin waistcoat. When dressed in his usual leather apron and rolled up shirtsleeves, hairy, brawny arms that bulged with muscle were revealed. Arms that, upon reflection, were quite capable of wielding a billy club to bring about a man's death. . . .

That, she realized thoughtfully, applied to almost all the men. In fact, given a hefty club and the element of surprise, even a man who was slightly built could have brained those weary, half-drowned sailors as they staggered ashore.

The parson, she recalled, had been much the worse for wear after several glasses of sherry.

As she recalled, Boreham, like most Cornish vicars and parsons, was not averse to a bit of wrecking himself when given the opportunity, despite being a member of the clergy.

The parson had taken a seat next to the Drakers' table. He had nodded to Draker and, as tipsy as a lord, had blown Lady Dinah a kiss by way of greeting.

His nod had not, to her knowledge, been returned by the squire, however, although she had noticed Lady Dinah in animated conversation with the parson later on that evening, and had been struck by the similarity of their coloring. Odd she'd never noticed before.

So many possibilities, and yet most of the men of Lizard's Cove were as familiar to her as her own family. She'd grown up among them, for pity's sake!

Whom did Morgan suspect? Whose name had he feared to entrust to her?

And who would be caught in his trap?

Her hands began to shake. Was her family the quarry he hoped to snare tonight? If not, why had he not denied it?

Because he didn't want her to warn them?

Perhaps.

Had he believed from the first that the Killigrews had killed the crew of the *Lady Anne*, exactly as Ashe had told him, but wanted to spare her?

Very likely, aye.

She swallowed over the lump in her throat. What other explanation was there? He would not have balked at saying Big Jan's name, or Thomas Tremayne's, nor the Coppingers,' surely.

They had no claims upon her heart or loyalty. He knew she would not rush to warn them, as she would most certainly try to warn her own flesh and blood!

But where should she go, she wondered as she quickly buckled on sturdy walking shoes. Should she take one of the coaching horses and ride to Eastmoor Farm, perhaps wasting precious time in the process? Or were her brothers, her father and the other reckless fools who plied the free-trade already out there on the darkened beach, drenched to the skin by the howling storm? . . .

She bit her lip. Her brothers and father were smugglers. Lords of the free-trade! Kings and princes of contraband! And as such, every one of them could be hanged at the nearest crossroads, if apprehended. But . . . they had never been wreckers. Nor cold-blooded murderers, either. Why, her Da' had said he'd rather be captured and hanged himself, than be a party to murder!

But did Morgan know the difference?

In his eagerness to bring justice to bear on those who had killed his friend and the *Anne's* crew, would he make such fine distinctions? Would he listen to her kinsmen's protests of innocence—or act first and ask questions later?

She shuddered. A short dance at the end of a rope awaited those smugglers the Preventives caught red-handed. A similar dance awaited the men who had murdered the *Anne's* crew.

The thought of her brothers and father—or herself!—dancing the hangman's jig made the blood turn to ice in her veins.

The beach, she decided, her mind made up. If they were not there, so much the better. . . .

Fully dressed, she slung a hooded cape over her shoulders, took up a candle, then clattered down the back stairs to the kitchen, fastening the cloak as she went.

Hastening to the pantry, she lifted a storm lantern down from the shelf, and lit it from her candle with a paper spill. Then, after hastily dousing the kitchen fire, she pulled her hood up over her hair and, holding the lantern aloft, fiddled with the hidden catch at the very back of the old brick fireplace.

A yawning black hole opened up as the door swung inward. The iodine, fishy stink of seaweed and salt water wafted out on the musty air.

The tunnel had hidden Royalists fleeing

Cromwell's Roundheads two centuries ago. It had hidden other fugitives since—and would, God willing, do so again tonight!

Gathering the folds of her cloak tightly about her in case a stray ember of the doused fire remained, she stepped over the sooty hearth into blackness.

Chapter Nineteen

An eternity seemed to pass as Morgan waited in the keeper's round room, high in the lighthouse, wondering if his ruse had worked.

Would someone come to douse the Argand and silence the lighthouse keeper, as he'd once tried to silence William Ashe? Or was he wasting his time waiting for someone who would never appear?

After standing in the darkness for some time, his thoughts began to wander. As they had so often lately, he found them returning over and over again to Miranda.

If he lived to be a hundred, he would never forget the desperation on her face, the naked anguish in her eyes tonight when he'd left her at the inn.

Leaving her had been the hardest thing he'd ever had to do. But he could not take the risk that she would follow him and put herself in danger. He had lost Jade Moon eleven years ago to a terrible disease. He was not about to lose Miranda—not to anything. Unfortunately, her greatest attribute was also her greatest flaw: She was loyal to a fault, as she had once been loyal to her dead husband's memory. He dared not take the chance that, believing her family implicated in Geoff's death, she would try to intervene. Nor could he allow her to inadvertently let slip his plans, if she knew whom he expected to catch. . . .

Midnight had come and gone before he heard a muted reverberation from the iron staircase outside his door.

His wait had paid off!

He quickly melted into the shadows as the door swung inward.

A slightly built figure, caped in black and wearing a black tricorn, slipped across the room to stand over the banana bunk in which Morgan usually slept.

"Looking for me, Squire?" Morgan asked from his hiding place.

350

In one hand, Alan Draker brandished a pistol by its heavy wooden stock.

Held by its barrel, the firearm would make a serviceable club. Had, in fact, served effectively as a lethal weapon on more than one occasion, Morgan reminded himself, leashing the rage that boiled through him now as he confronted Geoff's murderer.

A rough woolen blanket covered the lumpy form of a man asleep on the bed before Draker. And, although he stiffened at the sound of Morgan's voice, he did not turn around. In fact, only the man's rigid shoulders betrayed that he'd heard Morgan at all.

He flexed powerful fingers, itching to wrap them around Draker's throat. Wanting to knot them into fists and bury his knuckles in Draker's face.

"How did you figure it out, St. James? I was so very careful," Draker said huskily, still without turning around. His voice sounded high and strained, yet mocking.

"The pocket watch. I saw it in the taproom of the Gull the other evening. Remember, when I asked you the time? It belonged to Geoffrey Christopher. The captain of the *Lady Anne*."

"Ahhh."

"The timepiece was a gift from his bride. Geoff

351

carried it with him wherever he went, tucked in an oilksin pouch. You would have had to kill him to take it from him. *And you did.*"

Morgan's jaw was hard now. His green eyes were murderous, filled with deadly rage. Icy purpose. His hands were knotted into fists at his sides.

"Nonsense, dear boy," Draker insisted, still with his back to Morgan. "Your friend was the unfortunate victim of a shipwreck. Half-drowned, then dashed to death against the rocks, like so many other poor devils in these waters. It's not known as the Ship's Graveyard for naught, eh? At least, that's the story I gave the insurance investigators."

He turned to face Morgan, the pistol now held right way around. Its slim barrel was aimed directly at Morgan's heart.

But it was *Dinah* Draker's beautiful, mocking face that smiled up at Morgan from beneath the shadow of the tricorn hat. *Her* amber eyes that gleamed with mockery. *Her* expression that held no trace of remorse or regret, or even a pinch of compassion. Not her husband's.

As Morgan had once told Miranda, when speaking of the kittens, females made the best hunters. . . .

"I gave that stupid old man the watch as an anniversary gift. Even so, it was more than he

352

deserved! Ten years I've endured his disgusting attentions in my bed, gagging whenever he touched me—"

"Forgive me if I'm not sympathetic," Morgan cut in. "From what I've heard, you seem to have found other . . . divertisements."

"I did, didn't I?" A sly smile curved her lips. Her tongue darted out to moisten them. "You could have been one of them, Morgan, had you not rejected my offer."

He smiled thinly. "You, madam, are too well-used for my taste. Your favors are too often and too lightly bestowed."

Even in the shadows, he could see the anger that flushed her face.

"Step aside, keeper," she hissed, contemptuously gesturing with the pistol. "I have much yet to do tonight, once I've extinguished your wretched beacon. Don't make me kill you."

"As your fellows tried to kill Ashe?"

"Tried?" For the first time, she seemed genuinely unsettled. "What are you saying? Ashe *is* dead! Coppinger and his fellow killed him. Carl told me so—"

"Then he lied! The stupid oaf bungled it, as he bungles everything he does. He and his cronies set upon Ashe, beat him almost to death, then extinguished the beacon. But Ashe did the impossible! *He survived their beating*, saw what you

353

and your fellows had done, and lived to tell of it! To tell *me*."

"Shut up! Don't make me shoot you. It would be a pity to scar that broad chest. You really are a very striking man. We could have been perfect partners, despite what you think of me." She pursed her lips in a mocking kiss as she leveled the pistol at his chest.

A thin smile curled Morgan's upper lip. "Your wrecking days—and your days as a free woman—are ended, Dinah. If you don't hang for what you've done, I'll see you transported, by God! I didn't come alone. You may as well give up."

"A pity it's come down to this. I was so looking forward to taking you as a lover. Rage can be so . . . so sensual, don't you think? My husband's whey-faced daughters will be devastated to hear of your death. They had their eyes on you, you know, Morgan St. James. 'Husband material,' that's what they called you. We had that much in common. All three of us liked your pretty face." Dinah smiled and pursed her lips in another kiss. "Such a pity, hmmm, darling? Ah, well. Adieu!"

With that farewell, she held her right arm straight out, steadied it with the other, then cocked the pistol, ready to fire.

In the same instant, the rough blanket was

tossed aside. Rob Killigrew sprang from the bed, reaching for her weapon.

Dinah twisted away, but Rob grabbed her cape and hauled her back toward him. Desperate, she swung the pistol at his head, slamming it into his shoulder, instead.

"Bloody bitch!" he snarled, grasping his arm in pain.

"Bastard!" she screamed.

Knocked off balance, Rob toppled to the ground, knocking over the sea chest beside the bunk and the lamp, and dragging Dinah Draker down with him. Although slender, she was as wiry and lithe as a she-cat, and easily as strong as a small man.

They were both fighting desperately for control of the pistol when it suddenly exploded, filling the lighthouse with a flash and a deafening report.

Morgan, who was about to haul Dinah Draker off Rob, spun about as the red-hot ball gauged into his upper arm, then ploughed into the whitewashed wall behind him, showering crumbs of brick and mortar everywhere.

In the shock that followed the explosion, Dinah managed to squirm free of Rob. Still clutching the empty pistol, she sprang toward the open door, the cape fluttering around her.

Morgan hauled Rob to his feet.

"You're bleeding like a stuck pig, man!" Rob said hoarsely.

"Never mind. Let's go."

Dinah had dashed outside, and was quickly clambering up the wrought-iron staircase to the viewing level. Above a metal ladder yawned the trapdoor that led up to the Argand itself.

Thad and Gil Killigrew were waiting up there, ready to defend the massive light, and keep it from being extinguished.

Dinah saw them. With a furious squeal, like a desperate, cornered animal, she leaped up the ladder, taking the rungs two at a time, still bent on getting past the men to destroy the great light.

But while still only half way up, she realized she could not hope to force her way past them both and abandoned her efforts.

Trapped between Morgan, who was bleeding profusely, and Rob, coming up the stairs behind her, and Thad and Gil above her, she took the only way left and ran out onto the narrow catwalk.

Thad followed her out, as did Gil. Rob barrelled past Morgan to help them.

Morgan heard metal clanging and reverberating with the ferocity of the scuffle that was ensuing on the narrow walkway just out of his line of vision.

"Get back!" he heard Dinah cry, her voice high and desperate. "Get away from me! I'll jump!"

"Give yourself up, woman! Don't be a fool!"

Thad's voice.

Then there was a sudden high, drawn-out scream that carried over the moaning wind, over the clatter of the thunder, over even the boom of the breakers that battered the rocks below.

Morgan averted his eyes as a large black shape windmilled past him, the folds of the cape spread like the leathery wings of a giant bat.

And then, the ululating scream was abruptly cut off. The noise of the storm suddenly abated, and an eerie, ominous lull, a silence that seemed to last forever, took its place.

One life for so many, Morgan thought heavily as Thad and Rob clattered back down the stairs to tell him what he already knew: that Dinah Draker had fallen—or jumped—to her death, rather than been taken alive.

It was hardly justice.

He should have felt some sense of fulfillment that the woman who'd acted as ringleader in Geoff's murder was dead. Some small triumph that justice had prevailed, against all odds, over one who had engineered the deaths of so many. But only sadness remained.

His friend was dead and gone, as were the other good men of his crew—and who knew how many other good crews and good ships before them? But nothing, revenge included, could bring any of them back to their wives and children.

"Morgan," a white-faced Rob began. "She fell. She's—"

"Aye. But she wasn't alone. Her accomplices must also be held to account for their actions. Let's go after them."

"Where to, son?" Thad yelled over the wind as they followed him down the stairs.

"The shore," Morgan shouted back. "They're waiting for her to douse the Argand—and silence the keeper," he added grimly.

Just as they'd once tried to silence Ashe. . . .

As lightning flashed, all three of them saw the small vessel riding the heaving swells off Lizard Point.

"Sweet lord!" Thad breathed. "There's a schooner out there!"

Morgan nodded at the vessel as he bound a length of cord around his arm to slow the bleeding. " 'Tis the *Lady Jade Moon*. She's right on schedule, bless her! Now, let's find out what other rats have taken my bait, aye?"

Chapter Twenty

The gusty wind storm lifted the cape over Miranda's head the instant she stepped from the tunnel. Its heavy folds flapped violently, almost tugging her off balance. Needles of rain stung her cheeks and brow, and soaked the woolen cloth.

Fighting the tug of rain, wind and sand, she staggered down the shore, making her way toward the bulky shapes of the men silhouetted there.

Four in all, they held a storm lantern aloft and were signaling to a small sailing ship that rode the heaving black seas off the Point.

A single quick flash, three seconds' pause, then another quick flash.

Her stomach churned. The Lizard Light's characteristic! Were they signalling the *Lady Jade Moon*—or a smuggler's vessel?

Please God, let it be a smuggling vessel, she prayed silently, then realized that it didn't matter. Either way, the signal proved she'd found them in time! Morgan was not here.

Or at least, he was not here *yet.* . . .

"Da'!" she cried, cupping her mouth with her hands to make herself heard over the crash of the breakers against the rocks, and the moaning and whistling of the wind. "Rob! Gil! Come away! The bloody goods can wait!"

The wind snatched the words from her. Whirled them away like leaves in a gale. She'd almost reached the men before one of them turned and noticed her.

"Da'!" she yelled again, trying to brush the hair out of her eyes. "Rob! Come away, I tell you!"

The man who had turned raised his lantern aloft.

By its amber glow, she saw—to her horror—*Dane Coppinger's* face, not her father's, lit from one side like a grotesque mask with a single milky blind eye. The other, a rheumy blue, squinted at her.

"Well, well. Look who's here, parson!" Dane

roared over the storm. " 'Tis your bonny daughter, finished with her own dirty deed, come t'help us with ours! Is it done, Dinah, lass?" old Dane demanded eagerly. "Did ye silence the keeper?"

Silence the keeper? What was he saying? Did he mean what she thought he meant?

Miranda froze in her tracks. She stood, gaping in disbelief, at the quartet before her, her hand flying to cover her mouth in horror.

It was not her father. Not Rob and the others at all! Dear God, no! These four were more like characters from a nightmare!

The men luring the vessel onto the rocks were the Rev. Boreham, Dane and Carl Coppinger— and her own Big Jan. Jan Van Dyke who'd tended the bar and done odd jobs about the inn since before Daniel died.

Men she'd known all her life, and trusted, she thought, as dazed and deflated as if she'd been punched in the belly by a hefty fist.

Men, as it transpired, that she'd never really known at all. . . .

Thanks to the wild dark night and the fierce storm, they had mistaken her for Boreham's *daughter*, Dinah—or so Dane had said. Her thoughts raced. Dinah Draker must be Boreham's by-blow, since St. Breoch's parson had never been wed. Or at least, not that she knew of.

The old rumors that her father was a bishop were somewhat exaggerated, though she had been sired by a man of the cloth.

All of this hit home in a matter of seconds as she stood there, frozen. With it dawned the realization that her life was now in grave jeopardy. After all, she was not the person the wreckers had been expecting—not one of their number at all! And yet, she had seen them luring the ship onto the rocks. Had heard the question Dane asked. . . .

As she stood there, willing her feet to move, old Dane fell abruptly silent.

He'd realized his mistake, too.

"Well, I'll be! Look lively, now, lads!" he urged with a sly edge to his tone. "It ain't our pretty Dinah at all, but the Killigrew bitch! What is it ye're wanting, darlin'?" Dane chortled. "My Carl here? Or will his old Da' serve t'plow your pretty furrow? He! He! There's life in this old dog yet, ain't there, lad?" He grinned. "Aye, and in his cock, too!"

Their raucous hoots of laughter acted as catalysts, setting her feet in motion.

As she turned to flee, she heard Dane roar, "After her, lads! That un'll sing like a nightingale, 'less she's caught!"

Terror was all the prodding she needed.

Hurling the lantern like a fiery comet in their direction, she whirled and ran, haring back the way she'd come as if the hounds of hell snapped at her heels. Her numb fingers fumbled with her cape strings as she fled. She had to get the wretched garment off, before it proved her undoing.

The fierce wind took the wet, dragging folds the moment they were free, whirling the garment away, into the night.

Unhampered, she ran on through the stinging rain, cursing the wet sand and crunching shingle that slowed her steps, grateful only that her pursuers faced the same obstacles.

Every breath was an agonising sob. A sharp stitch was stabbing her side by the time she neared the crumbling path that led up the cliffs, and to the lighthouse.

She flung herself toward that path, forcing a last burst of speed from raw lungs and aching legs, willing them to carry her forward, just a little farther. Just another few feet, please God!

She was almost there when something caught in her flying hair. The sudden, painful tug stopped her dead in her tracks, and brought her to her knees with a yelp.

She screamed again as her assailant dragged her to her feet by her hair. Her scalp was afire!

"You ain't escaping me, gel, not this time," Carl ground through clenched teeth, dragging her up against him. "You've seen too bloody much, you have!"

"I won't tell! I swear I won't!" she lied.

"The devil you won't!" Carl growled, panting as he chivvied her down the beach, toward the cliffs, maintaining his cruel grip on her upper arms. "You're a nosy lot, you Killigrews! See something out o'the ordinary, do you turn a blind eye and go about your business, like decent folk? *Not bloody likely!* You stick your noses in as far and as deep as ye bloody well can!

"Like the night the *Anne* was wrecked. When I saw your blasted brother coming down the beach, I knew we'd never catch Ashe. 'Killigrew's coming!' I told the others. 'The game's up! Take what ye've got and run!' Got away that night, Ashe did. Crawled away and died like a whipped dog. Well, it won't happen again," he added with a threatening snarl.

"It didn't happen then," she panted, struggling to escape Carl's punishing hold. "Ashe isn't dead! He got away, and went to the authorities. He told them everyth—*ouch!* Let me go, damn you! Stop it! You're hurting me! They know what you did, Carl! It's no use. Don't you see? They know your names! They know everything about you! Everything you've done. They . . . they'll be here, any moment! They're going to hang the lot of you at the nearest crossroads!"

It was a desperate ploy, but what else could she do?

"Will they, now?" Coppinger purred nastily, curling his thick sausage-like fingers over her breast. "Then I'll have t'be right quick, won't I, Miranda, darling?"

"About what?" she whispered, chilled with terror. Faint with it. "Quick about *what*?"

But Carl only smiled. . . .

"What was that? *Miranda!*" Morgan thundered, forcing a burst of speed from his weakened body as he and the Killigrews scrambled down the steep cliff path to the beach. *"Miraaaanda!"*

He didn't care who the devil knew they were coming—not anymore. All he could think about was protecting Miranda.

Shingle and clods of wet, sandy earth scattered beneath his feet, sending him slithering several feet down the steep, mud-slick path, out of control yet still straining his eyes to see through the blinding rain and the darkness. Yet, try as he might, he could see little more than a foot or two in front of him without the moon's revealing light.

"Did you hear it?" he demanded. "A woman's cry?"

"Nay, lad. Besides, didn't ye say my lass was safe at the inn?" Thad murmured.

"Was, sir. I hope to God she's still there!"

"Me, too. She's terrible obstinate, though, my sister—whoa! What's this?" Rob cried, bending to pick up something in his path.

The lightning chose that moment to flash, bathing the shore and the cliff path in eerie purple light.

In it, Morgan saw a sodden black cape had wrapped itself about Rob's ankles. Tangled in its folds was a fringed silk shawl that was the vivid orange-red of poppies. Miranda's Spanish shawl! And the last time he'd seen it had been two hours ago—in her bedchamber at the inn.

That it was here could mean only one thing.

"She's out here!" he growled, furious and terrified for her safety at the same time. "That pigheaded little fool! She followed me!"

Or more likely, he added silently, she got away to warn her kin about him. . . .

"Go on back to the inn yourself, St. James. You're white as a bloody corpse!" Rob said gruffly. "Are ye still bleeding, man?"

Morgan could feel warm blood seeping from his wound, sapping his strength. But he was not about to run home like a whipped hound, its tail tucked between its legs!

"Like a stuck pig, Killigrew. But I'm not going

anywhere. D'you know why? Because even half-empty, I'm twice the man you are!"

Rob grinned and clapped Morgan's back. "Happen you are, keeper," he shouted over the storm. "Ye've lost buckets of blood, but ye've still piss and vinegar t'spare, by God!"

They burst from the other end of the tunnel, into the inn's kitchen, only to find it deserted and dark, the hearthstones grown cold to the touch.

The fire had been doused hours ago, Morgan thought, shivering more from blood loss and disappointment than the chill.

There were no signs here that Miranda had come back through the tunnel, willingly or otherwise. No puddles of rain on the flagstones. Nothing.

"Now where?" Rob wondered aloud, his expression strained and grim.

Before Morgan could reply, they both heard shouting from outside, the clatter of many hooves striking cobbles, followed by a hefty fist, pounding at the inn door.

"Dickerson and his men?" Rob asked Morgan, cocking a fair brow in his direction.

"Possibly. Or Squire Draker and his gardeners," Morgan added, distracted. He'd sent Simon to Windhaven with the message that he believed the wreckers would be out that night. He had suspected that instead of providing the help he'd promised, the squire would send someone to silence the keeper and douse the light.

But unless he was mistaken, Draker had known nothing of his wife's lucrative—and deadly—exploits as a wrecker, the income from which had allowed her to feather her rustic nest so elegantly. Nor did he know about the men she'd taken to her bed. The poor squire had clearly adored his much younger wife. He would be beside himself to learn she'd fallen to her death.

"The lighthouse!" Morgan declared suddenly, snapping his fingers. "Damn it, that's it!"

"What about it?"

"That's where Coppinger would take Miranda. That bastard would want me to know he could hurt her. He'd expect to find me there, right? He doesn't know what happened to Dinah yet. That's why we found Miranda's cloak and shawl on the cliff path! He was taking her there! We probably passed each other!"

Rob's expression was serious as he nodded. "All right. Let me tell Dickerson where we're going, then we'll go after her. Miranda's my sister, after al—*Morgan?* Morgan, wait!"

But it was too late. Morgan was gone.

Rob hoped to God he would be in time.

* * *

Morgan found Carl Coppinger, with Miranda held like a hostage before him, on the narrow catwalk below the lamp room, where Dinah Draker had met her end some while before.

"Is this what you came for, keeper? For Dan Tallant's whore? I'll give ye what ye want. Here!" With that, Coppinger shoved Miranda toward him.

As if motion were slowed, he saw shock change to terror on her pale face as she realized she could not stop. Heard her startled gasp switch to a high, desperate shriek that would stay with him forever as she lost her footing, slipped between the railings, and vanished.

"*Noooo!*" he roared, springing across the narrow walkway, certain she'd fallen to her death, as Dinah had done.

Instead, the fingers of one pale hand were locked in a desperate grip around the bottom of a metal post. A tenuous one-handed grip was all that kept her from certain death.

"Help me!" she pleaded. "Oh, God, *help me!*"

If he pulled Miranda up, Geoff's murderer would escape while his attention was elsewhere. Carl knew it. Morgan knew it, yet he didn't hesitate for an instant.

Leaning over the railing, he reached for her.

"Grab my wrist with your free hand!" he urged. "Good. Now let go of the post."

369

"I can't. I'll fall!" she whimpered, hoarse with fear. "Oh, God! Don't let me die!"

"You won't. I've got you. I won't let you fall. Grab my arm!"

To his relief, she found the courage to let go, trusting his injured arm as her only lifeline for what felt like an eternity before she made a desperate grab for his other hand.

Once . . . twice . . . the third time was the charm!

Her fingers wrapped around his wrist in a deathgrip, and—wondrously!—held.

Her entire weight dangled from his hands.

Sweat rolled off his brow in torrents. His wounded arm was bleeding again, and was shaking violently with the enormous strain. The veins down his neck and at his temple stood out, and he could feel more blood gushing down his arm as he heaved, using his last morsel of strength to drag Miranda up and over the rail, into the safety of his arms.

Relief set in.

His knees buckled as he folded to the walkway, Miranda cradled fiercely in his arms. She was weeping in reaction to her narrow escape, while he shook as violently as if he had malaria.

Sweet Lord! He'd come so close to losing her— too damned close for comfort. If she'd fallen, he could not have lived with himself or—

He rose abruptly, sweeping Miranda behind him as Carl, wearing the desperate look of a cornered animal, thundered back up the stairs. Hot on his heels came several dragoons, along with the Killigrews.

"Go ahead, lads! Fire your bloody muskets!" Coppinger jeered, beckoning to the soldiers, now ranged behind Morgan.

"Hold your fire, men!" Morgan countered, waving the men back. "Such an easy death's too good for this bastard! There was nothing quick about the deaths of the *Anne's* captain and crew. Now it's your turn. You're going to dance the hangman's jig at the end of a rope, Coppinger, so help me God!" Morgan swore with relish.

"Take him away!" He nodded at Harry's men.

Immediately, the four uniformed dragoons stepped forward. Grasping Coppinger by his beefy arms, they wrestled the hefty, struggling man down the clanging iron stairs to the keeper's cottage, where Dane, Big Jan and the Rev. Boreham were already in Captain Dickerson's custody.

Morgan swayed, his drained, exhausted body finally succumbing to the effects of blood loss. He felt lightheaded. Dizzy. Exhausted. Keeping Miranda from falling had taken everything in him. But it was over now. She was safe, Coppinger under arrest. Time for some badly needed sleep. . . . First, however, there was something he had to do. Something that couldn't wait till morning.

"Miranda," he began.

She turned, looked him full in the eye, then slowly and pointedly averted her face with a murmured, "Take me home, Rob. For pity's sake, take me home!"

"Miranda? Damn it, don't do—" Morgan began.

"Later, St. James," Rob murmured, shaking his head. "Get that arm seen to. I'll take Miranda home. When she's had a bit o'time t'think about what's happened, she'll be her own sweet self, won't ye, 'Randa, Love?"

"I hope to God you're right," Morgan ground out. For once, he was uncertain.

His gut told him Miranda would never feel the same again. Not about him anyway.

Chapter Twenty-one

"Why did you come here?" she demanded angrily, shrugging off his hand. "I told Rob I didn't want to see you!"

"That was several days ago. And I didn't give him much choice in the matter, I'm afraid," Morgan said with relish, and a smile that was very nearly evil. "I need to talk to you, Miranda. I want to know why you've turned from me."

"You're asking me? You know very well why! Don't play me for a fool, Morgan St. James. You lied to me from the very first! You used me. You hoped to make me betray my family. How can I ever trust you again? Come to that, why should I?"

"Because I love you," he said softly.

"Love?" She flung the word at him like a stone. "How can there be love when there is no trust, Morgan? Nor honesty? Tell me that, sir! Love cannot survive betrayal, nor lies, nor even half-truths."

"I did what I believed I had to do at the time. What I felt, in my heart, was right, and needed to be done to apprehend Geoff's murderers. I never intended anyone should be hurt, except those who deserved it. I'd sooner cut off my own hand than hurt you! How can I convince you of that?"

"You can't, so don't try."

"Ohh, I think I can. Do you know why? Because you love me, too. I know it. You're just too bloody proud—and too blasted obstinate—to admit it! You would never have given yourself to me unless you loved me. You're not that kind of woman, Miranda."

"That's where you're wrong," she flared. "I don't love you. I never loved you! Carl was right, all along. I just missed having a man in my bed. That's all it ever was."

The defiant tilt of her head, her jeering tone dared him to deny it. She wanted to hurt, to wound, he knew. Yet her turquoise eyes were bright with unshed tears.

"All of that's over now. Done with! I don't need

a man—any man, least of all *you!* I want you gone from here, do you hear me! Leave Cornwall, Morgan St. James. Get out of Lizard Cove and don't come back!

A muscle ticked at his temple. He looked ashen, almost white about the lips. Despite her promise to herself, his pallor pricked her with guilt. And filled her with concern. . . .

"That's what you want? You're quite sure?" he asked.

No, she screamed silently.

"Positive," she heard herself say aloud, yet she felt her heart shatter in her breast even as she said it.

After what seemed forever, he nodded once, very curtly. His green eyes were narrowed and dark with pain now. His rugged jaw was hard. The lips she'd love to kiss were compressed, set in a thin, humorless line.

"Very well, then. I suppose there's nothing more to be said. Goodbye, Miranda."

She didn't answer him. Couldn't have done so, even had she wanted to. Her tongue was tied in knots.

She turned her back, unable to watch him stride outside to his horse. Too shattered to watch him ride away, when inside her, that same desperate little voice was screaming, *You fool! What are you doing? Don't let him go! You love him! Go after him! Beg him to come back!*

After endless moments that seemed an eternity, she forced herself to turn. Found the courage to swallow her pride and whisper her plea aloud.

"I was wrong, Morgan. I don't want you to leave, ever. Forget what I said. Please, don't go. I don't care what you did, or even why you did it, because . . . because I do love you. Stay with me! Stay forever!"

But it was already too late.

Her words fell on silence. On an empty hush and a firewashed gloom that was scented with evergreen boughs and aromatic pine resin.

The scarlet and green holly wreaths and berries over the hearth, the mistletoe sprigs above the lintels, the bayberry candles, the scent of clove and cinnamon pomanders, as well as all the other wonderful scents of the Christmas season seemed to mock her as she stood there, alone and silent, save for the measured ticking of the grandfather clock.

They were empty wonders all, because Morgan was gone. . . .

"*No!*"

The solitary word of denial cracked on the silence, spurred her to action.

Picking up her skirts, she raced from the inn, slamming doors behind her, then flew across the yard, heedless of the icy cobbles there.

She ignored the team of startled chestnut horses, the scarlet mail-coach and the red-faced driver, who—muffled in scarves and greatcoat against the chill—clambered down from his perch and tipped his hat to wish her a good morning.

Instead, she began running down the lane toward the village, kicking up a trim pair of heels as she went. Her petticoats flew as she dashed full tilt down the steep, cobbled high street of Lizard Cove.

Villagers stuck their heads out of their doors, eyebrows raised as they watched her speed past. *No cloak, nor bonnet nor even a shawl on such a brisk December morn, Mistress Tallant?* The knowing looks they exchanged said it was past time Killigrew's lass came to her senses and realized she and the keeper were meant for each other.

Even the widow Pettit, Maisie's mother, agreed that a generous man like Morgan St. James was too fine a catch to let get away, newcomer or no. After all, he'd brought her and her Maisie fresh lobster from his own pots, had he not? Aye, and he was such a pretty lad, too!

Curious eyes followed Miranda as she ran down the stone quay, past the fishwives gutting buckets of pilchards and mackerel with cold blue fingers and rough red noses, to the stone bollards, where Morgan's schooner had been moored since the morning after the storm.

Her breath escaped her in great white clouds that billowed like smoke on the frigid sea air.

But long before she'd reached the quay, she knew in her heart she was too late.

Too late to take back the awful things she'd said. Far too late to make amends in any way, shape or form.

The *Lady Jade Moon* was already a child's toy ship on the distant horizon. She had sailed with the morning's tide and in minutes, had carried Morgan away.

Forever.

Chapter Twenty-two

Spring came late to Lizard Cove in the following year, 1793. She dotted the waving blond grasses along Gull Lane with pink thrifts and powder-blue sea-campions, and filled the hedgerows with white May blossom and birdsong.

Her Spanish shawl knotted about her shoulders, its long fringes fluttering in the wind, Miranda picked her way heavily down the rocky path to the beach, reaching for handholds in the tough sea-grass to help her climb down.

The narrow strip of sand was smooth and unblemished. A schoolroom slate, washed clean by each inland rushing of the sea. Perched on a handy slab of black rock, she tugged off her shoes and stockings and left them there, to continue barefooted, her pink toes curling over the damp sand as she walked along.

Bending now and then to toss a stray length of driftwood or a pebble into the lapping water, she could not help but remember the moonlit night last summer when she had strolled arm in arm with Morgan along this very stretch of beach, and how they'd stopped to enjoy stolen kisses in the lee of a leaky rowboat.

She remembered that night as vividly as if it were only yesterday! Remembered how Morgan had gazed into the green glass fishing float, his handsome face mysterious in the moonlight, for it had been that night her love for him was born. The night when she'd realized that, like it or not, trust him or nay, God help her, she was in love with him.

Seals basked on the rocks not far away, barking noisily, each cow protective of her big-eyed pup. If the comical creatures resented her presence so close to their nursery, they gave no sign of it. Mother seals watched while the little ones frolicked in the shallows, diving off their rocky shelf, then pulling themselves out and waddling back on ungainly flippers.

Miranda smiled at their antics. Seal children were not unlike human children, in all respects save one. Female seals kept their pups away from the dangerous bulls that had fathered them, for they would sometimes kill their own young, in order to mate once again with their harem of cows. The pups that survived seemed to flourish and reach adulthood without needing their fathers.

Human children, on the other hand, needed fathers as dearly as they needed their mothers, Miranda believed.

Where are you, Morgan?

She asked the question silently, her hands clasped over her belly as she shaded her eyes and gazed out to sea to where the dark dots and glinting white sails of several fishing boats were etched against the hazy mauve horizon and the glassy sea.

Had he sailed away to the fabled lands he'd told her of? To the bustling wharves of Hong Kong or exotic Macau? To the dreamy green isles of Tahiti, or the snowy wastes of Arctic? Was he holding in his arms a slender Oriental blossom, whispering in her shell-like ears the endearments he had once whispered in her own? Or was he making love to some dark-eyed Polynesian *wahine* beneath a swaying palm, threading scarlet hibiscus through her long dark hair?

The thought of him with another woman made her heart bleed. Scalding tears burned be-

381

hind her eyelids. What madness had possessed her to let him go? How could she have sent him away, after he'd bared his soul, swallowed his male pride and laid his heart upon the ground before her? What devil had prompted her to utter the words that would banish him forever?

"I don't love you. I've never loved you. I want you gone! Go—and never come back!

A shudder moved through her. Her punishment had been terrible, indeed. Would the agony of losing him ever dim? Would the pain ever become bearable? Would there come a time when she could spend a day . . . an hour . . . a minute . . . without some thought of Morgan intruding? Without the memory of her lost love turning every morsel of happiness to bitter ashes in her mouth?

She loved him! God, how she loved him! Ached for him!

She hugged herself with her arms, wishing with all her heart that his strong arms enfolded her.

Scalding tears slipped down her cheeks. More stuck in her throat like great rocks of sea-salt she could not swallow.

"Morgan! Oh, Morgan!"

She did not realize she'd screamed his name aloud until her cries were echoed by the keening of the great white gulls that wheeled overhead, riding the air currents on dazzling wings.

"Miranda!"

Stunned by the answering shout, she whirled around, unable to believe her ears as she squinted against the dazzling spring sunlight.

One of the gulls' screaming cries had sounded uncannily like a man's voice, calling her name! Or . . . had someone really called her name?

Wishful thinking on her part. A gull was far more likely.

She shoved red-gold hair from her eyes and looked back the way she'd come. Looked back to where the lighthouse tower rose from the craggy black point like a white finger that pointed to the cerulean blue of heaven, and there she saw—she saw—!

Morgan saw her turn and sweep her glorious hair away from her face in a graceful, fluid motion, like a beautiful sorrel filly tossing its flowing mane. He knew the very instant she spied him on the catwalk, for her hand flew to her heart, as if to still its sudden pounding, and the Spanish shawl she wore blew away, to float like a scarlet poppy with tissue petals upon the glassy sea.

It was not until she turned and he saw her body silhouetted against the pale sand, however, that he realized: She was heavily with child.

His heart skipped a beat.

His child!

It could be no other's.

Joy. Longing. Hope. All three sprang up inside him, like burned-out embers that burst suddenly into flame.

"Miranda!" he roared again. Turning, he started down the wrought-iron stairs, taking them two at a time.

In the same moment, she hoisted her skirts and began racing back up the beach toward the lighthouse, as swiftly as her bare feet and unwieldy condition would allow.

At the top of the path, she halted, her heart pounding, her breasts heaving, letting him close the gap between them with three last swift strides.

"Why didn't you tell me?" he demanded, cupping her radiant face between his hands. "Why didn't you send word to me? A letter . . . *something?*"

As his eyes searched her face for an answer, his other hand dropped down, to rest lightly upon her swollen belly in a caressing, possessive gesture that touched her heart, and said more than words ever could.

"Why did you send me away, when you must have known you carried my child?"

"Because I wanted you to stay because you

loved me. Not because you had to. Nor because you felt trapped," she began in a breathless, shaky whisper that was choked with tears.

"You bloody, wonderful little idiot!" he scolded, shaking her gently, holding her near, not knowing whether to kiss her or wring her neck for ever doubting him or his love. "I did love you—do love you!—more than anything in this world! With all my heart and soul! That's why I wanted to stay in the first place. To be here, with you. Geoff's death brought me to Lizard Cove, Miranda. But it was you—nothing and no one else!—who made me want to stay here forever. Just as it was my love for you that brought me back. . . ."

"But I'm nobody. Just an innkeeper! While you're—"

"You could never be 'just' anything. You are everything to me, my sweet and only love." He pressed a finger gently across her lips and softly repeated, *"Everything*. That's why I intend to make you my wife. To spend the rest of my life with you, sharing all the years have to hold, whether good or bad. Nothing else matters if we love each other, Miranda! That's all that will ever matter. That we love each other, and the children we have together," he murmured urgently.

Taking her in his arms, he held her, stroked her bright hair, cradled her close to his heart, where she had belonged for so long.

"After you sent me away, I thought that at sea, I could forget you. That I could leave the pain behind, as I'd once tried to leave the pain of my mother's death behind. It never happened," he explained simply. "Not this time, nor the last.

"Distance doesn't lessen one's loss, or make it easier to bear. Nor can you run from it, because no matter how far you go, you carry it with you. As a part of you. I know that now. You have to face it, accept it, learn to live with it. But . . . my heart wouldn't.

"I saw your lovely face in every beautiful woman I chanced to see. Imagined you with me in every port of call. Dreamed of you in my bunk each night." He kissed her lips, tasting her salty tears on his own. "My longing for you never left me, Miranda. It runs too deep.

"Soo, I'm back to stay, if you'll have me this time." He took her hand and gently rubbed the ball of his thumb over the back of it. "Do you remember what I told you, that night by the rowboat on the shingle? I said, 'Here's my hand,'" he quoted, lifting her hand to his lips and kissing her fingertips. "And you answered me—"

" 'And mine, with my heart in't'," she finished softly, her voice cracking with emotion.

"My heart's in your hand, too, Miranda. Handle it tenderly."

Cupping his beloved face in her free hand, and laughing through her tears, she looked up into his darkly striking face and knew she'd never been as happy as she felt in this moment.

"I will, my love. Oh, I will!" she whispered.

The wind off the sea ruffled his crisp black hair. Spring sunlight danced in his deep-green eyes and burnished his tanned, masculine features. A tender smile hovered about his mouth now, filled with love for her, and for the child they had made together. A child that would, she knew somehow, be a boy, with his Papa's striking looks and dark hair.

"Could you be happy married to a lighthouse keeper, Mistress Tallant?" he asked. His laughing green eyes searched her face, uptilted to his like a lovely, open flower, seeking the sun.

"Aye, I think I could, very easily. Especially since that keeper holds my heart," she added shyly, her face radiant with joy.

"You're my guiding light, my sweet. The bright star I intend to steer by for the rest of my life." He smiled, his handsome face no longer haunted. "Shall we go home, Miranda?"

The light in her turquoise eyes was all the answer he needed.

Arm in arm, her red-gold head on his shoulder, they walked back towards the lighthouse together, and into a future as bright and shining as its beacon.

Chapter Twenty-three

Lahaina, Maui
The Sandwich Isles,
January 1796

Legs braced akimbo, hands clasped behind his back, Captain Morgan St. James stood in the prow of the *Miranda*, enjoying the thrilling display of a pod of porpoises frolicking off the starboard bow.

There were six or seven of the amazing creatures cavorting this morning. Their sleek, glistening, gray bodies crested the dazzling turquoise Pacific one after another like an endless coil as they raced his schooner. Every line, every movement they made declared their sheer joy at being alive!

"Did I miss them, Papa?" cried his son, Geoffrey Morgan St. James, scampering across the decks toward him on sturdy, sun-browned legs. "Did I?"

"No, lad. They're still there. Look!" Morgan declared, sweeping the little lad up into his arms. He touseled the head of jet-black curls he'd barbered for the first time just the month before, when they dropped anchor in Tahiti. His tenderhearted mama had looked on, Morgan remembered, weeping as she collected their son's baby curls for her locket. "Six . . . seven . . . eight!"

"Hurrah, Papa! Eight biiiig fishes!" little Geoff declared, suitably impressed. He clapped his hands together. "Faster, Papa, faster! Geoff'y want to race 'em!"

Laughing, Morgan swung the boy up high, onto his shoulders. "We can't go any faster, son. How do you like this, instead?"

Geoff crowed with delight in his lofty perch. "Wheee! Look at meee, Mama! I'm up high! I'm high as a—a giant! Jack 'n Beeean Stalk!" his son squealed as Miranda, carrying the baby dressed in a lacy sunbonnet and lightweight muslin dress, like her mama's, joined them at the taffrail.

"So I see!" Miranda told her son, laughing.

"Look, Ariel! Look at your brother, darling. See what a big boy he is, up there on Papa's shoulders?"

"Boo. Ah. *Booooo*!" three-month-old Ariel burbled, completely unimpressed. She was far more intrigued with the lock of her mother's hair she'd managed to grab, and promptly stuffed into her mouth. Or in cooing at the spray of lavender orchids that danced like butterflies about the crown of her mother's hat, one that a native of the beautiful island of Hawaii had woven for her the day before.

Like her older cousin, Bianca, little Ariel had inherited Catherine Killigrew's flawless ivory complexion and dark-auburn hair, and already showed promise of becoming an exotic beauty some day.

Miranda kissed her daughter's round pink cheek, delighting in the wonderful, powdery baby smell as she carried her across the deck to her father.

"Well, there it is, Mrs. St. James! Lahaina, Maui. Have you ever seen anything quite so lovely?"

The Sandwich Isles, discovered by the British explorer, Captain James Cook, several years before, lay off their starboard bow like a strand of emeralds, set in a glittering turquoise sea. A sea the same color, Morgan insisted, as his wife's

391

lovely eyes. Even from this distance, he could smell the sweet, exotic perfume of tropical flowers, fruits and coconuts.

Soon, the native people of the island before them would launch their outrigger canoes and paddle out to greet the *Lady Miranda*, bringing flower garlands to drape about the newcomers' throat and heads, as well as fruits, necklaces of shells and other items.

So they had been greeted by native peoples all over the world, in countless different lands, from India to Madagascar, from South America to Yerba Buena—or San Francisco, as some called it. After Geoffrey's birth three years before, at Morgan's urging Miranda had surrendered to the restless, adventurous spirit that the standing stones had awakened in her, and gone to sea with her bridegroom.

Sailing with him was a decision she had never once regretted, not even when hatches were battened and they were forced to ride out some terrible storm, or when they lay becalmed off the tip of South America in sweltering heat without a whisper of a cooling breeze for days on end.

During the summer months, she kept the Black Gull Inn, while Morgan tended the lighthouse—a task he had grown to love. Then, when the first cold blast blew down out of the north Atlantic, they turned the lighthouse over to

Simon, and the running of the inn over to Gil, Kitty and their three children, Bianca, Titania and young James, and sailed for warmer climes.

It was as close to an ideal life as any woman could ask for!

Standing in the prow of the swift schooner as it raced like a flying fish over the glassy ocean was truly thrilling. A breathtaking, exhilarating experience, just as Morgan had promised the night he'd urged her to answer the call to adventure, to cast off her inhibitions and swim naked in the icy sea with him.

Sailing all over the world had answered something in her blood. It had satisfied the hunger for adventure and new experiences that she'd smothered for so many years.

Now the parents of two beautiful children, together they sailed the world over on the new St. James Shipping Line schooner, built in Scotland like the others by the Larsen Brothers. Morgan had named the line's newest addition the *Lady Miranda*. Another vessel, the *Lady Ariel*, was even now under construction.

Last year, Morgan's father, Sir Robert, had gone around the world with them, and had enjoyed himself immensely. Next year—if they could only talk Thaddeus into leaving dry land!— her mother and father might try the sea-wanderer's life. Miranda knew that her mama secretly hoped to visit Juliet, Harry, and their twin sons, little Harry and Peter, in India, where Harry, now a major, had been posted with his regiment soon after he and Juliet were married.

All in all, she had a life that any woman would envy, and freedom and adventure that most of her peers could only dream of—not to mention a handsome husband whom she loved beyond all reason. . . .

"Mama! Mama! Look!"

Geoff's excited squealing broke into her day-dreams.

"What is it, darling?"

"Whale ho! Off the starboard bow! There she blows!" roared the voice of the lookout from the crow's nest far above them.

Shading her eyes against the glare of sun off water, Miranda saw a fountain of spray shoot from the blowhole as a great humpback whale sounded. Then the huge, gleaming body slowly submerged, a vanishing trick that ended with a joyous flick of its enormous tail, before the massive creature disappeared.

"What a sight!" Morgan crowed, delighted by the display. "Happy?" he asked as he drew Miranda to him.

"Yes!" she murmured, smiling up at him. "Oh,

yes! If I were any happier, I'd burst!"

With Morgan's arm still around her, their children in their arms, they went to greet the first of the native canoes.

SCANDALS

PENELOPE NERI

Marked by unwarranted rumor, Victoria's dance card was blank but for one handsome suitor: Steede Warring, eighth earl of Blackstone. Known behind his back as the Brute, he vows to have Victoria for his bride. Little does she suspect that Steede will uncover her body's hidden pleasures, and show her that only faith and trust can cast aside the bitter pain of scandals.

___4470-6 $5.99 US/$6.99 CAN

Virtual Heaven
Ann Lawrence

The warrior looms over her. His leather jerkin, open to his waist, reveals a bounty of chest muscles and a corrugation of abdominals. Maggie O'Brien's gaze jumps from his belt buckle to his jewel-encrusted boot knife, avoiding the obvious indications of a man well-endowed. Too bad he is just a poster advertising a virtual reality game. Maggie has always thought such male perfection can exist only in fantasies like *Tolemac Wars*. But then the game takes on a life of its own, and she finds herself face-to-face with her perfect hero. Now it will be up to her to save his life when danger threatens, to gentle his warrior's heart, to forge a new reality they both can share.

___52307-8 $5.99 US/$6.99 CAN

Dorchester Publishing Co., Inc.
P.O. Box 6640
Wayne, PA 19087-8640

Please add $1.75 for shipping and handling for the first book and $.50 for each book thereafter. NY, NYC, and PA residents, please add appropriate sales tax. No cash, stamps, or C.O.D.s. All orders shipped within 6 weeks via postal service book rate. Canadian orders require $2.00 extra postage and must be paid in U.S. dollars through a U.S. banking facility.

Name_____
Address_____
City_____State_____Zip_____
I have enclosed $_____ in payment for the checked book(s).
Payment <u>must</u> accompany all orders. ❏ Please send a free catalog.
        CHECK OUT OUR WEBSITE! www.dorchesterpub.com

ATTENTION ROMANCE CUSTOMERS!

SPECIAL TOLL-FREE NUMBER
1-800-481-9191

Call Monday through Friday
10 a.m. to 9 p.m.
Eastern Time
Get a free catalogue,
join the Romance Book Club,
and order books using your
Visa, MasterCard,
or Discover®